She wanted to be touched...

Once in the sanctity of the house, Grace found she was shaking, shaking uncontrollably, shaking almost hysterically.

So it was just as she'd expected. An innocent touch, the beginnings of attraction, and she froze up. She balled up her fists and pressed them against her eyes. She would not cry. She would *not*. To do so would be to admit that Kristopher had won. Kristopher, who had spent years whittling her down until she was a miserable zombie to his violence, would be so pleased to know that his arm could still stretch out and hurt her now, four years later and three thousand miles away.

For the truth was, she *wanted* to be touched by Patrick. After four years of recovery, he was the first man in whom she was interested. And yet what happened the moment he touched her? Her mind shut down and her memories took over—memories that a man's touch was painful and vicious. For even when Kristopher hadn't been brutal physically, he had been mentally and emotionally vicious, telling her a packet of lies about herself over and over until she was forced to believe him. She *knew* Patrick was different—yet she'd behaved like a terrified rabbit.

Saving Grace

by

Patrice Moore

This is a work of fiction. Names, characters, places, and incidents are either the product of the author's imagination or are used fictitiously, and any resemblance to actual persons living or dead, business establishments, events, or locales, is entirely coincidental.

Saving Grace

COPYRIGHT © 2007 by Patrice Moore

Contact Information: info@thewildrosepress.com

Cover Art by *Tamra Westberry*

The Wild Rose Press
PO Box 706
Adams Basin, NY 14410-0706
Visit us at www.thewildrosepress.com

Publishing History
First Crimson Rose Edition, May 2007
Print ISBN 1-60154-030-2

Published in the United States of America

Dedication

For the love of my life, Don,
who makes my dreams come true.

Chapter One

Patrick Hess could not believe his good luck. It was the kind of luck that occasionally hits private investigators, the kind that is talked about in wonder around the water cooler after the case is long-solved.

The kind of luck that would go into the detective novel he'd always wanted to write...

And to think it happened in the middle of an office supply store!

The luck came in the form of a loudspeaker announcement. "Grace McNeil," announced the speaker. "Grace McNeil, please return to the Copy Department."

And Grace McNeil, he was pretty sure, was juuuussst the woman he was trying to find. Luck, pure and simple.

He hurried to arrive at the Copy Department of the enormous Staples store before Grace McNeil might get there. Picking up a random pack of felt-tip markers, he arranged himself next to the display of markers and waited.

Then his luck ran out. For not one, not two, but *three* women descended on the Copy Department, and not one of them fit the physical profile of the woman he was seeking.

The first woman was too old. Kristopher Lehrer hadn't married a woman approaching her seventh decade.

The second woman looked more the part, but she was shepherding three small kids with her. Patrick cocked his head, studying her over the display rack. Long blond hair—check—slightly on the heavy side—check—two earrings in both ears—check. But Kristopher Lehrer had told him that his wife had only one child, his precious little girl Jeannie. This woman had two young girls and an older boy with her, and from her affectionate behavior it was clear the woman wasn't babysitting. Patrick gave

1

Patrice Moore

an irritated shake of his head. This couldn't be Grace McNeil.

The third woman didn't fit the profile at all. She was about the right age—late twenties—but she was slim instead of heavy. She had chestnut hair cropped at the shoulders instead of long blond hair; she had no children with her; and she wore only one earring per ear. He watched the woman, pushing aside some pens to peer through the display. Her profile seemed wrong—the nose was a different shape, the shoulders hunched just a bit, the cheekbones too pronounced. Patrick was too far away to hear the murmured conversation between her and the clerk that might have confirmed her name.

But then the woman gathered up her copied materials, turned, and walked past him on his way out of the store. She didn't notice him—it was part of his job, not to be noticed—but for the first time he got a good look at her eyes.

Large, green, heavily fringed, without makeup...they had a haunted quality that pierced him viscerally. Sad eyes. Those eyes, though more troubled than his photograph depicted, looked eerily like those of the woman he was seeking.

He suppressed a twist of pity for whatever troubles had caused those eyes to be so haunted. It wasn't his job to fall for pitiful eyes. It *was* his job to find those eyes—if they were the right ones—and arrange for them to go back to where they belonged.

At random, he grabbed a packet of felt-tip pens and hurried to get in line behind her at the checkout stand. He didn't stand too close to her—he didn't want to be noticed in any way—but he was able to pick up the faint scent of gardenias and Jergens lotion.

"I can take you over here, sir," said a clerk, opening the next cash register over.

Patrick shook his head. "I'm fine, thanks. Just have one thing." He held up his pens.

"Well, I'll get you through quickly then," said the friendly clerk. She waved him over. "Come along."

Shut up, he thought desperately. He saw this Grace McNeil—if it was her—glance his way as she placed her items by the register. But the clerk was insistent, and

2

unless he wanted to draw further attention to himself, he had little choice but to go to the other check-out stand.

So, he missed seeing any identification she may have pulled out for the clerk. But he noted that she was wearing rather old tennis shoes, stained at the edges. Her jeans looked worn, and her short-sleeved plaid shirt was creased.

He shook his head. The one thing Lehrer had emphasized was that his wife, Margo, was a sophisticated sort who enjoyed the cultural benefits of an urban environment. Patrick wasn't sure Eugene, Oregon offered the cultural advantages that Margo apparently enjoyed, but he was willing to be generous.

She did, however, have a second pierced hole in her earlobe. If only the rest of her looked right.

She paid for her purchases in cash, so he wasn't able to glimpse a name on a check or credit card. She gathered up the bag holding her documents and departed the store. Outside, he saw her pause and glance around...the stance of a woman used to being followed.

His instincts were piqued. *Used to being followed...*

Patrick paid for his pens and hurried after her.

****

Grace emerged into the bright late-summer sunshine and blinked at the contrast. She stopped and glanced around, a habit that had never left her. She felt for "the prickles," but none came.

Satisfied, she stepped off the curb into the parking lot and crossed over to her 1985 two-toned brown Ford pickup truck. It was a vehicle so ordinary, so common, that it never caught anyone's attention. It was perfect.

She started the truck and then looked at the mileage odometer. The gas gauge was broken—it had broken two years ago and she didn't have the money to fix it—but she knew when it was time to fill the truck by how many miles showed on the odometer.

One-hundred eleven miles. Should be plenty of gas left.

She swung onto West Eleventh Avenue, then left onto Garfield. When Grace hit Highway 99, she took I-5 heading south. Once on the interstate, the tension she felt whenever she went to Eugene left her. She settled down

3

for the half-hour drive home.

Her home, thanks to Hazel. Grace let her mind drift as she drove in the right hand lane, never speeding, always following the traffic laws. Good old Hazel Flanagan. There had never been a spunkier, kinder, better woman, Grace was sure. For Hazel to take her in when she most needed it had been a blessing beyond all; but Hazel had done more, so much more for her. Even now, two years after Hazel's death, Grace could hardly think of her without getting teary-eyed.

Thirty miles south of Eugene was the town of Faucet, small and old-fashioned and obscure. Grace drove through the community and hesitated in front of the feed store. She needed chicken feed, but didn't have enough cash left. She'd have to come back later.

She waved at Dirk in front of the feed store, and then, since the car in front of her had slowed, she rolled down her window and called to him, "I'll be back in a day or two for chicken scratch!"

"See you then!" he called back, as he continued loading something for a customer.

Grace settled back and waited for the slow-down to clear. The traffic of the small town never bothered her. She loved Faucet, loved the small-town closeness of it, loved the welcoming feeling it gave her. She had been scared—terrified—to get to know anyone in town when she first arrived. Hazel had gently led her by the hand, almost literally, until she had emerged from her dazed shell and begun to live again.

The traffic cleared, and Grace made a left turn onto rural Highway 38 and left town. Two miles out of town, she took Hayhurst Road and wound her way into the mountains.

****

Following behind her in his car, Patrick noticed the man with whom she exchanged the pleasantries. A farmer's feed store. Interesting. She obviously knew the guy. Clearly, she was a regular customer. He made a note to come back and check on the situation.

He followed her, as far back as he could without losing sight of her truck, all the way through Faucet. *Faucet*, of all places. Criminy, the names these westerners gave their towns. Sounded like a piece of hardware, not a community.

Still, it seemed a pleasant-enough place. There was a combination liquor store and tanning salon—good grief, what a partnership—a grocery store, a number of antique stores, an absurdly large bridal salon, a fire station, a medical clinic...In looking around, he almost missed her sharp left-hand turn onto rural Highway 38. *Idiot*, he cursed himself. *Pay attention to what you're doing.*

The car in front cleared away, leaving him following behind her out of town. She slowed and turned left onto another road—Hayhurst Road, he noted. He made sure that he kept a discrete distance between their vehicles as he followed her.

For six miles he trailed her, past a gravel pit, past a scattering of small homes surrounded by broken-down debris and abandoned cars. He swerved to avoid a girl's bicycle left on the side of the road, its shiny pink-and-silver streamers fluttering from the handlebars. He glanced at the untidy yard where a woman was hanging laundry on a clothes line amidst a scattering of children's toys. What a mess.

Her truck continued down the road, past small ranches and farms. Six miles was a long time to follow a single car, and he was concerned she would notice him. He made a mental note, if he was able to find where she lived, to return the next time in a different car.

Would she notice she was being tailed and keep driving to try and shake him off? Or would she simply go home? That little edge of uncertainty kept him in this job; that little frission of excitement or tension kept his senses alert and his mind sharp. After five years as a detective, he now wondered if he could live without that sensation.

It didn't appear that she had noticed him. When she slowed down, he slowed too, just as if he was any old car on the road behind her.

She pulled into a semi-circular gravel driveway before a fenced yard. The house beyond was a pale blue, about seventy years old, and tidy. Patrick gave no more than a passing glance at it, acting just as if he were an ordinary traveler, before driving on. He noted the mileage on his odometer, and continued down Hayhurst Road.

The road wound in a large half-circle past fields and woods, bringing him, after another five miles, to the small community of Pincolla. *Pincolla*, he thought. Sounded like an alcoholic beverage. But, like Faucet, it was a small farming community with a smattering of cafés, a post office, churches, taverns, a community center, and a library.

This woman, hopefully the woman he was seeking, lived on a place halfway between the two towns. Patrick turned his car around and retraced his steps, slowing as he passed the place where Grace McNeil had pulled in.

Sure enough, her truck was still there, and she wasn't in it. Whether she lived here or was visiting someone would have to wait for more proof, but his instincts said this was her home.

He saw the fields stretching behind the house, the barn, a scattering of cows. The woman lived on a farm. Good. Excellent, in fact. He had spent many summers as a teenager working on his grandparent's ranch in Colorado. Farm work was not an unknown experience for him.

He noted the address, then sped up and began the drive back to Eugene, swerving wide to avoid a child on the pink bicycle he saw earlier.

It was time to switch cars...and create a new identity. Patrick needed to become a man with an excuse to spend time on a farm.

****

"Three bags of hen scratch, some fly powder, and four sacks of COB with molasses," said Grace. She pushed aside a strand of hair and smiled at Dirk Van Winden.

Dirk was graying at the temples but was handsome still, and he and Grace had been friends since she came to Faucet. There was no danger in Dirk. He was happily married to Ethyl, his bride of thirty-five years, and he had a boatload of strapping sons to take over his feedstore as well as a passel of grandchildren to spoil.

No, there was no danger in Dirk.

"You still interested in getting some help 'round your place?" he asked.

Grace pushed that annoying strand out of the way once again. "Might be. I tweaked my back last week while vaccinating the cattle, so a little help would be nice. I

6

don't know what I afford, though."

"You may not have to afford anything," said Dirk, tossing a seventy-five pound sack of corn, oats, and barley—COB—onto his shoulder as if it was a sack of feathers. "Fellow came through town yesterday, wanting to know if anyone was letting rooms." He dumped the sack in the back of her truck and went for another. "Seems he's a writer, and needs a quiet place to stay while he works on his book. He's willing to pay for his board plus do some work to earn his keep. I thought about you right away, keeping Hazel's farm running 'n all by yourself. You've got that little guesthouse arrangement you stayed in while caring for Hazel—ever thought about letting it out? For pay?"

"What on earth's a writer doing in Faucet, of all places?" asked Grace, loading the fifty pound sacks of hen scratch herself. Her back twinged, but she ignored it. After four years of farm labor, she should be able to handle the bags easily. "I would think one of those types would rather be in Eugene. Writers are supposed to be bohemian, aren't they? If so, Eugene's the place for them."

"That's what I asked him, but he said no. His book takes place on a ranch, he said, so he doesn't want the city surrounding him while he works on it. He's more interested in getting some real live experience with cows and such. Like I said, thought of you right away."

"That's nice of you, Dirk." Grace climbed over the back end of the pickup and hauled the bags of feed around until they were distributed to her satisfaction. "But I don't know...having a strange man about the place, with me out there by myself."

Dirk scratched the stubble on his chin. "I can appreciate that," he conceded. "Still and all, I suppose you can ask for references, that kind of thing." He shrugged and led the way back inside the store in order to ring up her order. "It's something to think about, after all."

Grace handed over four dozen eggs plus cash—no checks, no credit cards—to pay for the supplies, then got into her truck and drove home.

It *was* something to think about, after all.

****

And think about it she did. She thought about it

7

while she moved the irrigation pipes out of the north field and stacked them next to the pond, despite her aching back. The pipes weighed a good hundred pounds each and ran to twenty feet in length.

She thought about it while lugging a bale of alfalfa out of the haybarn and breaking it open for her herd of purebred Dexter cattle.

She thought about it when she fed and watered the chickens and gathered the eggs.

She thought about it when she sat down that night to fillet the two dozen catfish she'd netted in the pond and prepare them for the freezer.

And when she finally swallowed three aspirin and tumbled into bed that night, tired beyond all rational thought, she actually dreamt about it.

Dreamt about a tall, slim man, with high cheekbones and a shock of black hair, a friendly gleam to his hazel eyes and a quirky smile. A man who was surprisingly comfortable—for a city slicker—around her cattle and around a tractor. A man with a strong back and little curiosity.

She awoke the next morning and milked the two cows, strained and chilled the milk, separated the cream, then pulled the tractor up to the north pasture to mow it. One last cutting of alfalfa this year—that was it. She hoped she had enough to get the animals through the winter.

It took her three hours to mow the twelve-acre pasture. Then she pulled the tractor back into the utility shed, strode into the house, swallowed two more aspirin, and plucked her cell phone out of the kitchen cabinet where she kept it.

"Dirk?" she said. "Good morning, it's Grace. So tell me...what's the name of that writer fellow who wants a ranch job?"

****

She waited for him at Betty's Cafe in downtown Faucet. Betty's was a no-nonsense place with Formica-topped tables and cracked-vinyl stools in front of the counter. But it was cheap, and Sally, the waitress, was not the curious type.

Grace flexed her hands and tried to stifle her

8

nervousness. Men still made her edgy. When the tall, slim fellow opened the glass door to the café and stood for a moment inside, scanning its clientele, she told herself the reason her heart jumped was nerves. Just nerves.

It couldn't be his hazel eyes, the ones that turned up just a bit at the corners. It couldn't be his quiet demeanor, one of those still-waters-run-deep types. It couldn't be the comfortably worn clothes he wore—scuffed hiking boots, well-loved jeans, a faded short-sleeved red denim shirt. It couldn't be that he bore an uncanny resemblance to the man she'd dreamed about.

He looked, she must admit, like a country boy, a man used to outdoor work. He didn't look like an urban replant.

She waited for the 'prickles'—an awareness of something amiss, her only weapon of self-protection. But nothing came.

****

Patrick saw her sitting alone and watching him. He nodded his head gravely and strode over to her booth. "Miss McNeil?"

"Yes. You must be Patrick Hess."

"I am." He offered her his hand to shake, and she hesitated a moment before accepting.

He kept his handshake firm. "I'm pleased to meet you. May I?" He gestured toward the booth seat opposite her.

"Of course."

Sitting opposite, Patrick saw that she was anxious and unsmiling. She clasped her hands until the knuckles whitened, and there were tension lines around her mouth. Why?

The waitress came to take their order. Patrick ordered coffee, black. Grace ordered coffee with cream and sugar. Patrick made a mental note of that, and added it to his roster of details about her to check out with Kristopher Lehrer later on.

"So...are you from around here?" she asked.

"No. The Midwest."

She raised an eyebrow. "What brings you out to a place like Faucet, Oregon?"

Patrick quirked a small smile at her. "You really

9

want to know?"

"Well, sure."

Patrick traced the rim of his coffee cup with an idle forefinger. "I took a map of the U.S., closed my eyes, circled my finger—" He demonstrated, circling a finger above the table top. "—and plopped it down. It landed on Faucet."

"You're kidding!" A small smile started at the corners of her mouth, then vanished. To Patrick, it was clear she was controlling her emotions.

"Nope."

"So choosing Oregon was not specifically what you wanted?"

"Nope." He flicked hair off his forehead. He knew he was capable of smooth, realistic lying, just as he was capable of dressing the part to blend into whatever character he was required to role-play during the course of a job. He had raided a Goodwill store just this morning, to make sure he was dressed appropriately. "I just knew I was heading west, but I really didn't care where. That's the advantage of being a writer. I can go anywhere, set a book any place I choose. I just wanted a small ranch or farm-type setting." He gave a casual shrug. "And what better way to learn the ropes than to do the work?"

"But why Faucet? Why not Eugene? That town is crawling with writers."

He grimaced. "I'm not interested in crawling with other writers."

"Where are you from?"

"Chicago," he said, and gritted his teeth. He prayed she wasn't familiar with the city, since he'd been there only once. His parents had only recently moved there. "Hyde Park area. Ever been there?"

To his relief she shook her head. "No. I've never been to Chicago at all."

"Hot and humid in the summer, cold in the winter, but otherwise not bad," he commented.

"Now, you understand, Mr. Hess, my farm isn't very big. Thirty acres, fourteen head of cattle, that's about it."

"So I make my setting a thirty-acre farm. Nothing wrong with that. All I need is some privacy."

"What is it you write?"

"Detective thrillers. Y'know, those hard-boiled types." Might as well add a bit of realism to his alibi. God knows he knew enough about the detective part.

She raised a cool eyebrow. "A detective thriller? Set on a farm?"

"Hey, it stands apart from the crowd." He kept his voice light and teasing as he added, "I imagine that people living in rural areas are just as much in need of detective work as urban people."

Her mouth tightened. Patrick knew right away he had made a mistake. *Idiot*, he thought. *You're scaring her with all this talk of detectives.*

Her green eyes clouded with what looked like pain. She dropped her gaze to the tabletop and picked at a chip in the saucer of her coffee cup with a thumbnail. The silence lengthened as Patrick—for once unable to come up with a smooth cover for his blundering words—searched for something that would ease over his mistake.

She finally raised her eyes to his, and he marveled at the mask of coolness she now wore. It was a shame that she should look upon him with such...such neutrality. He wished she would look upon him as a man.

Get a grip, he told himself. *She's off-limits.* It startled him, this humanizing of his prey. He wasn't used to reacting that way.

He realized that he'd better just do his damned job, confirm her identity, and get the hell out of Oregon before he did something he might regret.

"...references. I'm sure you'll understand."

He blinked, realizing that once again his mind had wandered and he'd completely missed what she'd said. God in heaven, what was wrong with him? Show him one pretty woman with haunted eyes, and his entire training and sharpness and perception went down the toilet.

"Excuse me?" he asked, with what he hoped was a self-conscious smile. "I'll have to warn you, Miss McNeil, that I'm subject to wool-gathering at odd moments. I'll think up a sudden turn of phrase for a scene I've been working on, and my mind wanders as I mentally polish it. This is a way of apologizing for missing what you said."

She raised her brow again—whew, the woman could be frosty when she chose—and repeated her statement.

"I'm not in the habit of hiring strange men to work my farm, Mr. Hess. So I'll have to ask for references. I'm sure you'll understand."

"Of course," he said at once. He'd been expecting this, and had a list in his wallet for the occasion. He leaned over on one buttock, removed his wallet from his back pocket, and flipped open the leather. His badge and his driver's license were tucked out of sight, so she wouldn't glimpse the New York identification and panic.

He removed a type-written index card, folded once, and flipped it over on the table toward her. "Here are two guys I boarded with while researching my previous books. I can also give you my home address, if you like, although frankly I'm not there all that often. The phone's been disconnected—I use my cell phone when I crash there." His "references" were retired detectives, co-workers from years past, who had agreed to such a scenario. They were in different states, Florida and Arizona, and were well-coached with the story they were supposed to confirm.

His 'home address' was, quite simply, his parents' new address in Chicago.

He watched as she picked up the card, unfolded it, and scanned the names and addresses. He hoped it gave the casual appearance that a writer might portray. Nothing ultra formal, yet something for her to check up on right away.

"How many books have you written?" she asked.

"Two," he answered. "I'm starting to build a name for myself. *Jason's Big Day*—that's the name of my first one. You've heard of it?" He cocked his head expectantly, and just as he predicted, she shook her head. He was confident she didn't read detective fiction. "And that was followed by *Jason's Nightmare*. The one I'm working on now will be my third Jason book."

"Well, part of me is flattered, that you'd want to set your book on my little farm. But you understand I need someone who can do physical labor on the place. Have you ever worked with animals, tractors, that kind of thing?"

"When I was a teenager, I spent summers working my grandparent's place in Colorado," he replied. "They had a wheat farm in eastern Colorado, so I've worked with tractors and combines. I've ridden horses and even learned some roping, though I was never much good at it. I've had some exposure to cattle, but probably not as much as you'd like. I have a strong back, and I don't complain that much. The bottom line, Miss McNeil, is that as long as I have a few hours a day to write, I'm willing to pay five hundred dollars a month in board plus help with the heavy work on the farm."

As expected, her nostrils flared at the mention of the money. So, she was hard up for cash. Good. Much more likely to take the bait.

She picked up the index card and tapped it against the table with a distracted air. Her incredible green eyes focused on some point in the middle distance, and he could practically see the gears whirling in her brain. He was silent while she figured out her finances, knowing that the sum he mentioned would be enough to tip the balance in his favor. Heck, she might not even check out his references.

At last, she refocused on him. "Let me describe my setup," she said. Her tone of voice was still cool, calm. He rather admired her for that. "I have a guesthouse, a two-room building separate from the main house. It has a wood stove and a bathroom. No shower, but you can use the shower in the house. There's also no kitchen, so I can provide meals. Or, you can use the kitchen if you prefer to cook for yourself. I can't promise your quarters will be completely private, since there's a pantry next to your bathroom that I use. The rooms are furnished, and since they're separate from the house, you should have all the quiet you'd need."

He nodded but said nothing. So far, this was all working out better than he'd hoped. With some luck, he'd spend a week or two poking around the place. He'd confirm her identity, find out where the kid was, and get the hell back to Buffalo

"As for farm duties," she continued, "I would expect help during reasonable daylight hours. If I can get some work between nine in the morning and four or so in the afternoon, I would consider that adequate. Does this all sound suitable to you?"

"Yes," he replied.

"Naturally, I'll need to check your references first.

Where can I reach you?"

He hesitated. "Right now I'm staying in a motel in Cottage Grove," he lied. "I can give you my cell phone number, but it seems to get pretty spotty coverage out here. Can I call you instead? Say, in a day or two?"

"I don't have a phone, Mr. Hess."

Now it was his turn to raise his eyebrows in surprise. No phone. Interesting. "Then how will you—"

"I use payphones for whatever calls I need to make. I also have a cell phone for emergencies, but I don't give out that phone number."

"Of course. Well—" He scratched his chin, considering. He supposed he'd just have to find a motel in Cottage Grove, check in, and relay the phone number back to her. "You can just call me on the motel phone, then. I could leave the number with that fellow in the feed store. Would that work?"

"That'll work. Now, another thing, Mr. Hess..." She dropped her eyes to the coffee in front of her, firmed her lips, and raised her head again to regard him with that cool air. "I'll admit I have some concerns with the idea of a strange man on my place. My farm is not exactly isolated, but it's far enough off the beaten track that we will be essentially alone. A woman by herself is always vulnerable. I know you understand where I'm going with this—"

"Of course. Truthfully, Miss McNeil, I'd be surprised if that *didn't* bother you. I don't know how else to show my good intentions—give you my word, perhaps? That I'll behave myself?"

She probed him with her eyes for a disconcerting five long seconds. Criminy, the woman had eyes that could see into a man's soul. He held her gaze, for he would not let her think his intentions were anything but professional.

Finally, she gave a jerky nod. "Very well. Let me check out your references, Mr. Hess, and I'll be in touch."

She laid down a five-dollar bill on the tabletop, rose, and was gone. The small bells on the cafe's door jingled in her wake.

He gave a sigh of relief. He was in. The first step was done. With luck, he'd crack this case quickly and be gone—before his heart became involved.

Chapter Two

Three days later, Patrick drove down Hayhurst Road in a rented two-door Toyota Camry. He had debated whether or not to purchase a used vehicle, then rejected the thought. As a traveling writer, a rental would be easy to explain.

He caught a flash of pink out of the corner of his eye, and instinctively slammed on the brakes. The same girl on her bicycle he had seen before darted out of his way and wobbled into a ditch. Patrick yanked open the door and ran to pull the girl up. "Are you okay?"

The screech of tires brought the woman from the untidy yard running in their direction. "Andrea! Andrea, are you all right?"

The girl was crying and shaking, but appeared unhurt except for a few scrapes. Patrick led her across the road to the yard. "I think she's okay, ma'am. Just scared."

The woman snatched the girl in her arms and closed her eyes with relief. "Thanks, mister," she said. Patrick saw a gleam of moisture in her eyes. "She loves to ride her bike, but we don't have any paved area on our farm. She's always on the road."

"Hey, count your blessings. When I was a kid, I got a concussion when a car hit me, because I was doing the same thing." Patrick shoved his hands in his pockets because they, too, were shaking. "You sure you're okay, sweetheart?" he asked the child.

She buried her face in her mother's neck and sniffed. "Yeah. Thanks."

"No problem. Hang on, I'll get your bike for you."

Ten minutes later, having restored order to the family, Patrick pulled into Grace's driveway. He killed the engine and got out, examining his surroundings with the eye of a man accustomed to taking in details. A brook

15

burbled next to the road. Opposite the house was a forested hill that reared up with startling swiftness.

It took him a moment to realize what was missing—the sounds of traffic. The road was deserted, and in the absence of engines, he noted birdsongs. The air was clean and clear, with little of the humidity he was used to in New York.

The house was old, pale blue, and tidy. Roses grew along the three-foot high chain-link fence that enclosed the yard. Under the windows were a profusion of flowers—daisies, columbine, nasturtiums, and zinnias. He knew his flowers; his mother loved them.

There was no porch, just a concrete stoop in front of the door. He strode up the narrow walkway and knocked.

There was a long pause. He was just about to knock again when he heard the sound of footsteps, and another pause before she opened the door. He had no doubt that the second pause was for her to peer through the small peephole.

"Good morning, Mr. Hess."

"Miss McNeil." God, she was gorgeous. He blinked once or twice and tried to swallow whatever it was that suddenly choked his throat.

"Come on in. I was just setting some bread. Can you come back to the kitchen for a second while I finish?"

"Of course."

She was dressed in jeans and a loose baggy green T-shirt with sleeves that came down to her elbows. The blousy shirt came to almost the middle of her bottom, and he wondered why a woman with such an attractive figure would hide it under the shapeless, oversized shirt.

Her hands were dusted with flour. Her eyes, those haunted eyes, were more relaxed today. Her short hair was held away from her face with a green braided elastic band. A smudge of flour was on the lower part of her shirt, and another smudge on the thigh of her jeans.

She looked wholesome and entirely provincial. Patrick had a moment of serious doubt that this was the woman he was looking for.

Kristopher Lehrer had stressed the urban sophistication of his wife. She was used to the finer things in life, Lehrer had said. Designer clothes, the best silver and china, the service of a maid. And then there was the child...

He couldn't afford to screw up this case. He had spent weeks tracing a dead lead in Nashville, and Lehrer wouldn't tolerate another failure. Patrick desperately needed the money that solving this case would bring.

The living room was furnished simply—dark wood floors, an antique woodstove, pine furniture with plaid upholstery, bookshelves. Rural prints hung on the walls, framed with the kind of gilded wood popular in the fifties.

But—and here was a clincher—there was no evidence of a child anywhere. None whatever. No toys, no childish drawings tacked up, no photographs scattered about, nothing.

With the exception of those incredible eyes, he would have said right away that this Grace McNeil was *not* the Margo Lehrer he was seeking. But the only way to confirm it was to see her upper arms. Lehrer had told him about the thin jagged scars she bore from falling through a plate glass window when she was eight years old.

The kitchen was spacious and airy, white and pale blue. There was a breakfast nook at one end, and windows overlooking the backyard.

"Sorry for the mess," she said, and plunged her hands back into the huge lump of bread dough she had on a wooden breadboard set on the kitchen table. "Why don't you have a seat until I finish this? Take me no more than five minutes."

"Nice place," he said politely.

"Thanks. I like it."

She kneaded the dough, pushing and pounding the mass with vigorous strength. She didn't seem inclined to speak, so Patrick stayed quiet as well.

He used the time to examine her more closely, with the special technique detectives learn, the ability to note details without *looking* like he was noting details. He glanced around the kitchen while watching the muscles that roped her lower arms as she kneaded. He scratched an itch while estimating her height to be about five-feet-four inches. He stretched back and crossed his ankles while guessing her weight at about one hundred fifteen. He noted those empty second earring holes in her ears, next to the plain gold studs she wore. Her fingers were ringless. She wore no nail polish.

Finally she picked up the bread dough and plopped it into the greased bowl.

"There," she said, and went to the sink to wash up. "That's done."

"I haven't seen anyone make bread since I was a teenager," he said. "Grandma used to make it all the time."

"I enjoy it," she said. "There's something soothing about pounding the stuff. They always say it's a good way to get rid of aggressions."

He chuckled. "Are you in the habit of being aggressive?"

She gave him a friendly smile, the first he'd seen. "Not usually. But it's fun anyway."

He had to bite back a sharp intake of breath. Smiling made her shine, glow, with an inner strength he found appealing—and sexy.

She finished washing up, snatched a blue-and-white checked dishcloth out of the handle of the refrigerator, and wiped her hands and forearms. Then she flipped the cloth over the bowl of bread dough and placed the bowl on the windowseat in the breakfast nook, full in the sunshine.

"What do you do with it now?" asked Patrick, interested despite himself.

"Let it rise." She strode over to the refrigerator and lifted down a magnetized kitchen timer, which she set. "I'll punch it down in about two hours, then put it in pans for the second rising. Come on, I'll show you around."

She went out a second doorway from the kitchen, and he followed her down a short hallway. "Bathroom's here," she gestured. "It's the only tub in the place, so you can shower here."

He nodded. "Sounds good."

They emerged back into the living room. "This house only has two bedrooms," she said. "Mine, and then this bedroom that I use as an office." She stood in the doorway of the office. "There's no need for you to ever go in this room. I keep the farm records here, and do some desktop publishing to bring in extra money."

The room was clean and tidy, with a computer and printer, folders, a file cabinet, and a bookshelf filled with magazines and more folders. Patrick fairly itched to dig through the paperwork to try and find some identifying information.

"I see," said Patrick. He made a mental note to ask Lehrer if Margo knew desktop publishing.

"There's an attic storage room up there," she said, and opened a door. Steep, narrow steps led upwards. "It's not furnished. Not much up there. Come on, I'll show you the guesthouse." She closed the door again.

She took him back through the kitchen. "Washer and dryer over there," she said, pointing to an extra room behind the kitchen. "And your place is out back."

She opened a back door from the kitchen and walked down two concrete steps toward another building about ten feet from the house. Overhead was a roof of clear corrugated plastic, making a breezeway. The little building had an open shed attached to it, which was stacked high with split logs. There was a maul and a wedge stacked near a wall. Criminy, the woman split her own wood?

"This is the guest cottage," she said, opening the door and stepping inside.

It was a low building with two rooms. The first was a rather dark living room, long and narrow, with a squat bank of windows. Four armchairs of various degrees of decrepitude clustered around a slim pot-bellied woodstove. Surprising touches of femininity—laced trimmed curtains, floral slipcovers—saved the room from dreariness.

"This is the pantry I mentioned," she said, pointing to a door leading right off from the entryway. "A sort of deep closet I use for canned goods. In here's the bathroom." She whisked open another door next to the pantry to reveal a tiny room with a toilet and sink. "Nothing fancy, I'm afraid."

"Hey, it's adequate."

"The woodstove works fine, and I cleaned the chimney pipe yesterday." She pointed to a wooden box in the corner. "I stocked you with newspapers and kindling and some dry oak, so if things get chilly, feel free to start a fire. Matches are up here on this shelf."

Patrick nodded, though he was no more knowledgeable about woodstoves than he was about needlepoint.

"And over here—" She strode across the narrow room and opened the door at the end. "—is the bedroom. Watch your step," she warned, as he was just about to cross the threshold.

There were two steps leading down into a small bedroom about eight by eight feet. A double-sized bed took up most of the space, but there was also a small dresser with a mirror on top and a small bookshelf. She'd placed a vase of fresh wildflowers on top of the dresser. The only light to this room was from the glass-and-wood door leading outside.

"There's no heat in here," she apologized, "so if it gets cold, just leave the bedroom door open and you can get the heat from the woodstove."

Patrick nodded. "It looks great," he said.

She gave a brief laugh, the first he'd heard, a silvery sound that warmed his bloodstream. "It's dismal and dreary and a little dark," she said. "I should know. I lived in these rooms for two years."

He was startled. "Excuse me?"

"The old lady who left me this farm. I was her caretaker for two years before she died, and these were my rooms."

"Interesting way to obtain a farm," he observed blandly, not wanting to root the information out of her so fast that she became suspicious.

"I suppose. Hazel was a dear, wonderful friend. It was tough losing her."

"I can imagine."

"Anyway, as you can see—" She stepped back up into the living room. "—there's no kitchen facilities, or for that matter, a washer or dryer. You're welcome to use the kitchen or washer in the house. As for meals...well, what do you say I cook the evening meals, and we forage for ourselves the rest of the day?"

"Sounds fine with me. I'll do my share of cooking, and maybe I could be in charge of washing up."

She cocked her head at him as if this concept

surprised her. He sensed a softening in her, a trembling awareness that maybe he was more than just a monthly check.

"Thanks," she said softly. "Maybe I'll take you up on that."

Those enormous green eyes looked fathomless and vulnerable in the half-light of the room. Patrick mentally swore and made himself look away. He didn't want to start feeling warmth toward Grace. She was a case to investigate, that was it. Parental abduction, runaway wife. He didn't want to feel like a knight on a white horse coming to rescue her from whatever it was that gave her that haunted look. All he needed to do was confirm that she was, in fact, Margo Lehrer, and get the hell out.

"Well." Grace's brisk voice broke the moment. "Do you want to unload your stuff first, or see the farm?"

He considered. "Let me unload my stuff," he decided. "Won't take me long, and I'll change into something better for walking around a cow pasture." He briefly gestured toward his leather loafers.

She nodded. "I need to get something out of the freezer for dinner anyway. Do you like lasagna?"

"Yes."

"Great. Dinner's at six or so."

She left the guesthouse, closing the door behind her. He heard her footsteps on the concrete walkway up to her back door, and then the screen banged shut.

Patrick exhaled a shaky breath and sat on one of the cracked leather chairs. He dropped his head in his hands and closed his eyes.

What was wrong with him? What was it about this Grace McNeil that made him want to protect, not investigate? In the years he'd been a private investigator, he had never *once* become personally interested in any of his clients *or* the people he was investigating. He was too professional for that.

His business specialized in locating missing persons, especially missing spouses. It wasn't always a pleasant line of work. There were times when a lot of ugly emotions came up.

Frowning, he leaned back in the chair and gazed at the smoke-darkened ceiling. There were times when he

21

seriously thought about finding another line of work, one that was less dependent on people's darker sides.

And now, thanks to a frivolous lawsuit, his firm was in financial trouble. He'd cut the staff down to himself and one other detective. Kristopher Lehrer, hot-tempered though he was, at least paid well. Well enough, thought Patrick with a twist of distaste, to keep his business solvent for a few more months.

He looked out the window and saw an enormous garden and a nearby brook. There were flowers and a single lawn chair—peaceful, ordinary things. But there were no children's toys, no tricycles. He wondered where the little girl was.

It took only three trips to unload his belongings from the car. He swung his two suitcases and his laptop computer on the bed, and placed the six-pack of beer he'd purchased earlier on the dresser. He had a box of books as well, bought at the same Goodwill store that had supplied his wardrobe. He was squatting down and putting them on the small bookshelf when he heard a knock on the door.

"Come in!" he called.

She walked into the living room. "Mr. Hess?"

"Call me Patrick," he said, shoving the books onto the shelf.

She came to stand in the doorway to the bedroom. "Okay. Call me Grace." She cocked an eyebrow at him. "Do you go by Patrick? Or do you answer to Pat?"

"Only if you answer to Gracey-pooh." He grinned at her.

She wrinkled her nose. "Ouch. Point taken. Patrick it is—"

Her voice trailed off so swiftly that he turned, startled, to look at her. She was staring at the six-pack of beer as if it were a poisonous snake. Her face was pale.

"Grace?"

"Is—is that yours?"

"The beer? Yes. Why?" He couldn't understand the horror on her face.

"Get it out."

He raised himself from his squatting position, and looked at her with some concern. She looked ill—almost greenish, swaying as if she were close to fainting.

"You don't like beer?" He was genuinely puzzled. It was a fairly expensive imported brand, nothing cheap.

She blinked rapidly, and tore her eyes away from the bottles to look at him. Her face was wild-looking, almost frenzied, her eyes huge, and he saw her gulp. Before he could stop her, she turned and fled from the room. Distantly, he heard the back door of the house slam.

He was stunned at her reaction. Good God, was she *afraid* of beer? It was more than fear he saw—it was terror.

Shaking his head, he removed the offending beverage and placed it out of sight in the dresser. There was a lot more here than met the eye, and he intended to get to the bottom of it.

****

Grace ran into her bedroom and threw herself on the bed, shaking uncontrollably. Behind her eyelids, she saw jagged brown glass, saw the blood drip from her arms as she struggled, trying to escape the cutting edges. Four slashes if she screamed out loud, two slashes if she could stay quiet while under attack...

Kristopher had enjoyed that particular brand of beer, and enjoyed even more bashing off the bottle necks and slashing her with the sharp glass. It was his Friday-night ritual.

Kristopher was not a drinker. His drinking was a weekly event, and he rarely drank more than two beers. But for each bottle he drank, he took sick pleasure in causing at least one slash mark on her from the glass. Never her face, of course. That would be too obvious. He preferred her upper arms. A fastidious man, he always stripped off his shirt—lest he splatter blood on it—before approaching her.

Grace had come to hate the particular brand of beer he favored. With a typical battered-wife mentality, she attributed evil to the beer brand rather than to the perpetrator.

It took her ten minutes to calm down and get those images out of her head. *It's all in the past*, she thought. *He'll never hurt me again.* She went into the bathroom and splashed water on her face, and then felt embarrassed for overreacting. Patrick had done nothing wrong. He simply enjoyed the same brand of beer. That was it. There was nothing malevolent in his intentions.

She paused and felt inward, exploring, examining. Kristopher was not thinking about her, at least no more than usual. The 'prickles' didn't come.

"You're an idiot," she scolded herself, as she walked through the kitchen to the back door. "After four years, get over it." She gritted her teeth and prepared to apologize for her behavior.

She knocked on the door again, and heard Patrick's "Come in!" When she entered, she saw him sitting in one of the chairs, lacing up a pair of sneakers.

He hesitated and looked at her. "You okay?"

"Yeah." She took a deep breath. "I'm sorry, Patrick. I, um, overreacted."

"Are you afraid of beer?"

"No. No, not really. Just a bad memory, that's all."

"Do you want me to throw it out?"

"Of course not." She did, but she wasn't going to admit it. Valiantly, she changed the subject. "I need to feed the cattle—you want to come? I can show you around the rest of the farm."

She knew he was watching her closely, trying to fathom the reason behind her earlier behavior. She kept her face composed. Finally, he turned back to his sneakers. "Okay. Let me just finish throwing on my shoes—" He reached for his other sneaker, pulled it on, and tied the laces.

Grace felt calmer now, more in control. She wouldn't let that kind of reaction happen again. It was counterproductive and useless, Hazel had taught her. Look forward, not back. Kristopher may have weaseled his poisonous thoughts deeply into her, but he wasn't going to win. Not now, not ever. Unconsciously, she fingered the revolver that was constantly strapped at the small of her back under her shirt, and was reassured.

She watched Patrick lace up his footwear. Grace hadn't seen a man put on his shoes in four years. He slipped on the sneaker and then crossed his ankle over his knee in order to tie, rather than a woman's usual method of bending down to tie the lace. It was warming, somehow, watching the little domestic effort. Patrick seemed so...so normal. Not violent, not abusive, not sick. He just seemed like an ordinary guy, trying to make a living. It had taken quite awhile to realize that normal guys were more common than she had been led to believe.

She gave a brief shake of her head and looked up to see Patrick watching her.

****

"You sure you're okay?" Patrick asked softly.

She made a small gesture with one hand. "Yes, of course." When he looked doubtful, she added, "I'm just wondering if I've done the right thing, inviting a stranger onto my property. Oh, your references checked out okay, but still...it's a little nerve-wracking."

"Have I done anything to make you nervous? If so, let me know and I won't do it anymore." *She's been hurt,* he thought. *Badly. By Lehrer? By someone else?*

"No, you haven't. It's just the principle of the thing. I'm sure this arrangement will work out fine." She gave a nod toward his laptop computer. "That's what you write on?"

"Huh?" For the briefest second, his mind was blank. Write? "Oh. Yeah. That's what I write on."

"How long does it take you to write a book?"

"Um, about five or six months for the basic thing." He had no idea how long it took to write a book, so he hoped that sounded believable.

"It must be exciting, seeing your name in print."

"Yes. It is. So—" Anxious to get off the subject, he clapped his hands together and rubbed briskly. "Let me see the rest of your place."

They walked into the backyard and headed for an enormous fenced area.

"This is my garden," she said.

Patrick folded his arms and rested them on top the fence. "Nice. What do you grow in here?"

She pushed aside two buckets in front of the opening, and unlatched the gate. He followed her inside. "Corn," she said. "Tomatoes, pumpkins, raspberries, strawberries, carrots, broccoli, beans, peas, tomatoes, onions, garlic—"

She continued listing the vegetables while Patrick looked around in amazement. They all looked like a bunch of plants to him—except the corn, of course, and the tomatoes, which he could identify.

His certainty that Grace was Margo Lehrer slipped a bit. The picture Kristopher had painted of his wife was that of a woman who never gardened, never wanted to soil her hands with dirt.

Yet those eyes were so much like the photographs he'd seen, and the basic structure of the face...

"Woolgathering again?" she asked.

He looked up to realize that they'd completed the tour of the garden. Hastily he improvised. "Yep. Sorry. Just thinking how the ordinary part of a farm, such as a garden, could be implemented into the plot."

"Mayhem among the melons," she suggested lightly.

He forced a chuckle. "Yeah. Something like that."

Next she showed him the chicken coop, which was alive with cackling birds of every variety imaginable. Patrick hadn't seen chickens—real live chickens—since his teenage days on his grandparent's farm. They flowed and swirled and fluttered around them, cackling and clucking. Two roosters competed in a crowing contest.

"How many birds do you have?" asked Patrick, jumping back when a black-and-white speckled hen fluttered across his shoe.

"About fifty, although next week I'll have only half of that. See those enormous white hens over there? Those are Cornish crosses, a meat bird. They're just about ready to put in the freezer..."

He swallowed hard. "Do you...do that yourself?"

"Oh no. There's a service in town that will do that for you. You bring them your birds, they do the rest and give you back frozen chickens."

His shoulders wilted with relief, for he wasn't sure if he was up to butchering chickens in the interests of confirming Margo Lehrer's identity. *The things a detective is called upon to do*, he thought sourly.

"—keep the rest for eggs."

"Excuse me?" He *had* to stop his mind from wandering.

"I said, I usually cull about half the flock, and keep the rest for eggs."

"How many eggs a day do you get?"

Grace opened the door to the coop and returned to the yard. Patrick plucked a feather off his arm and followed.

"About two dozen," she replied. "I sell them in town to the grocery store, and I often trade them as well, for animal feed."

"So they about pay for themselves."

She flashed a smile at him that nearly had his knees buckling. "That's right. Over here—" She strode to an open shed, "is the tractor. Do you know how to operate one?"

"I haven't been on one since I was a teenager," he replied, "but I think with a brief lesson I could remember."

"I did the last cutting of alfalfa earlier this week," she said, resting her hand on the snub-nosed hood of the tractor. "The weather's been dry, so it's about ready to bale. I don't have a baler, so a neighbor comes in and does it for a share of the alfalfa."

"How many bales do you get?"

"About a hundred, per cutting. This is the third cutting of the summer, the last one. I don't have all my acreage in alfalfa, though, or I'd get more. See that building over there?" She stepped outside the shed, and pointed to a low-roofed building a short distance away. "That's the haybarn. I store the bales there."

"And what do you do with the alfalfa?"

She looked at him with some surprise. "Why, I feed the cattle with it."

"Of course." *What else would she do with it, you idiot!* he scolded himself.

"I usually have some extra to sell, too," she added.

"I see."

As they walked out of the machine shed, she stepped on a loose branch that rolled away from under her. She flailed, striving to regain her balance. Reflexively, Patrick reached out and clutched her arm to stabilize her.

She froze as he continued to grip her arm. Her eyes widened and her body grew still. Her gaze was fixed stiffly on the fenced yard ahead of them. Beneath his fingers, he felt the muscles in her upper arm, muscles defined by hard work, but also by something more. She

27

seemed rigid with fear. He removed his hand.

"Doing okay?" he questioned.

She swallowed and continued to stare straight ahead. "Doing okay," she confirmed in a quiet voice.

Something's not right, thought Patrick.

Chapter Three

"Come on, I'll show you the barn," said Grace.

Patrick turned, and they crunched over the rough road toward the bridge over the brook.

Grace's reaction to his touch continued to bother him. There was something evasive about her, something not quite right in her behavior. She freaked at the sight of beer; she froze at his chivalrous touch. Those were not normal reactions for a woman.

Yet she strode next him, quiet and calm and composed, as if nothing in the world was wrong. She was a walking contradiction.

He took a breath and focused on the bridge in front of them. "How far up does your property go?" he asked.

She pointed. "See that tree line over there? That's my boundary."

They stepped onto the bridge over the brook. "Ever go swimming in this?"

Grace paused and leaned over the balustrade. "Yes. That section of creek bank over there—where it gets sandy—makes a good swimming hole on a hot day."

Patrick had this sudden vision of her in a swimsuit, and had to choke back the resulting reaction. Still, he knew there were enough warm days left this season to suggest a swim. If she were in a swimsuit, he could check for scars on her arms.

And, he told himself, it was only for professional reasons that he wanted to see her in a swimsuit. Of course it was.

"So...any chance that there are enough warm days left to swim? That's one thing I love to do," he suggested.

She shrugged. "You're welcome to take a dip any time you want, of course."

He gritted his teeth. He could hardly say anything

29

along the lines of "Not without you." *Relax, Patrick*, he told himself. *You've barely been here an hour. You have weeks yet, if necessary, to find out if this woman is, in fact, Margo Lehrer. Take it slow.*

"Come on, I'll show you the cows." Grace boosted away from the side of the bridge and led him along a fringe of trees near the brook until they reached the barn.

Suddenly Patrick stopped. "Those are *cows?*" he exclaimed, and couldn't help but laugh.

She shot him a look that might have been amusement. "Yes, of course they're *cows*," she replied. "Specifically, Dexters."

"What are Dexters?"

"They're a small breed which—"

"Obviously. Very small." His words were wry.

For the cows, a good dozen of which were scattered about the pasture in front of the barn, were indeed small, no higher than his chest.

Within a few minutes, they were surrounded by a milling herd of the friendly animals. Their horns looked alarming as they pushed and swiped and butted their way around Grace. Quite a few thrust their moist noses at him too, as if expecting him to pat them or something.

He ventured a caress on a cow, and found that it was indeed what she was expecting. Her eyes actually closed in pleasure as he scratched her under the chin. He started to chuckle.

"Man oh man," he commented. "They're sure a lot friendlier than my grandfather's Jersey's."

"Oh, Jerseys are beautiful."

"Yeah, the *cows* are okay, but the bulls are meaner than spit."

"I've heard that. Now here, here's my bull, Chester."

"That's a *bull?*" Warily, he glanced down and confirmed that it was, indeed, an intact bull. "Are you sure he's safe?"

"Chester? Oh, absolutely. He's dehorned, of course. And I raised him myself, didn't I, you big lug." She put her hands on Chester's halter and swayed him back and forth, smiling foolishly at the animal. "Chester's my breeding stud," she explained. "He's fathered all the calves this year."

"Ouch." One overly friendly cow had poked him in the hip with a horn. "Stop that."

"Ruby, move off, you monster," said Grace mildly as she released Chester's halter and moved to shove the curious animal away. "They want dinner," she said by way of explanation. "They're friendly beasts, but not normally this—ow, stop it!—this sociable."

Watching her walk among the milling cattle, Patrick again doubted that this was Margo Lehrer. Kristopher's wife, he suspected, had never touched a cow in her life, and here she was saying she'd raised Chester herself.

"What do you *do* with these guys?" he asked.

"Some I eat, some I milk, some I sell."

He winced. "You *eat* them?"

"Of course." She raised an eyebrow at him. "I grow or raise just about everything I eat. All right, all right, I'll feed you," she said to the animals. She turned and began wading through the black fur toward the barn.

His doubts increased as he followed her into the barn. Margo Lehrer was much more likely to have a maid cook her food than to grow it herself.

He watched her heave a heavy bale of alfalfa onto a cart. "Hey, I'll do that!" he said, but it was too late. Criminy, the woman must be far stronger than she looked, if she was able to move around a bale that probably weighed as much as she did.

"No problem. I do this all the time." But he had seen her wince.

She hoisted her shirt a bit and fished a jack-knife from her pocket. As she did so, Patrick caught a flash of elastic gray material around her waist. *Kidney support*? he wondered. Somehow, he didn't think so. The flash of gray puzzled him, tickled at his mind, long after she had sliced the twine around the bale and returned the knife to her pocket.

Later they walked through the pastures, delineated by hedgerows of blackberry bushes. "I'm impressed," he told her, looking at the neat swaths of fresh-cut alfalfa. "There's a lot of work involved here."

"Yes. Especially this time of year, when there's grass hay and alfalfa to put up, the garden's at full blast, and I'm trying to can and freeze and dry and preserve everything at once." She kept her eyes straight ahead. "I don't know how long you'll stay, Patrick, but I'm grateful you're here." She glanced at him. "It's even nice to have someone to talk to."

He felt a twist in his gut. She was lonely. If this person *wasn't* the Margo Lehrer he was seeking, why on earth was she alone? She was beautiful and intelligent—why wasn't she married?

"Why are you doing this all by yourself?" he asked. "It's a lot of work for a lone woman."

"I know. But it's mine," she replied softly. Her eyes rested on the field before her, filled with such an expression of soul-soothing satisfaction and deep love that he swallowed hard. "I never thought I'd be a farmer," she went on in a low voice. "Never in a million years. But I find myself out here in these fields, and I know, God willing..." She stopped and bit her lip. "...I'll stay here the rest of my days."

His radar went up. *I never thought I'd be a farmer, never in a million years...*Could Lehrer's dainty socialite wife have found a new vocation as well as a new identity? One that had taken her literally across the country to find? It struck him as odd that a woman with no rural background whatsoever could settle and be happy in a profession like this.

He glanced at her profile, thinking again how different it was from the photographs he had. She was much slimmer than Margo Lehrer, but a person could lose weight. Her nose had a bump; it wasn't the dainty pixie nose in his photographs. That part was harder to explain, though plastic surgery was always a possibility. But it was those eyes that caught him, and made him strongly suspect that she was indeed Mrs. Lehrer. Eyes like that couldn't possibly be found on two people.

She turned and caught him staring at her. Those enormous eyes widened into something akin to fear. Their gazes remained locked for a few heartbeats, until she asked, in a shaky voice, "Is s-something wrong, Patrick?"

"No. Of course not." He turned away. *Don't scare her*, he chastised himself. *You're supposed to win her confidence, not make her think you're out to attack her.*

But he found to his distress that he *liked* looking at

her, and in a capacity far removed from his profession as a detective. In the short time he'd been in her presence, he was coming to admire her tenacity and spunk. Coupled with her physical attractiveness, it was only natural that the man in him should stand up and take notice.

So he forced himself to get back to work as a detective. He refused to think about the question that had been nagging him—*Why did she run away*?

"It's a beautiful farm," he said. "It'll be quite the thing to leave to your children." *There*, he thought. *Find out what happened to Lehrer's daughter*.

She turned to face the pasture once again. "Well, I'd have to *have* some first." This was said without guile, and apparently with complete truth.

It was all he could do to keep from staggering back and exclaiming, *"What?!!"* Lehrer had made it clear that his wife had fled with his daughter, who should be four years old now. Fled with everything, Kristopher had said. All photographs, toys...nothing left for a loving father to remember his daughter by. The child had been a small baby at the time Margo had disappeared.

He was able to tame his chaotic thoughts enough to comment, as if off-handedly, "What a shame. This would be a great spot for kids."

She gave him a strange look. "I suppose you're right. So—would you like to see the pond?"

"Sure." And they started walking.

Patrick's mind was in turmoil. No kid. Could Grace by lying? Could she have abandoned the baby, or adopted her out? Or—perish the thought—could the baby have died? But her few words hadn't suggested any of these possibilities. It was as if she were being completely truthful, which didn't bode well for his case.

Okay, so maybe this *wasn't* Margo Lehrer. Yet those eyes...

He vowed to search her office as soon as possible.

The pond was large and rectangular. "It was made about twenty years ago," she said, "for irrigation."

"Are those the irrigation pipes?" Patrick pointed to a neatly-stacked pile of twenty-foot long pipes.

"Yes."

"And let me guess: you moved them all yourself."

"That's right. I tweaked my back last week vaccinating the cattle, and I have to admit it hurt to move those pipes."

He shook his head. "No wonder you needed a man about the place."

She stiffened. "I don't know if I like your tone there..."

"Sorry. That didn't come out right. I didn't mean to imply that you haven't been doing an outstanding job here. What I meant is, everyone needs help every so often. No shame in that."

Her shoulders relaxed. "You're right. And it was after hauling these all back from the field before mowing the alfalfa that I realized it was stupid not to look at my options. When Dirk at the feed store mentioned that there was someone out there willing to work a farm..."

Patrick marveled how sometimes the most minor events in a detective's life can lead to such major clues. If he hadn't been right behind her car that day they drove through Faucet, if he hadn't seen her speak to Dirk as they'd slowed down, then he wouldn't have known to approach Dirk about finding a farm to work while he wrote his novel...

"Well, I'm glad it all worked out," he said. "This is beautiful, by the way. Look at those ducks over there."

"Canada geese," she clarified. "They nest here every year. And those are meadowlarks, western meadowlarks. They're the state bird of Oregon. Those little birds there, on top the bull thistle, those are lesser goldfinches. They eat the thistle seeds. And those are towhees. Can you hear the yellow-breasted chat? They sing at night, which is rather unusual..."

He watched her face, aglow with delight as she described the wonders of her little corner of the world. Her green eyes softened, her hands gestured as she pointed out the various birds. He could see calluses on those hands, hands accustomed to hard work. Unwittingly, he wondered what those callused hands would feel like on his body.

"...it'll work?"

Once again he had to emerge from his own thoughts to the uncomfortable realization that he'd completely missed what she'd said. "I'm sorry...?"

She smiled. "Woolgathering? You must be working out a scene."

"No. I'm, uh, working out the plot at this point, not the scenes. Er, what did you say earlier?"

"I asked if this farm will be good enough for your novel, if it'll work?"

"Oh yes. Yes, it'll be perfect." He forced his mind back into acting mode. "I'm envisioning a peaceful country scene like this, wholesome, provincial, but it disguises hidden motives for the characters involved. On the surface they're working the farm, but underneath they're working mayhem."

"Sounds exciting. Do you ever allow mere mortals to read your work in progress?"

"Nope. Never. Stifles the creative urge, you see."

"Of course." She glanced upwards at the sun. "Goodness, I'm talking too much. The lasagna's probably finished, and I've got chores to do."

"What do you need me to do tonight?"

They started walking across the pasture back toward the graveled road that led to the house.

"Not much," she said. "I have some canning to do tonight, but you can't really help with that. It'll all change tomorrow, though, when I'll put you to work."

****

"This is the best lasagna I've ever had," said Patrick. "Where'd you *get* this?"

Grace felt a niggle of pride go through her. "I made it."

"Yeah, but this cheese—fabulous..."

"As I said, I made it."

He paused, his fork half-way to his mouth. "You made the *cheese?*"

"Yes." She smiled a bit shyly.

He lowered his fork and began to pick apart the lasagna. "The mozzarella or the ricotta?"

"Both."

"The spinach?"

"From the garden. Along with the tomatoes and herbs." Her smile widened.

It was a game now, trying to guess what she *hadn't*

produced. She hadn't had a playful moment like this in years.

"The sausage?" he asked

"Last year's pig."

He peered at the lasagna. "The noodles!"

"My own eggs. I bought the flour, though," she finished in mock apology.

"You're amazing." He shook his head, forked up the last of his piece, and reached for more.

Grace felt a quiver go through her at the simple compliment. She didn't consider what she did amazing so much as a matter of necessity, yet the words were sweet.

Kristopher had never, ever complimented her, not after they were married. He'd complimented her constantly while they were dating; yet once the wedding vows were uttered, sweet words were rare indeed.

No, that wasn't true, she thought. In all fairness, he'd eased into that state of affairs, becoming more and more controlling over a period of time until one day she woke up and realized that sweet words were no longer a part of her marriage. Instead, constant suspicion on his part, constant vigilance to her every move, constant picking away at her friendships until she was isolated—all destined to make her completely dependent. And then the criticism had escalated into violence, and she had been trapped.

She focused inward, concentrating, checking. The 'prickles' came and went—mild and low. No danger, at least not yet...

"Hellooo...?" said Patrick softly.

Startled, she blinked a few times and looked at him. He was watching her with concern.

"You okay?" he asked.

"Y-yes. Of course. Why?"

"I thought I'd lost you there for a moment. You went off into your own little world."

"Sorry." Trying to hide her emotions, her memories, she lifted a glass of milk to her lips. "Not used to having people around, I guess."

She could sense that Patrick knew it was a lie, but he only said, "Dinner was wonderful."

"Thank you."

"How late will you be up tonight working?"

She felt a quiver of alarm. Questioning her every move had been one of Kristopher's methods. "I'm not sure..."

"Don't you have to milk the cows this evening?"

"No, I only milk once a day."

He lifted an eyebrow. "I may be a city slicker, but don't cows need to be milked twice a day?"

"They need to be milked. If the calf has the mother during the day but is separated at night, then the cow is satisfied with the schedule and I have more than enough milk for my needs."

"As I said, amazing."

"Well, I didn't think this one up. Hazel came up with the concept."

"So who was this Hazel, anyway?"

"The old lady who used to own this farm."

"And you worked for her?"

A shimmer of suspicion went through her. "Yes. She was widowed and in poor health. She needed help."

"And she left you the farm?"

"Yes."

"She had no kids, I assume."

"That's right."

"How did you hook up with her?"

She turned and looked at him. "Mr. Hess," she said in a soft voice laced with steel, "You're getting nosy. She just did. Let's leave it at that."

He lifted both hands up as if warding off a blow. "Hey, sorry! Just curious. Being a writer and all, I'm always asking questions, sometime to the point where they offend people. I apologize."

Her suspicion sank, like a crocodile sinking beneath the water—still there, but invisible. She nodded. "Apology accepted."

Patrick was a handsome man, Grace acknowledged. The small portion of her that was still a whole woman, rather than a battered ex-wife, was interested. But Grace had vowed to herself that never—*never!*—would she allow another man to have control over her.

Intrusive questions were part of the pattern leading to control.

"I've never met a woman as self-sufficient as you are," Patrick said.

The crocodile poked its nose above the surface of the water just a bit. "Is that a compliment?"

"Heck yeah. I'm trying to figure out now I can use that factor in my novel."

Alarm went through her, and she sat up straighter. "You—you're not going to feature me in this book, are you?"

"Hey, relax! Not by name or face, of course. But it's only natural that I should incorporate certain factors, including you, into the plot."

She wilted back against her chair. "Please don't. The thought of being i—" She stopped and bit her lip.

She saw Patrick glance at her sharply. "The thought of being...what?" he asked gently.

Grace could have cursed herself. She'd nearly said, "The thought of being identified." *That* would have a mistake. "The thought of being featured as a character doesn't hold much appeal," she finally said, rather lamely.

****

It wasn't what she was going to say, Patrick knew with a detective's instinct. She had been about to say "identified." He *knew* it.

To Patrick, some loose threads were starting to come together. Whenever someone was reluctant to talk about their past, his senses sharpened. It meant they had something to hide. And if Margo Lehrer had run away from her responsibilities and kidnapped their child, as Kristopher had accused, it was up to him to find her. Despite all the disparities, he was becoming more certain that this woman was Margo Lehrer. If only he could prove it...

The only damned confusing thing was that there was no evidence of a child. That was just about the only thing that made him think Grace wasn't Margo.

He couldn't afford to be wrong...again. Like he had been in Nashville. He *had* to see those scars.

Chapter Four

That evening, after Patrick left for the guesthouse, Grace canned up the last of the season's corn while she made a double batch of cookies for Lyle Coffer, her elderly neighbor.

As she baked, she thought about Patrick, residing not ten feet from her back door. She had spent the entire day in the company of a strange man. And she had enjoyed it.

She had to tread carefully around Patrick. He was attracted to her, she knew. Given the slightest encouragement, she might find she was attracted back. And then they might...*no!*

Her hands froze as she thought what might happen if she were attracted back. Rather than sweet expectancy, there was dread. A bitter gorge rose in her throat, a gorge of hatred so palpable that it nearly made her nauseous.

Kristopher was still haunting her. From all the way across the country, he could still affect her life and make her too frightened to think about the future with a new man.

Despite her complete change of identity, despite leaving her friends and home behind, despite four years of recovery, Kristopher still had the power to disrupt her happiness, and the fragile normalcy she'd built up around her. It wasn't fair; dammit, it wasn't *fair*.

With something akin to anger, she added the ingredients for the cookies and slammed in the blades of the mixer. Why was it that even burying herself deep in the countryside outside a small town in rural Oregon wasn't good enough to separate her from Kristopher?

She'd worked so hard in the last four years, guided at first by Hazel and then by her own impetus, to become self-sufficient, dependent upon no one—especially no man—to put food on the table or to supply her with happiness.

Oh, occasionally during the years, especially in the winter when there was less work to do and more long dark evenings to think, she would wonder if she was destined to spend the rest of her life alone. She was a normal woman, with a woman's needs. She wanted a husband—a sane one, thank you very much—and children someday.

It just seemed so unjust that the first man she had chosen had turned out to be so brutally dominating and emotionally devastating—and later, deranged and dangerous—that she could no longer pursue even the concept of a future marriage.

So Patrick would receive her gratitude, nothing more. She would allow no hint of attraction, no intimation of temptation, to tarnish his stay here.

She knew it was her job to keep her gratitude and attraction separate. The man was renting a room from her. He was not available to be the object of her famished affections. And though she had never experienced a faster or more enjoyable day since she'd had him to share it with, she knew that her judgment of men had been poor in the past. She was reluctant to test that judgment again.

Because, by God, the results in the past had been devastating and life-threatening.

****

Patrick awoke just as dawn was lighting the eastern sky. He lay in bed, listening to the early twittering of what Grace had called the yellow-breasted chat, which sang at night as well as during the day. He heard the deep bass voice of an owl calling, and a slightly higher-pitched response from another, by the brook.

It was so different from waking up in his Buffalo apartment. Here, there was no ceaseless bustling of the city. There were no buses, no exhaust fumes, no sounds of horns honking or people fighting. There were no sounds of anything, in fact, that were man-made.

Quiet. Peaceful. Dangerous...?

What could be dangerous out here in the countryside?

Well, what could? Lying there in bed, sniffing at the

cool morning air, Patrick began to formulate an idea. A plot. A story.

What the heck, he thought. *I'll have some free time around here, I may as well give it a go. It would add to my credibility anyway, if she catches me writing.*

To write a book. It had always been there, the idea, kicking around in the back of his head. God knows he had enough real-life experience as a detective to draw upon, enough to fill a dozen books. As he lay there, an idea started to organize in his brain. An idea about a story taking place on a farm, a plot involving a woman caught up in a maelstrom of...of...something rural...drug production, perhaps? A detective sent to crack the case and bring her to justice...

His mind swirled with bits and pieces of the cases he'd worked on in the past, or cases he'd heard about, picking bits here and pieces there. How could he bring all these loose threads together into something cohesive?

He threw back the covers and jumped out of bed. It took him only a few minutes to open his computer case and plug in his laptop. While it booted up, he yanked on jeans and a T-shirt. Then, wondering if he could do it, he sat down in front of his computer screen.

Wouldn't it be something, if he could really write a book?

****

It was in this position that Grace found him an hour and a half later. She knocked softly on the door to the guesthouse and heard the tappity-tappity of computer keys. "Patrick?" she called.

The tapping stopped, and she heard him say, "Come in!"

She opened the door and saw him crouched over a laptop. There was a dazed look on his face, as if he had been deep in contemplation. *What must it be like*, she thought, *to be a writer*?

"You're writing," she said.

"Yes." He gave his head a shake. "Sorry, I forgot the time. I imagine there are morning chores to do?"

"Well, Lyle's coming over around ten to bale my alfalfa."

"Lyle?"

41

"Lyle Coffer, my neighbor. He has a baler. He's coming round this morning."

"Anything I can do to help with that?"

"Yes. I'll pull the truck into the field while he's baling, and you can help me load it. Ought to take us through early afternoon. Keep those tough jeans on, you'll need them, as well as your long-sleeved shirt. Otherwise your arms and legs will get badly scratched. When's your best writing time? I don't want to interfere with your creative juices."

He flapped a hand. "Whenever the mood strikes. I've gotten a good start on this."

"Can you tell me what the plot is about?"

"Nope." Patrick leaned back and stretched his arms above his head. "First of all, it's not completely plotted out. Second of all, I make it a policy not to discuss my work in progress, just because I don't like having to defend or argue something so raw."

"I see. Sorry, I didn't mean to pry. It's just that I've never met a writer before."

"Yes. Well." He glanced at his empty wrist. "What time is it? How long before your neighbor comes?"

"He'll be here any minute. The fields are still damp—do you have rubber boots?"

"No."

"What shoe size are you?"

He looked surprised. "Ten. Why?"

"I think the boots that belonged to Hazel's husband's are still in the hall closet in the house. I can see if they'll fit you."

"Thanks. That'd be great."

****

Patrick breathed a sigh of relief when Grace left to look for the boots. He hadn't expected to get involved on his computer so deeply. But he had—and it surprised him. The rough idea he was getting for a story was beginning, just beginning, to make some sense.

She had asked about his plot. It was natural, he supposed, that she be curious. But he could hardly explain it to her, since his attempts at pulling something together were still too new to him.

He saved his work and shut down the computer.

Having Grace walk in on him while he was "writing" was an advantage. His entire credibility here depended on convincing her he was a writer. The more he was able to gain her trust, the sooner he could confirm her identity and be done with this case.

He heard the screen door slam, and a moment later she appeared in his doorway. "They're not in the hall closet," she told him. "Let me check in the pantry here. I know I've seen them somewhere..."

She began to rummage in the closet, and he walked behind her and stopped short, exclaiming in surprise.

The pantry was lined floor-to-ceiling with heavy shelves at least eighteen inches deep. Each shelf was completely filled with neatly-labeled jars of food. He saw peaches, pears, cherries, blueberries, blackberries, corn, beans, peas, soup, stew, chili, pizza sauce, enchilada sauce, plain tomato sauce, tomato paste...the different types went on and on and on.

"There must be a thousand jars in here!" he gasped.

"Here they are." She plucked a pair of knee-high rubber boots out of a dark corner. She glanced around at the shelves. "Yes, it wouldn't surprise me if there's that many jars here."

"When you said you stored canned goods here, I assumed it was stuff from the grocery store. But you did all this yourself...?"

"Of course. Here—try these on."

He ignored the boots, instead trying to understand the reason behind the jars. Something about it bothered him. *A woman prepared*, he thought. But it seemed more than that.

Staring at the jewel-bright jars, he sensed something—desperation, perhaps—behind them. Then he shook his head at his own folly. "Why do you have so much food tucked away?" he asked.

A veil came over her eyes. "It's what you do on a farm, isn't it?" she said, and he heard the forced lightness in her voice. "Preserve food?"

"But all this just for yourself?"

"I like to can." She dropped her eyes to the boots. "You might call it a hobby. Here, try these on. I think Lyle is here."

Patrick heard the sound of a large engine rumbling from outside somewhere. It was clear that Grace was avoiding the subject of the jars of food, and that bothered him even more. But he obligingly toed off his sneakers and slipped his feet into the boots. "They fit fine."

"Good. Let's get going, then."

He followed her through the house and out the front door, where she got into the cab of her truck.

"I hope there's enough gas," she muttered.

"Excuse me?" He slipped into the truck beside her and closed the door. Two pairs of leather gloves lay on the bench seat between them.

"The gas gauge in my truck is broken," she explained as she fired up the engine. "I can usually tell about how much gas I have left by the odometer, but I'm getting low."

"Why don't you get it fixed? That could strand you if you're not careful."

"I'm careful." She swung the truck around the barn and followed a green tractor up the road toward the fields. "And it's too expensive to fix."

No wonder she needs my rent money, thought Patrick, and briefly wondered if he had the wherewithal to fix the gas gauge for her.

They drove up the gravel road and pulled into the field of mowed alfalfa. The swathes lay in a squarish spiral pattern across the field.

Lyle was grizzled and elderly. He waved from the tractor and continued to twist in his seat, steering with one hand while monitoring the baler behind him. The baler clawed up the cut alfalfa and slowly spit out a bale behind it, dropping it onto the field.

"Oh good, he's using the three-strand baler," she commented.

"The three-strand?"

"Yes, as opposed to the two-strand baler. Three-strands mean heavier bales, but it's more compact when storing it in the barn."

"Oh great. And I'll be loading," he replied dryly.

"Oh, I'll be helping, don't worry."

He nodded. "After watching you lift that hay bale last night to feed the cattle—the one that weighed more than you did—I don't doubt it."

Grace raised an eyebrow but said nothing. She drove the truck alongside the first two bales and stopped, leaving the engine running. "Ready?"

"Ready."

They hopped out, slipped on their gloves, and seized the sturdy orange twine binding the bales. They hoisted the bales into the back of the truck, Grace just as quickly as he did. "You want to drive or stack?" she asked.

"Uh, I'll stack. I can't in good conscience leave that to you."

She grinned at him. "Never underestimate the power of a woman," she quipped, and he got the uneasy feeling that she meant more than just the physical strength necessary to lift a bale.

He was thankful for his heavy leather gloves as the twine cut into his hands. While he tugged and pulled the bale toward the front of the truck, she slowly bumped over the field to the next bale. By the time he had arranged the bale to his satisfaction, she had already hopped out and tipped the next bale up. She propped it against the lowered tailgate, then hoisted the bale onto the truck.

"Hey, I'll do that!" he said, feeling protective.

"Been doing it for years," she grunted, giving the heavy bale a mighty shove toward the front of the truck. "Just keep working. We'll set up a rhythm here pretty soon."

He had never seen such amazing strength in a woman. No wonder her arm muscles were roped. It crossed his mind that she would be a formidable opponent in a fistfight.

The sun grew warm. They did, as she predicted, develop a rhythm, where he pulled the bales into position in the back of the truck while she drove to the next one, and then hopped down so they could both hoist the bale into the truck at the same time. He didn't want her to lift those damn heavy bales alone just because he was slow to arrange them.

The truck held twenty-eight bales, stacked at angles across the sides and piled four deep, before it was full.

"Get off," she commanded suddenly.

He swung himself off the back of the truck and stood

by. "What's up?"

"I'll be right back. Take a breather while I go unload these."

Before he could react, she had jumped into the cab of the truck and started to drive away.

"Wait!" He ran to catch up with her. "Don't you want help unloading?"

"Nah. I'm just going to dump them in the barnyard. The hard part comes later this afternoon, when we have to stack them in the barn. Take a rest, be back in a minute. I'll grab us something to drink, too."

She drove off in a tiny cloud of dust while he stared after her, bemused.

This could not *possibly* be the elegant Margo Lehrer. Impossible.

In the sudden silence, broken only by Lyle's tractor on the far side of the field, he wandered over to the next bale and sat on it. His shirt clung to his back and the sweat dried on his skin. Somehow the morning's exertions so far made him feel—well, strong. Brawny. Virile. Like a man earning his keep.

"Just keep a lid on the testosterone," he murmured to himself. "Or that would *really* complicate this case."

He lifted his head and looked at the rural scene before him. The neat bales arranged in rows, the tidy swathes awaiting the tractor, the glossy leaves of the blackberries lining the field. The air was clean and smelled of fresh-cut vegetation, with just the slightest tinge of diesel from the tractor.

Unexpectedly a sensation of peace descended on him, a sensation so foreign to his occupation that he was forced to examine it.

He hadn't experienced much peace since he'd left off working his grandparent's ranch as a teen. Four years at West Point. No peace there, not really. Then four in the military working in special intelligence. Ditto. Five years as a private investigator. A lawsuit that had all but brought his firm to bankruptcy. Nope. No peace there...

He opened his eyes.

And now he was here. Here, sitting on a hay bale in rural Oregon. Here, fighting off an unholy interest in a fey, independent woman. Here, trying to prove that Grace

McNeal was in fact Margo Lehrer.

What strange twists of fate life could sometimes offer.

Grace's truck and Lyle's tractor came together at the same time. Grace hopped out of the cab while Lyle idled his tractor.

"Morning, Lyle!" called Grace above the noise of the tractor's engine.

"Morning. Fine day for haying."

"Yep. Might as well enjoy it while we can."

Lyle had a leathery face seamed from hours in the sun. He had small blue eyes that missed nothing, and darted back and forth between Grace and Patrick.

"Lyle, this is Patrick Hess. He's a writer, believe it or not, who needed farm experience for a book he's working on." She grinned. "Thought I'd introduce him to farm work with loading alfalfa. You know, a sort of trial by fire."

Lyle cracked a grin and reached down to shake hands with Patrick. "And how's farm life so far?" he inquired.

"Difficult. One of those you-never-appreciate-it-until-you-experience-it situations."

"What sort of books do you write?"

"Detective thrillers."

Lyle's eyebrows shot up into his scanty hairline. "On a *farm?*"

"That's what I said," inserted Grace.

"Hey, it sets me apart from the crowd."

"I suppose." Lyle chewed meditatively on a strand of alfalfa. "Well, to each his own. Me, I ain't got the time for much reading, 'cept the evening paper. Grace, I'll have this done in another three, four hours, then I was hoping for some of your cookies."

"Got three dozen oatmeal-raisons waiting for you at the house. Made them last night. They're in bags on the front porch."

Lyle nodded. "Thanks." His gaze shifted to Patrick. "Grace, she makes the best oatmeal-raison cookies for miles around. Lost my wife a couple years ago, and miss her home cooking. Grace here helps me through."

Patrick experienced a twinge of sympathy. "I'm sorry," he said sincerely.

Lyle's eyes shifted to the horizon. "Well, the Lord saw fit to take her. I'm just markin' time till I can join her. Nice to meet you, Mr. Hess."

"Likewise."

They stepped back as Lyle opened the throttle and began bumping over the field again, slowing spitting bales out behind him.

"Sad," commented Patrick.

"No kidding," agreed Grace. "It was rather unexpected. It was cancer that had progressed so fast that she had only two weeks after it was diagnosed before she died."

"Well, I suppose if you have to go, go quick."

"With enough time to say good-bye."

He turned to Grace. "Cookies?" he asked. "That you made last night?"

"That's right. I knew Lyle was coming today. He loves them."

"You must have been up pretty late doing that."

"I had some canning to do, anyway." At his raised eyebrows, she added, "Well, I had to do *something* while the corn was processing."

"So you made cookies for an old man who misses his wife."

She eyed him. "I made cookies for a neighbor who's doing me a favor by baling my hay."

"Even though you pay him by giving him a portion of your crop."

"Even though. This is the country, Patrick, and neighbors help each other out. Next time my truck is on the fritz, it'll take one phone call to Lyle, and he'll be here with his head under the hood. For no pay."

"Hey, I'm saying I think it's terrific!"

"Yeah, but don't elevate it to sainthood. It's just a neighborly thing to do."

But the trouble was, to Patrick it *did* smack of sainthood. It also didn't fit the image Kristopher had created for him of Margo, his ex-wife. Margo had been shallow and vain, Kristopher had said. The implication was that she would never take time to bake cookies—if she even knew how—for an elderly widower.

"Come on. I brought something to drink, then we'd

better get back to work," she said.

She handed him a cold bottle of juice. He unscrewed the cap and tipped his head back. The berry juice was cold and refreshing, tasting of hot summer days and cool moonlit nights. Patrick lowered the bottle and backhanded his mouth, then glanced at Grace.

Her mouth was open, her cheeks flushed. It was as if she suddenly had become aware of him as a man. He slowly recapped his bottle, keeping his eyes on her. "Good juice," he said.

He watched her Adam's apple bob as she swallowed. Then she dropped eyes and stared at her own bottle, still in her hands. After a moment she remembered to take a drink, then she reached out to take his bottle. "Let me have yours," she murmured. "I have an ice chest in the truck."

Patrick understood her avoidant stance, her averted eyes. That little tug of attraction between them wasn't just on his part.

So what. It didn't matter if there was any attraction or not. He wasn't free to act on anything, so he would just play his role, find his evidence, and get out of here.

He ordered his body in check, wiped his sweaty forehead with his shirt, and got back to work.

For the rest of the morning and past noon, they loaded alfalfa. By the time the field was stripped of the crop, Patrick was exhausted. So was Grace, he knew, though she wouldn't admit to it. But her shirt—even baggy—was just as sweat-soaked as his.

"A good morning's work," she said at last, sagging against the side of the laden truck. They had just loaded the last bale. Lyle had gone ahead, telling her that he'd pick up the cookies and come back the next day for his share of the bales.

"What's this afternoon?" inquired Patrick from on top the stack in the back of the truck.

"Stacking the bales in the haybarn. We got about two hundred, so Lyle gets around sixty-five or so."

Patrick looked at the empty field. "A swim is beginning to sound good," he said. He was hoping to see her in a bathing suit—purely for professional reasons, of course—to try and see the scars on her arms. "Maybe I'll try out that swimming hole you mentioned."

"I'd wait until after we stack the bales if I were you," she replied. She gave a tired sigh. "Well, let's get started."

The front of the haybarn was scattered with dozens and dozens of bales. With a sinking feeling, Patrick knew it would take hours to stack the damn things. His muscles were aching. His shirt was soaked with sweat. *The things I do to prove a case*, he groaned to himself. *There's gotta be an easier way to make a living. Lehrer, I hope you appreciate this.*

They went into the house for a late lunch of ham sandwiches. The milk was fresh, the bread was homemade, the ham was homegrown, the cheese was homemade, and even the mayonnaise, he noticed, came from a canning jar. She made her own mayonnaise? He wondered but was too tired to ask.

And after lunch they stacked alfalfa, bale after bale after bale in an endless succession. "You have to stack them so the bales won't tip and fall," she said, and grunted as she heaved a bale up higher. "A hundred twenty pound bale falling from fifteen feet up could kill you."

"If I remember right, you stack them brick-fashion, right?"

"Right. Hand me up another."

Patrick slid his gloved fingers under the twine and yanked it off the ground and up the growing stack. His muscles protested, but he couldn't stop. He had a feeling that if he did, then Grace would uncomplainingly take over and do the entire job herself.

But there was satisfaction in the work as well. When the job as finally done, they stopped for cookies and juice and sat on two of the bales reserved for Lyle.

Patrick stretched out his legs in front of him and leaned back against the barn wall. "I think I got my second wind while stacking," he commented. He bit into a cookie and instantly understood Lyle's penchant for them. "I'm tired but not exhausted anymore. There's something to be said for manual labor."

Grace leaned her head back and closed her eyes. He saw that her mouth was lined with fatigue. "Sometimes there's *too* much of it," she murmured. "Manual labor, that is."

"I don't know how you did all this yourself."

"Took a lot longer, that's for sure," she said. She raised her head and smiled at him. "You were a trooper, Patrick, really you were. I think haying is about the hardest job there is on a farm, and you certainly got that trial by fire I mentioned to Lyle."

He felt a warmth of appreciation. Her praise shouldn't make a difference; he was just investigating a case, that was all. But it did. It did, and that worried him.

He smiled back. "I'm still interested in that swim."

"Help yourself."

"Care to join me?"

She met his eyes briefly and skittered away. "Maybe."

His heartbeat thickened. The closing of this case could come as soon as she set foot in the water wearing a bathing suit. Viewing those scars would be sufficient evidence to prove her identity, and he could immediately report to his client that he'd located his wife, though he didn't know what happened to the child.

The thought filled him with far less enthusiasm than he wanted, but he mentally shrugged. *Them's the breaks.*

He stood up. "Well, no time like the present. I'm going to change into shorts and take a dip. See you at the brook." With what he hoped was nonchalance, he started back toward the house.

****

Grace had begun to gather up the remains of their snack when she froze, watching Patrick's retreating back. *See you at the brook*, he'd said. *Brook*, not *creek*. Grace was fully aware that people on the east coast tended to call a small stream of water a *brook*; people on the west coast tended to say *creek* or even *crick*, if you were of Lyle's generation.

But he was from Chicago, he said so. Her eyes narrowed. Still, she couldn't deny that slight broad twang in his speech, a certain pronunciation of the short "a" sound that was prevalent in such cities as Buffalo. Why hadn't she noticed it before?

She shook her head in confusion. She was unaware of any peculiarities of pronunciation from Chicago, never having been there. Was there such a thing as a midwestern accent?

You're just suspicious, Grace, she scolded herself. *The man's a writer, you checked out his references, he's certainly earning his keep, and it's been four years since you've heard from Kristopher. Don't be paranoid.*

Mostly convinced, she walked back toward the house. Now that she thought of it, a quick dip in the creek did sound rather good.

****

"Damn," breathed Patrick when he saw Grace walking toward the sandy bank of the brook. "Short sleeves."

Sure enough, rather than the hoped-for bathing suit, she wore frayed cut-offs and a snug short-sleeved shirt.

Still, after his initial disappointment, he noticed how her legs were long and lean. For once she wasn't buried in an oversized shirt. Her breasts were small and uptilted, and he could tell that she modestly wore a bra under her shirt. No wet T-shirt contests for her, it appeared.

Her short chestnut hair was spiky in places from the day's sweat, but she looked unbelievable wholesome and provincial and sexy. She looked like every man's dream woman.

"Come on in, the water's fine!" he called from the depths of the pool.

****

Grace was feeling naked and exposed, not because of her clothing but because she had taken off her gun belt. Still, she could hardly swim with it on...

She saw that Patrick was chest deep in the water, against the far bank where the gravel was deep and the trees arched over the creek. Briefly she wondered if he wore anything at all, and was conscious of a fluttering sensation inside her at the thought. His chest was lightly haired and hard-muscled. She noticed a light scar, about an inch long, on his right pectoral muscle, and wondered how he got it.

She kicked off her rope sandals and waded into the water. Rather than joining him in the pool, she satisfied herself with standing in water up to her thighs and dunking up to her neck. The water was cool and refreshing after the day's exertions.

She watched Patrick swim the two or three strokes it took to get to the end of the pool, then back. "If I had a bar of soap, I could take a bath," he commented.

"I'd go get some, but I'm not sure about adding soapsuds to the water."

"Home-made soap?" he teased.

"Nope. Store-bought. Still, I'd like to try making soap—I have a book on the subject."

She saw his teasing expression fade. "Dammit, Grace, I was joking."

Surprised, she looked at him. "I thought as much." Why was he annoyed?

"What's with all this independence stuff, anyway?" he asked. "Why do you work so hard to make all these things yourself? Cheese, pasta—even soap, if you could?"

She hardened inside, a sensation that she couldn't help. Out here, few people questioned her motives. All the farmers in the area—and even the townspeople in Faucet and Pincolla—were of similar ilk, independent souls who preferred to do for themselves. No one was curious about her past, about the road that had led her here, about the circumstances leading to this drive for independence. How could she explain this to a city boy, a stranger, a writer?

Ah, a writer. Of course. That accounted for his curiosity. She relaxed slightly, though the hard edge of caution remained. As a writer, no doubt he wanted to know the mentality of her and the locals in order to implement them into his characters, or whatever writers did.

She stood up, water sluicing down her soaked shirt. She waded back to the creek bank and sat on the sand, wringing water from her shoulder-length hair. She wrapped her arms around her legs and looked at him in the water.

"You haven't answered my question," he reminded her.

"No, I'm trying to think how best to reply," she said. Goosebumps rose on her legs as a slight breeze touched the wetness. "You really, honestly want to know?"

"Well, of course." He waded out of the water. Grace saw that he was wearing shorts, cut-off jeans similar to

53

hers. His abdomen was firm, his legs well-muscled. He was gorgeous, beautiful, an unbelievable specimen of manhood. She closed her eyes and let her chin rest on her upraised knees.

She heard him seat himself on the sand beside her, taking advantage of the late afternoon September sun. She kept her eyes closed, though his very nearness made her heart speed up and warmed her chilled skin.

"So what's with the self-sufficiency bit?" he prompted. "Aren't you taking it too far?"

"What's *too* far?" she asked instead. What she couldn't say was, *No, it's kept me safe all these years.*

"Too far would be killing yourself to make something that can be bought for very little money. Like soap."

She shrugged and tilted her face to the sun. "It gets self-feeding after awhile. You start with one thing, say milking a cow, and before you know it you start wondering just how much you can do."

"Just to say you can do it?"

She opened her eyes but didn't look at him, preferring instead to pluck a leaf from a nearby plant and strip pieces from the veins. "Perhaps. But if there's one hard lesson in life that I've learned, it's that you should *never* depend on anyone else. To me, that's come to mean just about every aspect of my life. Food. Water. Shelter. Eventually even things like soap. It's a continual learning process, and one I like doing, even if it's extremely hard work."

He gave a slight snort, though of amusement or contempt she couldn't tell. Out of the corner of her eye, she saw him lean back and prop his arms behind him, stretching his legs out toward the water. The pose emphasized the masculine lines of his body. "Sounds to me like you've been reading a little too much about the early homesteaders in these regions," he commented.

"No. I just—just like the independence, that's all."

"But how far do you take it? Even the early settlers had each other. They had other people banding together to bring in the crops, or whatever. No one could expect you to do it all by yourself."

"I don't do it all by myself. That's why Lyle bales my alfalfa."

"But—let me guess—you *would* do it all yourself if you *could*."

She looked at him, noting how a ray of late afternoon sunlight slanted into his brown eyes, lighting them and making them look almost feral. Yet those crinkles were around his eyes, the laugh lines around his mouth. *This man isn't dangerous*, she reassured herself. *Just remember that.*

"That's right," she said quietly. "I would if I could."

A cicada started to shrill in a maple tree across the creek, and encouraged by their immobility, a daring robin hopped to the edge of the water and began taking a bath in the shallows. But they remained suspended in their poses—he leaning back, she clasping her legs—watching each other.

Grace found herself enchanted by those laugh lines around his mouth, lines that bespoke humor and a good-natured personality.

A delicious, pungent smell arose, and she lifted the leaf she'd been stripping and held it below his nose. "Lemon balm," she said. "It grows wild here, all over the place."

He lifted his hand to take the leaf, but instead his fingers closed over hers. The sweet odor of the leaf drifted around them. Her fingers tingled against his and she sat as still as a statue, her heart thumping.

Almost without realizing it, they began to lean closer, experimentally, straining, until their damp bodies were nearly touching. Her eyes fluttered once or twice and then closed as Patrick's lips hovered nearer, his breath warm on her cool cheek.

Their lips were a hairsbreadth away when a sudden hysterical laugh-like birdcall shattered the quiet.

They jerked apart.

"Good God, what was that?" he exclaimed.

She drew a shaky breath. "Pileated woodpecker," she muttered. She cleared her throat and pointed. "See it? The large bird with the red crest?"

A woodpecker the size of a crow gave a resounding drumming noise against the trunk of the maple across the creek, and then tauntingly serenaded them again with its harsh rapid kik-kik-kik-kik-kik call.

She stood up.

He scrambled to his feet. "Listen, Grace, I'm sorry," he said. "I didn't mean for that to happen—"

"Forget it. Nothing happened."

"It most certainly did."

But she refused to look at him. She scooped up her sandals and turned away.

"Damn it, Grace, look at me." He swung her around and gripped her by the shoulders. "You made it clear when you brought me on that you were worried about being alone with a strange man. I promised to keep my hands to myself, yet I just broke that promise. I want to apologize, I—"

His voice trailed off, for the expression on her face was one of stark fear.

Chapter Five

He drew a deep breath. "What's the matter?"

"Take your hands off of me." Her voice was a whisper, her eyes enormous.

He dropped his hands, noting with alarm that he'd left prints in the damp fabric on her shoulders. "I'm sorry, Grace, I didn't mean to—"

She blinked once, did an about-face, and began walking up the bank toward the house. He trotted after her, more worried at her silence and somnambulist stance than anything else.

"Grace?" he probed. Then louder, *"Grace?"*

No response. It didn't seem as if she were ignoring him. It was as if, literally, she didn't hear him. Unwilling to grab her arm to slow her, he stepped in front of her and planted himself in her path, careful not to touch her. "Grace, answer me! What's wrong?"

Her glazed eyes focused on him, as if seeing him for the first time. "Nothing."

"That's bullshit and you know it. Will you *please* tell me what's wrong?"

"I don't like being touched."

"Oh." He pulled himself up, deflated and puzzled. "Why not?"

The shutters pulled over those staring eyes once again, leaving behind nothing but a robot, a shell of a woman. "I just don't."

She sidestepped him and kept walking toward the house. He followed, watching her rigid back as she walked into the house and disappeared, never looking back.

He was left in the backyard, staring at her, wondering what in hell just happened.

****

Once in the sanctity of the house, Grace found she

57

was shaking, shaking uncontrollably, shaking almost hysterically.

So it was just as she'd expected. An innocent touch, the beginnings of attraction, and she froze up. She balled up her fists and pressed them against her eyes. She would not cry. She would *not*. To do so would be to admit that Kristopher had won. Kristopher, who had spent years whittling her down until she was a miserable zombie to his violence, would be so pleased to know that his arm could still stretch out and hurt her now, four years later and three thousand miles away.

For the truth was, she *wanted* to be touched by Patrick. After four years of recovery, he was the first man in whom she was interested. And yet what happened the moment he touched her? Her mind shut down and her memories took over—memories that a man's touch was painful and vicious. For even when Kristopher hadn't been brutal physically, he had been mentally and emotionally vicious, telling her a packet of lies about herself over and over until she was forced to believe him. She *knew* Patrick was different—yet she'd behaved like a terrified rabbit.

Mechanically she stripped off her wet clothes and changed into dry. She slipped on an oversized T-shirt, and strapped on her gun belt as usual. Then she started to prepare dinner.

She expected Patrick any time. She knew he was hungry. But he didn't come.

With the meal on the table, she paused a moment, then stepped outside and knocked on his screen door.

"Yes?" he called.

"Dinner's ready," she said. "Are you hungry?"

He came to the door, his eyes sober. "I wasn't sure I'd be welcome," he said quietly.

"Patrick, I'm sorry for what happened." She met his eyes without flinching. "Just some...old hang-ups I'm working through, I guess you could say."

"And I'll apologize too. Here I was just saying that I wasn't going to press anything on you, and the next thing we know..." His voice trailed off, and he fell silent.

So did she.

Finally he heaved a sigh. "The truth is, Grace, I'm

58

finding myself attracted to you, and I promised you that I wouldn't do anything to make you nervous. Yet I have, and I'm sorry. That's why I didn't want to impose on you for dinner."

She nodded. "I appreciate your honesty. I wish I could say I'm attracted back—well, that is, I *am* attracted back, but...um...dammit, this isn't coming out well." She rubbed her eyes in a gesture of fatigue, and realized how bone-weary she was.

"But there are things preventing an interest from forming," he supplied helpfully.

She dropped her hands. "Yes. You could say that."

"That's just as well, frankly," he said. "I'm in somewhat the same predicament."

This news startled her so much that she jerked. Of course...he might well have a girlfriend somewhere, or for that matter a wife. Good God, what did she really know about the man? Maybe it was a good thing she had frozen up, after all...

It was if he read her thoughts. "No, there's no one else," he said quietly.

Relief flooded her. She stepped back from the doorway. "Well. Anyway, dinner's ready," she said. "Chili with garlic bread." She turned and fled.

Dinner was awkward. Toward the end, her spoon suddenly clattered down and she glanced at the darkening evening in some alarm. "Oh damn, I forgot that I let the cows into the upper pasture. I have to get Bossy and Ruby in for the night so I can milk them tomorrow morning."

"They won't come in automatically?"

"Not if they're in a new pasture." She pushed back from the table and snatched a large flashlight off a shelf. "I'll have to go get them. Back in a while." And she was gone.

****

Patrick stared at the screen door as it slammed behind her. In the sudden silence, it occurred to him that she would be gone long enough for him to make a hasty search through the paperwork in her office.

From the living room, he looked through the large picture window and could just make her out in the dusk, crossing the bridge over the brook. He turned and darted into her office. Hoping the small desk lamp wouldn't be noticeable to her from the distance, he flipped on the light and began to rummage.

He found some of the newsletters she did with desktop publishing. He found stacks of materials concerning bloodlines and breeders with Dexter cattle. He found literature on farming and pasture management. And at last—eureka—he found a stack of bills.

Yet as he rifled through them, he became frustrated. For every single bill—every single last one, and there weren't that many—was made out in the name of Two Creeks Farm. Electricity, garbage service, vet. There were no credit card bills, no mortgage bill, no car bills. It appeared that she had no debt whatever, and any bills sent were only in the name of the farm.

He opened the top drawer of a two-drawer file cabinet. He found past issues of newsletters she'd worked on, folders of farm receipts neatly divided into months, bank statements—all in the name of the farm.

He slapped the folder shut with aggravation.

He opened the lower drawer of the file cabinet. Here he found paid invoices from the local vet, fat files containing instructions from various household and farm appliances and equipment, and a folder containing, of all things, cartoons cut out from various magazines and newspapers. He glanced at one. It was an old *Far Side* cartoon, yellow with age, entitled "The Ice Crusades." It showed a bunch of burly crusading knights on ice skates, dancing in an intricate formation.

He smiled and slapped the folder shut with a little less frustration this time.

He slipped the folder back in the file, glanced at his watch, and was just shutting the drawer when he noticed the section way in the back: Medical Insurance. Medical Receipts.

Aha. Something *not* in the name of the farm.

He glanced at his watch and swore. She'd been gone fifteen minutes. He didn't dare take any more time. He rearranged everything the way it was, switched off the light, and headed back in the kitchen.

It was full dark now, and he noticed a bobbing

flashlight coming down the gravel road from the upper pasture. He suspected the flashlight was followed by two obliging cows and their calves.

He hoped that when he could get his hands on her medical receipts, he might find some clue about her past. One thing was for sure—if she *was* Margo Lehrer, she was damned good at hiding it. There was nothing to indicate what kind of past life she'd had. There were no family pictures of any kind around—not of her parents or siblings, grandparents, aunts or uncles. No one. There *was* a picture of an elderly lady on her desk, but he'd hazarded that it was the esteemed Hazel, not a relative.

Who was she?

And where was Kristopher Lehrer's child?

Some detective *he* was—he couldn't even pry out where her kid was located.

Of course, she'd said she had never *had* any kids...maybe she was telling the truth, in which case she couldn't be Margo Lehrer.

The bobbing flashlight disappeared into the barn. With a puzzled frown, Patrick went back into the kitchen and began cleaning up the dinner dishes.

The chili had been homemade, he was certain. No doubt she had grown the tomatoes and chilis and onions and beans, and she'd made the cheese as well. The milk was fresh, of course. The garlic and butter and bread were also home-produced.

He looked critically at the soapsuds rising in the sink. The soap, at least, wasn't homemade. But how in the world she managed to accomplish all this food production and still be walking upright was simply beyond him.

By the time Grace came in, he was elbow-deep in bubbles and half-way through the washing.

"Oh Patrick, you didn't have to do that," she said, a note of deep gratitude in her voice.

"Oh sure. You spend your day haying, you fend off assaults from your tenant, you cook me dinner, you go off in pitch darkness to get the cows...and you expected me just to leave the dishes to you?" He aimed a cocky grin in her direction as he rinsed off a bowl and stacked it in the drain rack.

"Well, I'll dry." She made to snatch up a towel, but he

was too quick. He grabbed it up first and flipped it over his shoulder.

"You'll do nothing of the kind. If you want to do anything, you'll make coffee. I could use a cup, and I imagine you could too."

"Coffee." She sighed. "Yeah, that sounds fabulous."

"Got the cows in?"

"Yes. No problem. They'll follow me to the ends of the earth for grain, so it was just a matter of waving a bucket under their noses. The hard part was keeping the rest of the cows from coming too."

He swirled the soapsuds around a plate. "Do you have enough alfalfa stacked to get your cattle through the winter?"

"I should." She filled a kettle with water and put it on the stove, then pulled a bag of coffee out of the refrigerator. She poured some into a mesh standup filter.

"Does it snow much here?"

"Not too much, not like they get in eastern Oregon or in the mountains. We get a couple good dustings a year, that's about all. Enough to look pretty."

"Do you miss the snow?"

Startled, she looked at him. There was a momentary silence.

"Miss it?" she asked at last. "How do you mean?"

"Didn't you used to live where there was a lot of snow?"

"No. I grew up in southern Oregon. We didn't get much snow there."

"Southern Oregon?" commented Patrick. "Sorry, for some reason I thought you grew up with snow. Me, I'm wondering if I shouldn't get away from those Chicago winters. I wouldn't mind missing the snow..."

****

Inside her head, alarm bells were clanging. Grace knew damned good and well that she had never, during their brief acquaintance, mentioned where she was from. Never. It was second nature to her not to discuss her past.

So why did he ask about growing up with snow?

"Last winter an early snow-fall caught me without my snow tires on," continued Patrick, rinsing a pot. "I nearly slid into a tree. Of course, I wasn't the only one.

Lots of cars were in ditches..."

The crocodile within her subsided again, barely poking above the water, and her racing heart slowed to normal. *You're too suspicious*, she scolded herself. *Patrick isn't any threat.*

She wondered if she would ever be able to stop lying.

****

The kettle began to whistle. Patrick chattered on about his close encounter with the tree while watching Grace out of the corner of his eye. Her hands were steady as she poured the boiling water through the coffee grounds and into the mugs. But he'd bet his bottom dollar she was lying about being from southern Oregon.

She was cool, he admitted. But her avoidant stance and the too-calm demeanor perked his senses.

"So—what's the agenda tomorrow?" He rinsed the sink, strung the dishtowel through the refrigerator handle, and joined her at the kitchen table.

She took a sip of coffee. "Not nearly as harrowing as today. I want to give the barn a good cleaning, as well as the chicken coop. I also want to walk the fences and check them, now that the cows will be in the upper pastures. I'm about done with the tractor for the winter, so I might give it a quick tune-up and close it down as well..."

He stared at her. "This is an *ordinary* day?"

"Well, yes."

"Man oh man." He shook his head and wrapped his hands around his mug. "I'd forgotten how hard farmers work."

She shrugged. "It's a living. We work hard three seasons of the year, and hardly work during the fourth. Once I have everything harvested and either in the barn, in the freezer, or in the pantry, I have a lot more free time."

"How did you get into farming, anyway?"

He felt rather than saw her stiffen, almost as if she were raising her shields.

"Hazel," she replied shortly.

"You worked for her, but what did you train in, get your education in? Clearly you've been to college, it shows in your voice and vocabulary."

"Psychology. Though I never did much with it."

A piece clicked into place for Patrick. Margo Lehrer had majored in psychology. "So farming was never a dream for you?"

"Not at first. After I started caring for Hazel's property, and hearing all about her life, I became more and more interested. And as she became less able to take care of this place, it fell more on me, and I grew to love it. By the time she'd passed on, I was running the farm, learning as fast as I could." Her voice grew soft. "She was a good teacher."

"Sounds like she was quite a lady."

"Oh, she was. I wish I could have known her husband as well."

"When did he die?"

"A good ten years before I knew her. Ten years—that's how long she kept the place up on her own before she finally admitted she needed some help."

"So she didn't hire you as a personal caregiver, in a nursing sense, but to help with the land instead?"

"That's right. The nursing was something that grew as she became more frail. Always kept a sharp mind, though, and a sharp wit. She had a sense of humor that wouldn't quit." He watched as she dropped her eyes and picked at a chip in her mug. "She had more than that, too," she continued in a low voice. "She had a tender heart and infinite patience..." Her voice trailed off.

Patience for what? wondered Patrick. But it was not the moment to ask. Instead he said, "Makes me hope I'm that way when I get old."

"Me too." She took a breath. "So anyway, about tomorrow, there's not much you'll need to do, unless you want to help clean the barn and chicken coop. You'll have some time for your writing."

"I might put some time in tonight." He lifted the mug to his lips and swallowed.

"So how did you get into writing, anyway?"

He nearly choked, hastily putting his mug down. Uh-oh, here it came, the natural curiosity on her part, wondering about his past. It was only normal, of course, to exchange histories over coffee. He could hardly keep it one-sided on his part. He crossed his toes inside his sneakers and prepared to lie through his teeth. He had already thought out a past "history" for himself, so it was only a matter of elaborating on the basic foundation of falsehoods.

"I used to be an insurance salesman, believe it or not," he said. "But I was one of those frustrated writer-types who always knew I could write a better novel than whatever I was currently reading. So one day I decided to put my money where my mouth was, and do it. Well, it was a pretty mediocre attempt—writing is a learned skill, just like anything else—but I took a bunch of writing courses and learned how to fix my problems." He gave her what he hoped was a self-deprecatory smile. "So I started sending it out to agents. One picked it up, sold it to a publisher, and it allowed me to quit my insurance job."

"It must be wonderful, to have a creative skill like that."

"Don't you? Have a creative skill, I mean?" Neatly he turned the tables.

"No." Her eyes dropped to her coffee cup.

She does, he knew instantly. *She does, but her confidence in her own ability has been undermined.*

"None?"

"None."

"I find that hard to believe. A woman as talented and intelligent as yourself..." His voice trailed off.

There was an odd look on her face, and he knew that she was no longer listening to him. He watched as an expression of searching, then of concern, then of pain, crossed her features.

"Grace?"

There was no answer. She sat stock still, staring at some point in the middle distance, with her hands still holding her coffee cup. The steam rose undisturbed from the hot beverage, but her fingers were rigid around the ceramic. Then her nostrils flared, she went very pale, and blinked rapidly.

"Grace?" His voice scaled up in alarm.

"What?" She focused on him.

"You okay?"

She blinked again, and gave a tiny shake of her head. "Yes. I'm okay."

"What's wrong?"

"N...nothing's wrong."

"You're lying." His voice was rough with concern. "Something *is* wrong."

He watched the shutters drop over her beautiful eyes. She firmed her lips and raised her chin. "It's nothing, Patrick. Nothing that concerns you."

The simple statement silenced him, for it was the truth. But he was left shaken by that expression on her face, the pain that had crossed her features. "Well, if you're sure..."

"I'm sure." She lowered her head and looked into her coffee cup. "Very sure."

He stared at the top of her bowed head.

There was silence in the kitchen. At last she raised her face to his, and he saw that the cool, controlled expression was back. "I'm tired," she stated. "I think I'll go to bed."

He took the hint and stood. "Good idea." He drained the last of his coffee and put his mug in the sink. "I'm pretty tired myself. See you at, what, eight o'clock?"

"That will be fine." She rose and turned away from him. "Goodnight, Patrick."

****

Patrick lay in bed, hands stacked beneath his head, and stared up at the dark ceiling. Cool air blew through the screen door to the backyard, and the sounds of crickets and the occasional great horned owl. Fall was in the air, the smell of drying leaves and the end of the ripening fruit. He could hear the brook burble past the house. Such different noises than he was used to. Peaceful sounds, restful sounds. At first, he thought he would be wakeful because of the lack of traffic and the usual city noises, but such did not appear to be the case.

He was wakeful for an entirely different reason.

Something wasn't right with this case. Working with Grace today, watching her react to his presence, his actions, that near-kiss before they were interrupted by the bird...these were not the behaviors of a spoiled woman who had fled her socialite responsibilities or the pressures of wealth.

Her actions were of a frightened woman used to physical abuse. Patrick had worked with too many such cases not to recognize it now. It was just that...well, it didn't sync with the story Kristopher had told him.

Kristopher had said that his rich little wife had fled with their infant daughter, apparently to spite him after the divorce. Margo Lehrer had been temperamental and unpredictable, he'd said, and he had concerns about the safety of his baby.

And where the hell was the baby?

And why had she dyed her hair? When she lowered her head over the coffee cup a couple hours ago, he noticed the blond roots.

Yes, there was a lot of stuff that wasn't adding up. He made a decision.

It was time that the very rich, very powerful Kristopher Lehrer had a little investigation done on *him*. Patrick decided it was time to call his partner, Jim, back in Buffalo.

Chapter Six

"Morning, Jim, it's Patrick."

The cell phone crackled and fuzzed. "Patrick!" boomed Jim. "How ya doing? How are things way out there in Or-ee-gonn?"

"Fine. I think I've located the woman, but I'm still working on trying to confirm her identity." The phone crackled some more.

"*Still?* How long does it take to figure out if she's the right one?"

"It's been harder than you'd think." Patrick ran a hand through his hair. "She's incredibly secretive. If she's Margo, she must have read the damn book on how to change identities, because there's nothing—and I mean *nothing*—to link her with her old life."

There was a crackly pause. Finally his partner said, "...can barely hear you. Where the hell are you calling from—the dark side of the moon?"

Patrick walked to the other side of the bridge that crossed the brook. He didn't want to risk being overheard in the guesthouse, so he was out in the pre-dawn stillness, well away from the house, in order to call his partner. He knew that with the three-hour time difference between Oregon and New York, his partner would be in the office by now.

"Sorry, cell phone coverage seems to be spotty here," he said. He stopped forty feet into the pasture as the interference on the phone lessened. "There—that seems to be better. Can you hear me now?"

"Yeah, okay I guess, but where are you?" Jim persisted.

"On a farm in Faucet, Oregon, about thirty miles south of Eugene," said Patrick.

"...on a farm...?" Jim's voice scaled up in disbelief.

"Why are you on a farm?"

"Because this woman I'm checking out, Grace McNeal, has a farm. I've told her I'm a writer who needs a little farm experience to add realism to my book. And, to prove my point, it's barely dawn here and I'm out standing in a pasture, cheek-by-jowl with a bunch of cows."

There was a fairly long pause and Patrick smiled, fully aware that his partner was experiencing disbelief warring with the urge to laugh hysterically at the situation.

"You're kidding," said Jim at last.

"Nope."

There was a subdued chuckle. "Good grief, the things detectives have to do."

"That's what I thought. And the funny thing is, I've hatched an idea for a book and may actually give it a go. Gotta do *something* to pass the time on these long country evenings."

"I suppose. You always did want to write the Great American Novel. So...what's up?"

"This case, that's what. Did you ever meet Kristopher Lehrer?"

"Lehrer? The one funding this investigation?"

"Yeah."

"No."

"Oh. Well I have, and he seems like a straight-shooting kind of guy. He's rich, he races cars for a hobby, he owns a chain of auto dealerships, and he's hot tempered."

"And you're tracking down his ex-wife and daughter," added Jim.

"Right. It's the same woman that at first I thought had gone to Nashville."

"Lehrer was pretty pissed, as I remember, when that turned out to be a dead end," added Jim.

Patrick experienced a spurt of temper at the memory. "Right. Though Lehrer's the one that told me his wife dreamed of being a singer and was probably in Nashville giving it a shot. Wasted three weeks chasing the elusive Margo all over the city only to find it was the wrong woman."

"So what's up now?"

Patrick began to pace, his usual stance when thinking things through. However, the cell phone crackled again, and he resumed his spot where the cell phone coverage was adequate. "What's *up* is that I want to make damn good and sure this woman is the right person before I notify Lehrer of anything, and the woman isn't admitting a thing. It's a little more complicated than I thought it would be, and I don't want another dead-end situation or another piece of Lehrer's temper if I'm wrong about her."

"Sounds logical. So what's the problem?"

"The problem, assuming that this woman is indeed Margo Lehrer, is two-fold. First, there *is* no kid, and she claims to never have had one. Yet all other signs indicate that she's the right woman. Second, and here's the thing that bothers me: she doesn't act like a disgruntled wife. She acts terrified. It's starting to look like an abuse case."

There was a muffled curse at the other end of the line.

"Yeah, I feel the same way," said Patrick. He pinched the bridge of his nose. "I'm getting sick of this kind of case. I sometimes wonder if I'm in the wrong line of work."

"Must be the rural life that's getting under your skin," quipped his partner. "Abuse cases are just part and parcel for a detective, and always have been."

"Yeah. Whatever." Patrick lifted his head. "Listen, I need you to do a little checking on Kristopher Lehrer while I continue checking out Margo. See if you can find birth records for the child—she's supposedly four years old now—and any legal or police records on Lehrer. The child could have been fostered out—remember the case where that happened a few years ago?—or put up for adoption, though I haven't picked up on any of that. And if in fact he's been beating Margo, obviously I don't want to let him know where she is."

"Obviously."

"Not a huge rush, but not a case to sleep on, either."

"Okay, give me a couple weeks and I'll have everything you'll need."

"Thanks, buddy. Oh, and don't call me, I'll call you.

Cell phone coverage is pretty iffy out here, so I have to pick a spot in this pasture to call."

"No problem. Give the cows a pat for me."

"I'll do that. *Ciao*, man."

Patrick turned off his phone and slipped it into his shirt pocket. He turned and surveyed the view before him.

The early morning was glorious, with small poufy clouds turning peach and gray and cream. The temperature was nippy and his nose was cold, but the air smelled fresh—like mown fields and sun-ripened berries and just a little bit like cow patties.

He could almost grow to like it out here.

The peaceful vista was so much in contrast to the gritty nature of his job that he felt a moment's envy of Grace. Wouldn't it be something to wake up to this kind of scenery on a daily basis?

He glanced at the thick hedge of blackberry bushes. The berries gleamed, large and ripe. He reached out, plucked one, and found it to be juicy and sweet. *I could pick some,* he mused, *and surprise her.*

He didn't want to be caught wandering the property at this hour of the morning, and then have to explain himself. He knew Grace would be out shortly to milk the cows. But if he were caught picking berries...well, that would be a good excuse. And he remembered seeing a bucket in front of the garden gate.

It only took twenty minutes to fill the bucket. He picked and plucked and began thinking about the book idea he was hatching. Before he knew it, his mind was off, charting possible twists and ideas, mentally recording scenes and possibilities. It was an exciting concept, the idea of actually writing a book. He was pleased with his efforts yesterday morning, and suddenly found himself anxious to get back and try putting more ideas into his computer.

He placed the bucket of berries on the back step on the house and hurried into the guesthouse.

For the next two hours he found himself alternately pounding the keyboard and staring vacantly at the middle distance, thinking, contemplating, plotting. He was writing a sketch of the story, just skimming it with ideas and putting thoughts on paper.

So when Grace knocked on his door, he went through the same procedure of blinking himself back to reality and calling for her to enter.

"You must be a morning person," she observed.

She was dressed in jeans and an over-sized blue sweatshirt—the air was still chilly—and looked like something out of an Ivory soap commercial. Her brown hair, with those blonde roots, was tucked behind her ears, and she looked fresh and wholesome and downright delicious.

"Excuse me?" he said, still emerging from his make-believe world.

"You must be a morning person," she repeated. "I found the blackberries, and here you are writing." She propped a shoulder against the doorframe.

He leaned back, then remembered to press 'control-S' on the keyboard to save his work, and leaned back again. "Apparently I am. I never really noticed it in the city. But I found this berry-picking to be rather good for plotting. Who'da thought?"

She chuckled. "For me, it's milking time that I find good for thinking. But I appreciate the berries. I'm going to can them this morning."

"Is that something I can help with?"

"Not really. Canning berries is simple. Are you finished for now? Or do you want to keep working?"

He shook his head. "No, I'm a little drained. I don't think I could get back to this for awhile."

"Is that how writers work? Drain themselves, and then do something else to recharge?"

How the hell would he know? "Well, it's how *I* work. I suppose every writer is different."

"I suppose. Well, breakfast is ready. Potatoes and eggs. I came to ask you how you like your eggs."

"Scrambled is fine, especially if you have a bit of onion you can add." Patrick rose and gave a mighty stretch, tipping this way, then that, bending at the waist. When he lowered his arms, he saw her look away, her cheeks pink.

Strictly off-limits, Patrick, he reminded himself.

They stepped into the house, where Patrick was assuaged with scents of bread baking and potatoes cooking and coffee brewing. God in heaven, it smelled wonderful. His life was a cycle of bachelor cooking. He hadn't experienced the simple joys of homey odors and delicious food since his teenage years. He suddenly realized he was starving.

He gave a small grunt as he sat down at the table and reached for the pepper. Grace looked up. "What's the matter?"

"Sore from yesterday," he muttered, rubbing his arm muscle. He flashed her a grin. "I'm not used to all the hard labor." He reached again for the pepper, being more careful this time. "I was a little stiff when I woke up this morning."

"Me too. Haying is hard work."

"I can't imagine you doing this all yourself." He peppered his eggs and forked a bite into his mouth, noting the incredibly fresh flavor. "You're one of the strongest women I think I've ever seen."

She kept her eyes on her plate and gave a small shrug. "I'm not sure if that's a compliment or not. I guess I'm strong, but it's only because I have to be, to get the work done."

There was a knock at the door, startling Patrick but not Grace. "That'll be Anna," she said, and rose to answer it. Patrick could hear a flurry of greetings at the door, and in a few moments, she returned to the kitchen with a middle-aged woman in tow. The woman had perfectly coifed hair, well-pressed clothes, nail polish, and a wide, friendly smile.

"Anna, this is Patrick Hess, he's staying in the guest house for awhile. Patrick, this is Anna Steele. She also raises Dexter cattle."

Patrick rose and shook hands. "How do you do?"

"Fine, thanks. What brings you out here to Faucet, Mr. Hess?"

"Call me Patrick, please." He reseated himself as Anna, clearly from long habit, helped herself to some coffee and joined them at the table.

"He's a writer," Grace told Anna.

Her eyebrows rose in surprise. "A writer? Here? Why not in Eugene?"

"That's what I said."

73

"What are you writing?" she asked Patrick.

"A detective thriller," he replied.

"But why are you here on Grace's farm?"

"Well, I needed a farm setting for my book."

"A *detective* book? Set on a *farm?*"

Grace laughed. "That's *also* what I said."

"Hey, it's how I set myself apart from the crowd." Patrick wondered why the comment about the setting for his book was starting to irritate him. Okay, he wasn't *really* a writer, but the plot that he was working on seemed to be going well. And so what if it took place on a farm?

The conversation settled on general comments about cattle, clearly a mutual love between the two women. They discussed meat prices, inoculations, de-horning versus polled cattle, the price of grain, something called a meat-to-bone ratio, milking techniques, and the next regional meeting for the cattle association they were in. Anna rose to refill her cup of coffee.

Grace scooped some blackberries into a bowl, washed them, and sprinkled them with a bit of sugar. She set them on the table along with spoons and bowls.

"Gorgeous!" exclaimed Anna.

"Patrick picked them."

"Thank you, Patrick." Anna dug into the berries. "I love blackberries, and never seem to get around to picking them."

"You have them at your place?"

She chuckled. "There's hardly a rural spot in western Oregon that *doesn't* have blackberries. Why, where are you from?"

"Chicago."

"Ah, a city boy."

"That's me." Patrick wiped his mouth and stood to clear his dishes from the table. "I'll let you two get to work," he said. "Is there something I can do while you're busy?"

"Would you like to walk the fences?"

"Sure. What am I looking for?"

"Just make sure everything is sound. Make note of any spots you think cows might be able to get through— sagging places, areas pushed down, that kind of thing.

"Will do. It was nice meeting you, Anna."

"Same here."

****

After Patrick's departure, Anna raised her eyebrows. "Nice butt," she said.

Grace burst out laughing. *"Anna!"*

"Well, it's true. I consider myself a connoisseur of nice butts."

"Well, I don't."

"You like him." It was a statement.

Grace sobered. "Yes. Unfortunately, I do."

"Why unfortunately?"

"Because I'm not free to pursue an interest in any man. *You* know that, Anna."

"You've been here four years. Do you think your ex is still looking for you?"

"Yes." From force of habit, Grace focused inward for a moment, then emerged once again. "Not at the moment, but yes. I still get the 'prickles' on a regular basis. He's thinking of me, Anna, and that's not good. Even after four years, he wants to find me. I can't risk getting involved with anyone, nice butt or not."

"Ah. Yes, I can see how that would put a damper on you pursuing another relationship."

"Yes." She used her spoon to trace a pattern in juice at the bottom of the bowl. "Kristopher wants to hunt me down and kill me. I can't get involved with someone else. I can't drag them into something like that."

"But Grace—does this mean you'll *never* be free to get married again?"

She raised troubled eyes to her friend. "God help me, I don't know. It's been four years, and I've stayed hidden all this time with never a peep from Kristopher. But I know he isn't done with me yet." Her hands clenched. "I get the 'prickles' fairly often, enough to know that someday, he's going to do something climactic for revenge. He's a stubborn man, is Kristopher, stubborn and obsessed and smart. And I have no doubt that eventually he'll find me." She unconsciously fingered her waistband. "And when he does, he'll kill me. Or try to. I don't know if I'll *ever* be free of him."

Anna sighed heavily, with deep sympathy. "You

should have hired a body guard, not a writer, to work your farm," she said.

Grace gave a snort. "Hire, nothing. The man's paying *me*. C'mon, Anna, do you really think I could have afforded to hire anyone?"

"I suppose not. I'm glad I sold those steers for you, then. The selling price will be a nice shot of income for you."

"You've got that right. Oh Anna, you've been such a help. I don't know what I'd have done without you."

"You'd have survived. You'd have survived." She cocked her head to one side and Grace saw a gleam come into her eye. "Still, take a look at that man's butt one of these days—it's not bad."

****

Patrick donned his rubber boots, grabbed a pair of leather gloves from yesterday's haying, and started out across the bridge. Once he was over the brook, he wondered where to start. Then he shrugged, turned to the right, and followed the fence line.

The property was fenced with field fencing, sturdy four-foot high wire square mesh spaced with T-poles. It was not the most durable of materials, he noted, as he donned the gloves and pulled off a branch that had fallen across the top of one section. He wondered how to improve it.

Some of the fencing was overgrown with blackberry bushes. He skirted these, figuring that even if the fences were flat on the ground in those areas, the cows wouldn't be able to penetrate it. He saw one or two spots where the T-posts were listing over, and reminded himself to mention them to Grace.

It was a pleasant day for a walk. The mid-September sun arced overhead, gilding the maple and black locust leaves a golden color. The blackberry leaves were starting to turn as well. But there were no overwhelming, dramatic explosions of color as was found on the east coast, where the forests would turn crimson and scarlet and orange. Here there was a general goldening of the landscape.

He walked along, eyeing the fences, thinking about Grace, wondering what in the world there was about the woman that made him want to protect her and comfort her. Not investigate her. Not confirm her identity. In his brief acquaintance with the woman, he knew that, should she turn out to be the Margo Lehrer he sought, she had left Kristopher for a good reason, not a flighty one. Of that he was certain.

What was *uncertain* was his personal interest in her. Professional indifference warred with his very male response to a beautiful, spirited woman. The fact was, he wanted to get to know Grace much, much better—and *not* with an eye toward reporting her whereabouts to a husband all the way across the country.

He doubted she realized it, but he could tell when she wasn't telling the truth. Yesterday, for example, when he'd tried to trap her into admitting that she came from a snowy climate. He had to admire her coolness and lying ability about being raised in southern Oregon. There was a manner about her when she lied—she became almost *too* confident, *too* cool, *too* innocent, *too* straightforward in meeting his eyes. It was an interesting skill, but it didn't fool him.

He finished walking the fence line along the lower pasture, and stepped onto the gravel road and through the gate into the second pasture, retracing the fence on the other side in order to walk the perimeter. Here, tucked into a corner, were a series of large wooden boxes on four legs, painted white. What were these?

He walked closer out of curiosity and saw a small opening at the bottom of each box. A noise warned him in time and he stopped. Of course—bee hives. There were ten hives, each bustling with activity. So Grace produced her own honey, too. He shook his head. Amazing woman.

If Grace was indeed Margo Lehrer, she had learned a stupendous amount in the four years since leaving Buffalo. One of the reasons Kristopher had been unable to locate her under his own steam, Patrick suspected, was that he'd been looking in all the wrong places. He'd been looking in cities, whereas this was about as far from a city as you could get.

She produced nearly everything she ate or used. Patrick found this strange. What was with the siege mentality? Unless...

Unless she was hiding.

A piece clicked into place.

He stopped dead in the grass, his hand gripping a fence post. Of course. *Damn it, Patrick, what took you so long?* he scolded himself. *She didn't get into town much, she said. It could be because she was hiding.*

From Kristopher.

****

When he returned to the yard, he noted that Anna's truck was still in the driveway. Rather than go into the house and disturb them, he instead went into his rooms and fired up his laptop. With the concept that Grace might be hiding out from Kristopher, he wanted to add that twist to his character and incorporate it into his plot. His heroine became a battered woman hiding from an abusive husband.

And now he had an opening scene, too. He bent over the little keyboard and started working out the images playing in his head.

> *It was one of those autumn days where the sunlight forced its way past the tattered curtains of the office window, lighting the dust motes which ebbed and flowed with the sweep of a cheap rotating fan. The kind of day where the smell of the fireweed in the vacant lot next door blended with the scent of hot asphalt and car exhaust, creating the perfume called This Is The City. Even the honking horns of the cabbies rising up four floors to his open window sounded fatigued and hesitant, like the end of a jam session by a pick-up band*
>
> *The man who came to Charles Pollock for help was strong. In control. Used to being obeyed. And willing to bankroll Pollock's Agency for another three months. It was an offer Pollock couldn't refuse.*
>
> *Oh, the job seemed easy enough: locate the guy's wife and child...*

There was a knock on his door, and Grace called out, "Patrick?"

He lifted his head and blinked, now familiar with the process of emerging from his writing world into the real world. "Yes? Come on in."

She swung open the screen. "Boy, you writers don't quit, do you? How's it coming?"

"It's coming well. Better than I hoped."

"Would you let me read some of it sometime?"

"Nope." He reached over and pressed the buttons to save his work. "Um, call it modesty, but I have a thing against anyone reading the unfinished product." *Especially since it's your story*, he thought.

"So—what did you think of the fences?"

"Overall, they looked good. A couple areas where the T-posts were pushed over somewhat, but nothing that looked urgent."

"Good. It's a constant job, keeping the fences up."

"I found your beehives."

She gave a delicate shudder. "They're not *my* beehives. I'm scared to death of them."

He raised an eyebrow. "Why do you have them, then?"

"They belong to a beekeeper working out of Eugene. He has hundreds of hives scattered around two counties. I'm just one of the many people who have his hives—they're wonderful for pollination and all that, they keep my fruit trees and berry bushes healthy—but I wouldn't touch them. He pays me about four gallons of honey a year as 'rent' for keeping the hives here."

"You're afraid of bees?"

"Wasps, actually. My first year here was a bad one for yellow-jackets. I stepped on a couple of nests and got stung at least eighteen or twenty times altogether. Ever since then I freeze up whenever I'm around a stinging insect."

"Interesting. You seem so strong and independent—I find it less intimidating that you have a fear, just like us ordinary folks."

She stared at him. "Me—intimidating?"

"Oh sure. It seems there's nothing you can't do. Except, I suppose, keep bees."

She gave a forced chuckle. "You're flattering me. I'm just as ordinary as can be."

"Yeah, right. Ordinary, when you produce things that no normal person would attempt. Like cheese."

"And lunch. Hungry?"

"Starved."

"I threw together a stir-fry."

****

After lunch, Grace prepared the berries for canning.

"What can I do to help?" he asked.

"You can wash the jars."

So he washed jars while she rinsed the berries. Grace enjoyed having someone to talk to during the mundane chore.

"We're ready to pack the jars now," she said, and handed him a wide-mouth funnel. "Fill the jars to about a half-inch from the top," she instructed, "but don't pack them down. The berries will squish if you do. Here's a slotted spoon."

She handed him the spoon, and his hand curled over hers. Startled, she froze and met his eyes. The power and electricity surging through her at the simple contact stunned her. It coursed through her body in the space of a heartbeat, centering down low, intense, and instant.

His hand stayed on hers until her eyes widened in alarm. Oh no, she wasn't the only one feeling it...that much was apparent.

"Grace," he whispered. Still holding the spoon, his hand tightened on hers, and he pulled her toward him.

She resisted, gently at first, then more firmly. It was almost as if they were having a tug-of-war over the spoon, when in fact it was a tug-of-war over whether she would walk into his arms or not.

That scared her. The last time she'd walked into anyone's arms, she couldn't get away until her very life was threatened.

****

Patrick saw the fear in her eyes, and he cursed himself. He removed his hand from hers. "I did it again," he murmured, and took a half-step backwards, putting distance between them. "I did it again. I'm sorry, Grace." He took a deep breath, trying to calm himself. "It appears that I can't seem to keep my hands off you."

She shut her eyes and turned away. She placed the

spoon on the cabinet. Then she gripped the edge of the sink, and leaned over it with her eyes closed. To Patrick it appeared she was in pain, and he became alarmed.

"Grace?"

No answer.

"Grace, are you all right?"

"Yes."

"Then look at me."

Slowly she opened her eyes and turned her head. When he saw the shimmer of tears, it felt like a fist had punched him in the gut. He felt like the lowest scum on earth.

"Grace, do you want me to leave?" he asked gently. "I can have my things packed in ten minutes, and then I won't bother you any more."

She blinked once—spilling one single tear over the edge and down her cheek—and her eyes widened. "N-no," she said. "No, Patrick, I don't want you to leave. I'm sorry for my overreaction. It's just that—"

"That someone's hurt you. Physically."

If possible, her eyes opened wider, until they seemed to dominate her face. "How did you know?" she whispered.

If this was indeed Margo Lehrer, Patrick vowed to himself, there was no way in *hell* he would ever let Kristopher Lehrer know where she was. "I've seen it before," he said briefly.

Relief flickered over her. She closed her eyes again for a moment, then nodded. "It's true," she murmured. Then she turned and handed him the spoon, and began filling the jars with berries. "It's true," she said again, and Patrick knew what kind of effort it took for her to act so nonchalant. "But I thought I was over the effects. It appears I'm not." She removed the funnel from a full jar and placed it over another, then stopped and rested the heels of her hands on the counter top. Then she turned her head and looked at him.

"The trouble is, Patrick, I find myself very much attracted to you. That worries me, and not only because of my past."

"Why?" He held his breath.

"Because I'm not free to look at another man. You see, it's the same as if I were married."

81

Chapter Seven

"Married." Patrick's mouth felt dry.

"Yes."

"The same *as if* you were married."

"That's right."

"To someone who abused you." His fingers clenched the spoon he still held.

"That's right."

"Yet you've been here what—four years?"

"That's right." She picked up her spoon and began filling another jar, but not before a spasm crossed her face, a hunted expression that turned his stomach.

He unclenched his hand and picked up a jar. For a few moments they worked quietly, spooning berries into jars as if that were the important thing.

"Did you divorce him, since he was beating you?" he asked at length.

"Yes. But he wouldn't let me go." She plucked the funnel off a full jar and placed it over an empty one.

Patrick worked efficiently, neatly, while his mind filed away her every word, her every nuance. She was scared. She hid it well, but she was very, very scared. He felt nauseous about his role in her life. "What do you mean, he wouldn't let you go?"

"He didn't want the divorce. He wouldn't sign any papers. Absolutely point-blank refused to even consider it."

"So you just up and left?"

"No. I wouldn't have been divorced then. But when he wouldn't sign the papers, I made him appear in front of a judge. I had to convince the judge that one of the fault-based grounds for divorce had occurred. It didn't take the judge any time at all to grant us the divorce, but my ex-husband was...was..." She stopped and took a breath. "He

82

was furious. He vowed he would get back at me for exposing his abuse, even if it was in the privacy of a courtroom with only a judge present. You see, he's a prominent figure in the community, and this just didn't fit his image. So he set out to make my life miserable. I stuck it out for a year, but he was becoming increasingly dangerous and obsessed. So I left."

"Did you get a restraining order against him?" Patrick's mind reeled. Lehrer had been insistent—had been *very* insistent—that Margo and he were currently married. Not divorced.

That meant Grace was a free woman. Whether or not she was Grace or Margo, she was a free woman.

"No, I never got a restraining order," said Grace.

"Why not?"

Her voice remained admirably controlled. "Have you ever known a restraining order to work against anyone except the law-abiding? He knew perfectly well that stalking me was against the law. And I knew perfectly well that a restraining order might be just the thing to tip the scales. We had one last encounter before I realized I needed to get away."

"Does he know where you are?"

"No."

"Do you plan on going back?"

"No." The simple word underscored the strength that Patrick had come to admire.

This was why he was beginning to hate his job. He asked his next question as casually as he could. "But are you far enough away from him? After all, you're only a few hours away from southern Oregon, where you lived."

"I'm far enough away," she answered without hesitation. Without missing a beat.

Man, the woman was an accomplished liar—if she was lying.

And that was the Big Question, wasn't it? Was she lying?

Okay, what did he have so far? He knew that Grace had been beaten by her husband. He knew that she had been here in Oregon about as long as she had been missing from Buffalo. He knew that some of her background—such as majoring in psychology in college—

83

coincided with Margo's background. She had the eye shape and color, and healed-over ear piercing, and apparently a natural hair color—the blond roots—that correlated to the photos he'd seen of her.

What didn't he have?

He didn't have an admission that she came from Buffalo. He didn't have any indication whatever of the presence of a child. He didn't have any evidence that her background story—that she was raised in southern Oregon—was not true. Her facial profile, especially her nose, differed from his photographs. There was the weight difference—Margo had been plump, Grace was slim. There was the matter of her legal status—Grace claimed to be divorced, Lehrer insisted they were married. And there was the very unusual occupation she'd chosen—farming. By all accounts it was the last thing Margo Lehrer would have done.

Which might, in fact, be why she was doing it. He glanced sideways at her, wishing he could see her arms. Scars? No scars? Therein lay the question to her identity.

Why don't you just come out and ask her, you idiot? he remonstrated with himself. After all, if he assured her that he wouldn't tell Kristopher Lehrer of her whereabouts, she would feel safe enough...

No she wouldn't. Of course she wouldn't. Patrick had enough experience with abused women to know that trust was a rare thing among them.

And she would never, ever trust him again if she learned who he was. To his dismay, he *wanted* her to trust him, and not just for professional reasons. This job was rapidly becoming a personal one as well as a professional one.

"You're awfully quiet," she said, slanting a side glance at him.

"Just wondering how I could alter history," he said. God, she was beautiful.

"History?"

He cleared his throat. "Yours."

"Ah."

"Meaning, I wish I'd met you before your husband did."

Her hands shook a bit as she kept spooning berries

84

into jars. "I wish that too," she said, in that same artificially-maintained conversational tone that he was beginning to recognize as disguising deep emotion. "I wish I could go back and never have become involved with my ex-husband to begin with."

"What was his name?"

She flicked a glance at him. "It isn't important."

Damn. Stymied again. "And you never had kids with him?"

"Nope. I love kids—enough that I could never hurt them. I had to hide the birth control pills, you understand, but I couldn't possibly bring children into that kind of environment."

Mentally he shook his head in bafflement. Kristopher Lehrer had been so terribly concerned over the fate of his baby girl...yet this woman was standing here denying not only having a child, but ever getting pregnant to begin with. Doubt flashed over him, doubt that she was indeed Margo Lehrer.

"God, I'm so sorry," he said hoarsely. He put his spoon down for a moment, and turned his head to look at her. "No one should have to put up with that kind of situation."

"No one should, but some of us do because of stupid, stupid decisions," she replied. He wished he could pierce that pitiful nonchalant tone of voice she was using. "But it's also my decision to never, ever become involved with that situation again."

"Meaning you're swearing off men?'

"Not necessarily, though I don't know if I'll ever feel free to become involved with one again. But obviously I have doubts about my judgment where men are concerned."

Guilt stabbed him. She would go ballistic if she were to find out why he was here, for it would prove, once again, her poor judgment...

"I can understand that," he said. He filled the last jar and noted that there were still enough berries left to fill another six or eight pints. He laid his spoon down and turned to face her. She started to rinse her hands in the sink. "And I apologize once again about making you uncomfortable. I'll make a promise to stay away from you, at least in ways that would be considered—inappropriate."

If his masculine ego was hoping she would protest this declaration, he was disappointed. For as she wiped her hands on a dishcloth, she met his eyes gravely. "Thank you," she said.

****

So he stayed away from her over the next two weeks, at least in terms of physical touching. It proved harder than he thought, but he stuck with his promise.

Still, she was everywhere, even when they were apart. The clear green in the sky during a colorful sunset reminded him of her eyes. The silky tassel on the cornstalks reminded him of her hair. The smell of crushed lemon balm recalled the feeling of her holding the plant under his nose that day. He feared he was becoming obsessed with her.

He saw her in the tangle of his bed sheets. His mind was full of that possibility, of seeing her in his bed. Yet such thoughts always brought a knot of dread to his stomach, for he knew for certain that once she found out why he was here, she would damn him into eternity.

That didn't stop him from molding the heroine in his book after her. He used Grace lavishly—her eyes, the steel in her spine, her physical strength, even that tendency to hunch her shoulders occasionally. And, in his book, he was going to damn well make sure his hero had a crack at the heroine in bed. Someone deserved some pleasure around here!

The weather grew chillier. The leaves turned brown and gold, and the wind gusted them off the trees.

"*More* berries?" she exclaimed. "You've been picking berries four mornings in a row!"

"It helps me think," he confessed. "I do a lot of…well, plotting, while I'm picking them." Oh, he thought and plotted, all right, with all thoughts focusing on the woman before him. Knowing her pleasure in getting the berries, he rose in the cold dawn to pick them for her. "What are you going to do with so many berries, though?"

She gave him a dazzling smile that buckled his knees. "Give me an hour, and I'll show you."

What she "showed" him was the most incredibly

batch of blackberry muffins he had ever tasted.

If Patrick sometimes worried that he was wasting Kristopher Lehrer's money by taking so much time investigating this case, he salved his conscience with the fact that he'd never enjoyed himself so much. It surprised him, this ease with which he slipped into the routine of provincial life. He brought his laptop outside in the afternoons, and typed while listening to the brook murmuring and the meadowlarks still calling their melodious song. He smelled the cows and felt the warmth of the autumn sun, and felt whole.

"How's it coming?" asked Grace. She placed a plate of shortbread cookies on the patio table next to his computer, and dropped onto the lawn next to him. She stretched her legs in front of her, and Patrick watched the sunlight burnish the artificial brown highlights of her hair.

"I'm getting far more work done on this book that I ever thought possible," he replied honestly. He took a piece of shortbread. "I've never written in the country before. It's always been in the city. I'm finding it's making a world of difference."

And it was. To Patrick's utter surprise, he found that writing came naturally to him. He explored to intricacies of dialogue, the depths of foreshadowing, and the pleasure of intrigue.

But it was the psychology behind the characters that he found most fascinating. In turning his novel into a thriller, with the heroine being stalked by her ex-husband, he found it interesting to examine the motives for his characters.

He looked at Grace, sprawling on the lawn beside him. She had her eyes closed and her face tilted to the sun. His throat closed. She was so beautiful...so beautiful...

He felt his body stir, and he ordered it in check. He promised to keep his hands to himself, and he'd stick with that promise. But the woman sitting beside him so innocently made that promise weigh like a stone around his neck.

****

September progressed into early October and the

mornings grew darker.

Grace caught Chester, the bull, in the act of breeding one of the cows that had come into heat.

"The timing's good," she murmured, as they watched the awkward coupling between the two animals. "She'll calve some time in July, which is fine with me."

Standing beside Patrick, with their arms resting on the top rail of the fence, Grace found the situation oddly carnal. They didn't say anything as they watched the bellowing and pumping animals. But Grace felt a flush of heat spreading upward, tingling over her body in a way she hadn't felt in years. Years.

She didn't dare glance at Patrick. But she heard his breathing take on a rapid pace, and knew that he was affected too. That realization brought a stab of lust to her midsection. She felt her cheeks flush scarlet. If she were to turn to him this moment and flow into his arms, there would be no turning back. They would be mating as surely as the cattle. And God, how she wanted that...

She forced herself to turn away and unclench her fists. "Well, I'd better go feed the chickens."

From behind her she heard a small noise, almost a groan. "Right," he said after a moment. "I'll, um, go change the oil in your truck. I've been meaning to do that."

They parted, leaving the cattle to their pleasure while the humans denied theirs.

****

They pulled up the last of the garden plants. Then they spent two entire days loading the back of the pickup truck with partially-composted manure and straw from an enormous pile next to the barn, and spreading it on the garden. By the time it was finished, the garden lay two feet deep in the stuff, and the pile was gone from next to the barn.

"It'll compost over the winter and leach nutrients into the soil," she said, leaning on a rake and perspiring freely despite the October tinge to the air. "We can let the chickens out too, and they'll help dig things in."

"Should I do that now?"

"Let the chickens out? Sure."

Patrick walked toward the coop. Grace watched him

go, admiring the butt which Anna had so indelicately pointed out. She couldn't believe how helpful he had been. Spreading compost on the garden, for instance, usually took her a full week to do, and here they'd done it in two days.

She wiped a trickle of sweat from her forehead and looked at the winterized garden with satisfaction. The squashes and corn and tomatoes and beans and onions and carrots—all were put up for the winter, much of it with Patrick's help. Yet it was more than his physical assistance, though that was no light thing. It was his presence.

He was someone she could talk to. Having had no one since Hazel died, she hadn't realized how painfully lonely she'd become. Anna was the only other person who knew her background, and Anna was busy with her own life. Grace's isolation was self-imposed, yet that made it no less difficult to bear. There were times, especially in winter when the rain came down incessantly, that she would sit by the flickering flames of the woodstove and wonder if she would be alone the rest of her life.

Then Patrick had come. Patrick, with his ever-helpful interest in everything she did. He had accepted her story about her background, and didn't probe much when she fed him the lies she had perfected four years ago. Patrick, with his lean frame and wonderful butt and high cheekbones and black hair that became shot with a bit of auburn in full sunlight. Patrick, with his quirky smile and strong hands. Patrick who was, miraculously, interested in her. Interested enough, as well, to respect her limitations and not push himself on her.

She closed her eyes and cursed Kristopher Lehrer for stalking her.

Then she opened them again, seized the rake, and started smoothing the bumpy mounds of half-composted material in the garden. Uselessly. Purposelessly. Because work, of course, was the universal remedy. Work was what she needed and craved to keep the memories and the grief at bay.

****

"I need to go in to Faucet this afternoon," Grace told him. "Do you want to come? You haven't been off the farm since we returned your rental car last week."

Patrick recognized an opportunity when he saw it. He wanted to rifle through her office, and this was his chance. He shook his head. "No, if there's nothing you need me to do while you're gone, I thought I'd do some writing."

"Sounds good. Anything you need?"

"Just you, home safe." He smiled into her eyes.

She paused as if startled, then gave him a slow smile back.

She was ready to go within ten minutes. "Do you have enough gas?" he asked.

She started the engine and glanced at the odometer. "Looks like it. I might fill up in town, though."

"Grace, you really should have that gas gauge fixed. It could strand you one day."

"Can't afford it," she said. She buckled herself in. "I'll be back in an hour or so."

Patrick watched her drive off, then turned and headed straight for her office.

After half an hour of thorough searching, he found nothing more interesting than references to follow-up care for a broken nose four years ago. That might explain the small bump, and possibly even the difference in her facial profile from his photographs...but it was all done under the name Grace McNeal. There were no references whatever to a Margo Lehrer, or to any life prior to her arrival at Two Creeks Farm.

If this woman was indeed Margo Lehrer, she had done a damn fine job of changing identities and covering her footsteps.

He left the office and hesitated by the small door leading up to the attic room. Then, shrugging, he climbed the steep flight of stairs and poked his head up into the room.

It was warm and stifling. A fly buzzed with monotonous regularity into the window, around the room, and into the window again. It was empty except for three boxes in one corner, which he examined.

Clothes. Nothing but winter clothes.

Turning to go back downstairs, he noticed a half-sized door inset into the wall at chest level at the top of the stairs. Clearly it was access to the rest of the attic section of the house.

He opened it, noticed a string hanging down from a light bulb, and pulled it on.

It was hot and uninsulated. Rafters, beaded with resin sweat, arched low overhead and came down to meet the plywood floor. He noticed one or two old mud-dauber nests.

The space was stuffed. Toilet paper, paper towels, feminine protection, reams of paper, shampoo and soap and cream rinse. Kitchen dishsoap, laundry detergent, strike-anywhere matches. Gallon-sized jugs of Worcestershire sauce and soy sauce, jars of honey, bags of rice, and jugs of imitation maple syrup. There was even—and he blinked when he saw this—two boxes full of .38 caliber ammunition.

Full-metal jacket *and* hollow-point.

Two boxes. Each box held—he peered at the printing on the side—twenty-four smaller boxes of ammunition. And each small box held fifty cartridges. Let's see—twenty-four times fifty was twelve hundred. Of full metal jacket cartridges. And there were another twelve hundred hollow-point cartridges, a far more deadly and powerful option.

Slowly he reached up and pulled the string to turn off the light. Then he closed the door and headed down the stairs.

Okay, so she must have a gun in the house, at least one .38 revolver. Well, why not? On a farm, there must be any number of instances in which a gun could be handy. Besides, she was a woman living alone...

He hesitated in the middle of the living room, looking it over with a critical eye. There was nothing out of place, nothing out of the ordinary. Her books were mainstream. Her furnishings were mainstream. Everything about her was so very, very ordinary—almost calculatedly so.

Except for those boxes of ammunition.

Conscious that Grace might be returning at any moment, Patrick decided to do his laundry. He gathered his soiled clothes and loaded the washing machine.

He was turning to go when something caught his eye.

There was a pile of Grace's laundry in the corner. On

top of the pile was the pair of shorts she had worn that morning.

Puzzled, he picked them up. There was a wide band of sweat saturating the top of the shorts, about five inches wide. Sweat. Five exact inches of sweat. Interesting.

What would cause such an unusual pattern? It was far too wide for a belt, which she didn't need anyway since the waistband was elastic. But what else could it be?

He remembered once glimpsing what he thought was a kidney-protector under her shirt, a logical thing to wear during the heavy lifting of the day. But they hadn't been doing any heavy lifting today.

There was something compelling about the pattern, something unusual and, he felt, important. He furrowed his brow and absently rubbed a thumb across the dampness, but found no answer. Finally he laid the shorts back on the pile of clothes and left the room. But it continued to nag him.

****

Patrick rose before dawn the next morning with a craving for coffee. He figured Grace would be milking the cows, but she wouldn't mind if he helped himself.

He opened the door to the guesthouse and stepped out into the breezeway. The sky was indigo blue, lighter toward the east, and stars still lingered overhead. The air was chilly and fresh, smelling of the coming winter.

He was just about to push open the door to the house when he stopped.

She was sitting at the kitchen table, writing something, bent over in concentration. A single wall sconce lamp lit her face, throwing it into attractive planes and angles. Her collar-length hair fell over one shoulder as she worked.

He watched her for a few minutes, admiring the sheer beauty of the woman. She wore a terrycloth bathrobe tied in the middle, pajama bottoms, and fuzzy slippers, yet the appearance was somehow seductive—as if she'd just risen from bed, a sight any man would find erotic. The bathrobe tie loosened, resulting in an intriguing shadowed V at her chest before she absently gave the tie a yank. He wondered what she would do if he were to undo the tie and slip her out of the robe.

A steaming cup of coffee sat at her right elbow.

He felt it would be rude to just walk inside, so he raised his hand and tapped lightly on the glass window of the door.

Her reaction stunned him. She gave a wild jerk and clapped her hand to her lower back in a reflexive gesture, as if she'd wrenched it badly. Then she whirled around, clutching the back of the chair with one hand and the table top with the other. He glimpsed a look of stark terror on her face, all out of proportion to the situation, a fear that was pitiful to behold.

When she saw him, she relaxed and smiled shakily, then motioned him in. He watched as she rearranged her face into a casual expression. "You startled me!" she exclaimed.

"I guess I did. I'm sorry, I didn't mean to. Your back okay?"

"My back?"

"I saw you grab your back. I hope you didn't pull a muscle or anything."

"Oh. No, thanks, my back is fine. Is—is there anything you needed?"

"Coffee." He tried to break her tension with a warm smile, but the strain lingered in her eyes. "I woke up with this urgent need for some caffeine."

"Coffee. Fine. I'll get it for you—"

"Grace, I frightened you. Sit down—I'll get my own coffee."

She all but collapsed in her chair. He noted that her face was still pale, and he could actually see her pulse beating in her throat.

She had been terrified. His mouth compressed.

"Actually, I need to get dressed and go milk the cows," she murmured. She gathered up what he saw were farm receipts and fled to the bedroom.

He poured himself some coffee and departed for his guesthouse. He vowed not to bother her again that early in the morning.

****

The winter rains started. The brown, dry slopes and hills around them soaked up moisture like a sponge.

Grace found Patrick standing in the breezeway,

93

listening to the pattering of the rain on the clear corrugated plastic overhead.

"What are you doing?" she asked.

"Listening to the rain," he replied, and smiled at her. "I realize how long it's been since I've heard any."

She smiled back. The sweetness of his action touched her. He was listening to the rain. Just standing there, listening. And he was willing to admit it, too. She didn't know why, but his simple pleasure struck her as profound. He was so different from Kristopher. She was enchanted.

The moment grew and lengthened, as they smiled at each other and listened to the tin-roof-sound of drumming overhead.

Finally she realized she must break the reverie or risk looking lovesick. "I was going to start a fire in the woodstove," she said at last. She closed the door behind her and descended the two concrete steps to the breezeway. "It's starting to get chilly. You'll want a fire tonight too, I'm sure."

They gathered wood and kindling from the woodshed next to the guesthouse, and carried them to the woodstove in the living room.

"Do you heat only with wood?" asked Patrick.

"Yes." She opened the side door to the stove and checked it, then adjusted the damper before starting to crumple some sheets of newsprint.

He crumpled too. "And it keeps the house warm?"

"Mostly. It tends to get cooler in the corners such as the bedrooms and the kitchen, but not overly so. The fan helps," she added, pointing to the ceiling fan. "I can turn it on low, and it helps push the heat around the house."

They crumpled a small pile of paper, and he watched while she heaped the paper inside, stacked thin strips of wood over it, and struck a match. Within moments the fire roared up, consuming the paper, and she shut the door and adjusted the damper.

"There." She crossed her arms and watched the flames through the isinglass windows of the stove. "I love the first fire of the season," she said with deep satisfaction.

Patrick loved watching the play of flames on the

planes of her face, reflected in those incredible eyes. But he only said, "What about the chimney? Won't it need to be cleaned?"

"Oh, I did that yesterday."

He stared at her. "You did? When?"

"When you were writing."

"How did you do it?"

"Like I do it every year. Put a ladder up the side, climb up with the brushes, and clean the stovepipe."

"You amaze me. I would have thought that was a man's job."

She looked at him. "But you forget," she said gently. "I don't have a man to do it."

"You have *me*."

"I have a tenant who is helping with the farm work. I didn't presume that would include climbing onto the roof and cleaning the stovepipe."

"Well, it would have." He set his jaw. Somehow it bothered him that she hadn't asked for his help.

"You've been so obliging—"

"Dammit, Grace, I don't want to be *obliging*..."

She stared at him in surprise, and he cursed under his breath and turned away. What *did* he want?

This is a job, he reminded himself. *You're turning it into something personal.*

But that's what it was becoming. Something intensely personal, something *unbelievably* personal.

"Patrick?" came Grace's voice from behind him. "What's wrong?"

What was wrong? What was wrong...was that he found himself afflicted with a desire to possess her. Physically, mentally, emotionally—everything—he wanted to twine himself with her until there was no way they could be separated. And this worried him. Not only was it against every professional ethic he knew about, but she was just as unavailable to him as he was to her.

Besides, some might call those feelings obsessive. And if there was one thing that would make Grace flee, it was another obsessive man.

That didn't stop the feeling, though. And it was up to him to control himself.

"Nothing," he said, fists clenched, staring at the wall.

95

She gave a small laugh, a sound of tinkling bells, as she bent to open the stove door and add more wood. "That's the biggest lie I've heard you say since you've come here," she commented.

He turned to answer her, and then caught his breath and stopped dead.

She was bent over, peering into the stove, and the oversized sweatshirt she wore was hitched up a bit, stretched across her back. And he saw it.

A gun.

A small .38 revolver was strapped upside down into a wide band around her waist so that it rested in the small of her back. It was a handy position, requiring her only to reach behind and yank the gun out of its Velcro straps. The steel caught a flash of flame before it was covered again by her shirt as it fell back below her waist when she straightened.

Apparently unaware that he'd glimpsed the weapon, she stood a moment, watching as the flames caught, before securing the door again.

In his experience, women carried guns for only one reason. They were afraid.

Suddenly, the little mystery of her sweat-soaked shorts came clear. He knew what caused it. Her type of holster was made of a flexible material called neoprene, the same stuff used to make orthopedic knee braces. It was designed to secure around the body in a flexible band about five inches wide, with the gun resting in the small of the back. That would also explain her reactive clapping of her hand to her back that one time he startled her early in the morning while seeking coffee.

His anger died, along with all physical desire. Instead, he felt a protective instinct well up, a wish to keep her from all harm, from all the reasons why she might feel the need to wear a revolver at all hours of the day or night. She looked at him, expecting an answer to her earlier comment.

"Nothing's wrong," he replied, this time in a soft voice, "except what's been wrong since I've come here." He reached out and brushed a strand of hair behind her ears. "You. That's all." Then he tucked his hand into his back pocket, as if he didn't trust what it might do on its own.

Chapter Eight

Grace found she and Patrick worked well as a team. Whether it was tightening up the fencing or making butter or cleaning the barn or making pasta or halter-training a calf, the work flowed as they chatted and learned about each other.

He kept his hands to himself. She kept hers to herself. It wasn't easy—that spark of attraction hadn't died—but they did.

She was amazed by his willingness to help with anything on the farm. He was as interested in the mechanics of a pressure canner as he was in the mechanics of the tractor as she showed him how she winterized it. He tried his hand at giving a shot to one of the cows. He took his turn cooking, and to her surprise made some delicious meals. He attempted to make cheese, and produced a mozzarella that proved tolerable, if a bit on the runny side.

He even offered to learn how to milk, coming down to the barn in the darkness of early dawn.

"They'll be leery of you," she told him, as she unlatched the barn door. "Cows are creatures of extreme habits. Any change in the routine throws them off."

The cows didn't appreciate a stranger in the barn with them. They backed away toward the end of their stalls and wouldn't turn around to settle down and eat their grain without some coaxing. Grace finally got Bossy into position first and showed Patrick how to milk.

He wasn't very good at it, so mostly he stood and watched, not talking much.

"Talking will disturb them, since I never talk when I'm in here—after all, I don't have anyone to talk *to*..." she said.

****

Patrick watched Grace as she milked the animals. Her hair fell over her shoulders and bobbed a bit with her rhythm. The dim overhead light threw shadows across the planes of her face, highlighting a cheekbone while leaving the temple in darkness. Her eyes were lowered, watching her hands, and her lashes created a dark chaos of shadows across her cheeks. Patrick felt his throat close. She was so very, very beautiful.

The calves bawled in hunger and Ruby, the second cow, shifted and bellowed. Grace finished milking Bossy and, hardly missing a beat, she emptied her milk into a bucket, swung the crate around, gave Ruby her grain, and settled in to milk the second cow. Each animal took a mere fifteen minutes. At the end, the bucket was nearly full.

"You can see why I need to make cheese and such," she said, as she emptied the last of the milk into the bucket. "This much milk, day after day, would overwhelm me in no time."

"Yet these guys don't give nearly as much as a commercial dairy cow."

"Oh no, not a fraction as much. I get a little over a gallon between the two of them, and I only milk them once a day. It's more than enough for me. Lyle, he comes in about once a week and takes home a gallon or so."

She covered the bucket with a clean cloth, let the cows out, and then let the calves out. Once the cows were in the barnyard, the calves dashed up to their respective mothers, fiercely butted the udders with their heads, and began nursing with gusto.

Patrick chuckled. "Hungry, aren't they?"

"Yep. That one—" She pointed to Ruby's calf. "—is a steer. I'll keep him and either sell him for meat or keep him for my own freezer. Bossy's calf is a heifer, and is more valuable. She's got good bloodlines, and I'll probably sell her as a breeder."

They watched the animals a few minutes longer, and then headed into the barn to clean up the night's mess and spread fresh straw in the stalls.

She sighed with satisfaction as they crossed the bridge and skirted the garden to walk up the back steps to the house. "I love milking," she confessed. "The smell of the cows as I milk, the satisfaction of producing—or maybe I should say harvesting—something so elemental to my diet, making butter and cheese with it...it's just so *satisfying*."

He chuckled. "Not bad for a city girl," he teased without thinking.

Immediately he knew he'd made a mistake. Even without looking, he could feel her stiffen, and when she answered, she spoke in the nonchalant voice he'd learned meant she was hiding something. "I'm *not* from the city," she replied, opening the back door. "That is, unless you could call a suburb of Medford, in southern Oregon, the city."

"Well, I meant you'd never worked on a farm before."

"Now *that's* true..."

And he dropped the subject.

****

He borrowed her truck and went into Faucet. He bought a cordless screwdriver and a bag of screws. It was amazing, the number of little fixes he could make with so elemental a tool. He spent an entire afternoon with Grace trotting beside him in a haze of gratitude, showing him the things that needed tightening. He had rarely felt so satisfyingly *manly*.

****

Even from fifty feet away, the hum of the bees was pervasive.

Grace gave a shudder. "I simply don't understand how he can do that," she said.

They sat on a slight rise of ground. Grace had her arms clasped around her knees. Patrick lay with his legs sprawled in front of them. The October day was snappy and gorgeous, with the sun shining through the yellow leaves.

The beekeeper was harvesting the supers of honey from the hives. A cloud of bees whirled around him, despite the smoker he used to calm the majority of the insects. He was well-attired in thick coveralls, heavy gauntlets which he had rubber-banded around the wrist, and of course the bee veil zippered to his collar. She noticed him jump once or twice as the occasional bee managed to get through, but mostly he was well-protected

99

from stings.

"Oh, I don't know," mused Patrick, watching the beekeeper. "There's something fascinating about them. The idea of a domestic insect has always been interesting."

"Well, have-at. Me, I'll stay away from them and just be grateful that I don't have to risk the stings he's getting."

Patrick brushed his shoulder against hers. "I'd rather be stung by bees than endure some stings by people."

Grace had no answer to that.

****

Grace lay in bed, tired as always. She *always* tried to be tired by bedtime. An exhausted body succumbed to the blessings of sleep faster.

But sleep eluded her tonight. Bitterness, overwhelming at times, took a new direction this time. Yet another one of the many reasons to curse Kristopher—because now he was preventing her from taking a second look at the best man she'd met in years. A man who was sympathetic, who was gentle, who was understanding. A man who had a great butt, as Anna had so succinctly put it.

A man who, apparently, found her attractive as well. After years of being told that no one would ever be interested in her except Kristopher, she had doubted her own looks and talent and esteem to the point where she was a shadow of her former self. These, she now knew, were the classic tactics of a batterer: to reduce the self-respect of the victim to the point where she wouldn't dare to seek help because she was convinced she was scum.

Well, he'd done that. The only difference was, she'd left anyway. And Kristopher couldn't abide that. One day, she knew, he'd come after her. She fingered the revolver she kept under her pillow at night.

But Hazel had helped her grow beyond that mentality. Dear, darling Hazel, bucking her up on her bad days, filling her mind and her heart with a healthy ego boost.

And now there was Patrick.

She closed her eyes and focused inward, seeking, probing. Kristopher wasn't thinking of her at the moment.

Of course, it was three hours later in Buffalo than it was in Faucet, Oregon. No doubt Kristopher was sound asleep right now.

But he *had* been thinking of her lately—a lot. The 'prickles' had been coming thick and fast in the last few weeks, catching her at odd moments and giving her the shivers. Something was going to happen.

Something big.

****

For Patrick, the point of no return came on a drizzly, warmish afternoon, when he raised his head from his writing and listened.

He heard singing.

He crept out of the guesthouse and listened. Grace *was* singing. It *had* to be her. But oh God, that voice...he never knew she had it in her.

He pressed his nose against the screen and peered into the house.

She was wearing an oversized sweatshirt, as usual, and he knew the shirt was hiding her holster. Her back was toward him as she kneaded bread dough.

She was singing along to a CD as she kneaded. It was an eerie song, Celtic in tone, about a woman driven mad by grief from a lost romance.

Some women had silver voices. Grace had a golden voice—deep, clear, pure unalloyed gold. Shivers ran down his spine. It was a staggering talent—stunning, magnificent, brilliant. Just listening to her transfixed him, making him as incapable of stepping over the threshold as if his feet were in concrete.

Whatever emotion she couldn't, or wouldn't, express in life came out in her singing. Patrick stood frozen on the steps, pressing his nose against the screen, listening like a man in a dream.

The song ended, and another came on that made his skin go cold. He listened to the words of a woman abandoned by a man she thought loved her.

"No one noticed when she died—" sang Grace with deep pathos, and his throat closed up. "Something gone within her eyes...her battered soul was lost, she was abandoned—"

He shut his eyes in pain. The purity, the perfection of

101

her voice only made the words harder to bear. Had that happened to her? Was her battered soul lost, was she abandoned?

The song ended. Grace finished kneading the bread dough and turned around, her heart still in her eyes from the words of the song.

Their eyes slammed together and held, and in that moment he fell irretrievably in love with her.

Time stood still for a few moments while he swallowed hard. Finally he spoke, and his voice was hoarse. "Is that what happened to you?"

She lowered her head and didn't answer. Patrick yanked open the screen door and stepped inside. "Well?" he demanded.

She spared him a glance. "Maybe."

"Maybe? That's all you can say, is *maybe?"* He ran a hand through his hair, frustrated. Grace began to wash her hands, scrubbing off the dough, her lips compressed together. "Something lost within your eyes, a battered soul, abandoned?"

"Leave it be, Patrick. It's none of your business." She turned off the water and grabbed a kitchen towel.

"I'm falling in love with you, and you tell me it's *none of my business?"*

She dropped the towel and her hands went up to clutch her neck in alarm. Her eyes grew enormous and dark as coal. *"What?"* she whispered. "What did you say?"

He heaved a sigh. "I'm sorry, Grace. I didn't mean to say that."

"Patrick, did I hear what I thought I heard?"

He met her eyes unflinchingly. "You did."

"But you *know* my circumstances...you *know* how complex my life is right now."

"Knowing and feeling are two entirely different things, Grace. Listen...I've never come right out and asked you, but—are you in hiding?"

There was a long, very long silence while she probed his eyes as if seeing into his soul. For once, Patrick wasn't asking because he was a detective. He was asking because he was a man.

Finally she spoke. "Yes."

He nodded gravely. "And do I have any hope?"

"I doubt it."

Again he nodded. "And is that because you don't have feelings for me? Or is it because of your ex-husband?"

"My ex-husband," she whispered.

"I see."

"Patrick, please try to understand." She lifted her chin, and he heard a thread of steel in her voice. "He'll kill me. He'll honestly try to kill me if he ever finds out where I am. I can't possible involve another human being in those kinds of complications. It wouldn't be fair."

"I can take care of myself."

"I don't doubt that you can. But is that what you want, Patrick? A woman connected to a deranged man who is just mad enough to be clever and not draw attention to himself until he commits the final act?"

"And you really think he'd try to kill you?"

"Yes." The single word, uttered with surety and dignity, convinced him.

Almost, *almost* he told her then. Almost he just came right out and asked her if she were Margo Lehrer, and confessed his real reason for being here. But he stopped just in time. Instinct told him that she would bolt if he confessed.

"What about legal action?" he asked her. "You could have gotten a restraining order. There are anti-stalking laws in every state now."

"A restraining order wouldn't have worked with my husband. You don't know him the way I do—it would merely have inflamed him and crystallized his desire to kill me." She held herself straight and still. "Besides, have you ever known anti-stalking laws and restraining orders to really work," she added, "when the person is not only obsessed but unbelievably intelligent? My ex-husband is very rich, very powerful, and can pull all the legal strings he wants. I didn't dare to get a restraining order against him. It—it would have been counterproductive. So I've learned to cope on my own."

"By wearing a gun everywhere you go?"

She went pale, sheet white. For a moment he thought she was going to faint. He reached for her, but she stepped back, and his hand fell away.

"How did you know?" she whispered.

103

"Last week. Your sweatshirt hitched up for a moment, and I saw the revolver."

She touched her waist, and he could see her calming herself. "It's necessary."

"Necessary?" he snapped. "Is it *necessary* to live your life under a cloud of fear? So much so that you wear a gun even when you're way out here in the country?"

"Yes."

How was it that the simplest syllables from her lips were as convincing as an oratory? He had come to learn that Grace was not a woman to dramatize anything. If she thought it necessary to wear a revolver for her personal safety, then it was. It was as simple as that.

"And this will prevent you from ever living a normal life? A life in which you can pursue a relationship with a normal man?"

"It might."

"Even though you're divorced?

"*Especially* because I'm divorced."

"Why is he so obsessed with you that he won't let you go?"

A spasm crossed her face. "I wish I knew."

"You must have *some* idea..."

But she shook her head. "Beyond the concept of a puny, helpless woman crossing wills with the all-powerful, no. He considers himself above the law. He thinks himself so superior that he will squash anyone in his way that becomes an irritant. I became more than an irritant—I was defiant. And I had the audacity to leave before he wanted to let me go. I must now be squashed."

Patrick felt a shudder go through him at the hopelessness of her words.

"So you see, Patrick, it's not that simple," she continued. She picked up the kitchen towel and began to crumple and uncrumple it. "If I were an ordinary battered woman, I could leave, go to a shelter, get a restraining order, all the things the law provides for. But I'm not. I am the obsession of a brilliant, sick man, a man who is rich enough and powerful enough to make me spend the rest of my life on the run. And *that* is not something I would impose on anyone else." She met his eyes gravely. "No matter how I felt about him."

He exploded then. "Dammit, Grace, how can you say that so *calmly?* What are you going to do—live in limbo for the next forty, fifty years, never relaxing, always on the lookout for when he'll come hunting for you?"

Her face contorted with anger, and her fists clenched the towel. *"Calmly?"* she spat. "Don't you *dare* stand there and accuse me of being *calm* about this! Do you have any idea of what it's like to live under a reign of terror? It alters your whole personality, your whole outlook on life. I've changed. I don't trust people, it's hard to smile at strangers..."

"Yet you took me in...!"

She recoiled as if he'd threatened to hit her. "So I did." The anger died from her voice. "God knows I had my doubts, but there's something about you, Patrick. I trusted you. I don't know why, but I did. I—I trust you enough to tell you I'm in hiding. I've told that to very few others." She turned and hung the kitchen towel on a hook.

A powerful jerk punched his midsection. If he'd toyed with the notion of telling her who he was before, it died a swift death now. For she would never, *ever* trust again if he told her at this moment...

He shoved his hands in his pockets so she couldn't see them clench into fists, then took a deep breath. "I suppose I should apologize again."

"For what?" She picked up the large bowl that had held the bread dough, brought it to the sink, and began to clean it.

"For further complicating your life. I suppose the last thing you need is a lovesick writer hanging about your neck."

She closed her eyes for a moment, even while her hands continued to scrub at the bowl. "I know I sounded ungrateful—"

"Ungrateful, nothing. You sounded confused. Angry. And rightfully so." With his hands still in his pockets, he leaned the small of his back against the kitchen counter.

"You've given me something very important, Patrick. Hope."

"Hope?"

"Yes." She was busy, rinsing off the bowl, letting the excess water drain off it for a few moments, wiping it down. "There's a common mentality among battered women about their own importance. You begin to doubt everything about yourself. Your talents, your accomplishments, your worth. Your attractiveness."

She took a paper towel, wrapped it around her hand, and dipped it into a container of shortening on the counter. She greased the bowl, tossed the paper towel into the garbage bag under the sink, and carried the bowl to the kitchen table. She hoisted the bread dough into the bowl and flipped the dishtowel over it.

"You're kidding," said Patrick. For some reason he couldn't credit her with those concerns. "You mean to tell me that you have doubts about yourself?"

She faced him and crossed her arms. "Yes."

"You sing with one of the most beautiful voices I've ever heard, you single-handedly run a farm, you have a brain that won't quit, you're beautiful beyond compare, and you *still* doubt why I'm attracted to you?"

She flushed, and he was certain he saw a shimmer of moisture in her eyes. "I'm not fishing for compliments."

"I'm not offering any. I'm merely stating the truth."

She whipped around and picked up the breadboard and took it to the sink for cleaning. The way her head was bowed over her work, Patrick had no doubt that she was fighting tears.

Finally she murmured, as if to herself, "I *knew* there was a reason I could trust you."

Now he felt like a troll. How on earth could he confess to her that her ex-husband was the one who had hired him to find her and confirm her identity? Yet, he consoled himself, he had not yet proved beyond a shadow of a doubt that she was Margo Lehrer. Not yet. Not until he found corroborating evidence, such as paperwork. Or her scars...

All he could answer was, "I hope I'm worthy of it."

She didn't look at him. "Why wouldn't you be?" She rinsed off the board and propped it behind the faucets to drain. Then she took a dishrag, wet it and wrung it out, and went to wipe the excess flour off the kitchen table.

"Grace, will you stop with the damn busywork and look at me?"

Startled, she paused in the act of wiping down the

table. He walked up to her, removed the cloth from her hand, and dropped it on the table. He turned her toward him. "I've wanted to do this from almost the first moment I saw you," he murmured. "Will it frighten you if I—"

"No." The word escaped her lips quickly. "No, it wouldn't."

"Good." And he lowered his head to hers.

****

He was so gentle that Grace instinctively knew he was holding himself in check. Her hands came up to his chest in an unconscious gesture as his lips skimmed hers, teasing, tasting, tempting. The tip of his tongue flicked out and touched hers, sending an unexpected shaft of longing spearing through her loins.

One of her arms crept around his neck as he angled her head into the crook of his shoulder, deepening the kiss in a manner that sent visions of glory beyond her closed eyelids.

She was aware of the point when lust hit him, for his body tightened and went almost rigid. Yet he kept his desire in check, treating her like dainty porcelain. She longed to tell him that she was a hell of a lot stronger than that.

She caught a flash—just a flash—of what joining with him might be like when her other hand came up and gripped his hair, drawing him in closer.

He gave the tiniest inarticulate moan at that, and yanked her close to plunder her mouth brutally. Yet it wasn't the brutality of hate and anger, as it had been with Kristopher.

This was the honest passion of a good man, and it sent rivers of gold through her veins as she responded with equal fire. Her blood sang in her body and she could feel how she affected him—his hardness pressing against her, the pounding of his heart, the strength of his arms.

He didn't go any further. He withdrew by degrees until they were merely leaning against each other, pressing forehead to forehead, eyes closed, lips parted, panting as if they'd been running.

"A very good reason to keep my hands to myself," he murmured at last.

"Why is that?"

"Because if I don't, I won't be able to contain myself next time. Good night, Grace. I'm getting out of here while I still can."

And he was gone, the screen door slamming behind him.

Grace stared after him, and felt like weeping.

Chapter Nine

She lay in bed, her fingers linked across her chest, and stared at the dark ceiling.

I'm falling in love with you, he'd said. She had tucked those words away inside her brain, too occupied with the emotions of the evening to examine them more closely. Now she mentally took them out, handling them carefully as if they were precious jewels.

She took out his kiss and examined it, too. She realized with some astonishment that she hadn't flinched when he kissed her. She hadn't been frightened. She hadn't thought his kiss would end in violence.

Instead, he had raised a latent passion in her, a physical desire that she hadn't felt in years. It had been there, briefly, with Kristopher, but he had extinguished it so thoroughly that she thought she was incapable of feeling passion anymore.

But it wasn't gone. It flared up now, all the more bright from being smothered. And coupled with those fateful words...*I'm falling in love with you...*

She closed her eyes and felt the sting of tears. If she were just an ordinary woman, she would take what Patrick had to offer with greedy hands. Take, and give back. Give and take. That was the way things were supposed to be, weren't they? But she couldn't. She was crippled with fear, and that fear had given her years of aching loneliness. She didn't want to be desperate and assuage that loneliness with the first decent man who crossed her path.

She shook her head. No, her feelings for Patrick weren't desperate. Her feelings felt like the mature love of a mature woman.

But how could she be sure? Her judgment about love had been poor in the past, and she'd spent years paying for it. Kristopher, too, had convinced her that he loved her after only a few weeks of dating. And she, a foolish young thing, had fallen for it. It was only after the ceremony that he'd turned into the possessive monster who broke ribs and noses and psyches.

And here was Patrick, after only six weeks of knowing her, saying that he loved her. Just like Kristopher had done.

She tossed and turned. The hours crept by. She turned on her bedside light and read for an hour without getting the least bit sleepy. She turned the light off again and thought about Patrick, lying not fifty feet away in the guesthouse. She turned onto her side and tried to punch the pillow into a more comfortable shape. She looked at her clock and realized that it would be time to get up in an hour and milk the cows.

She sighed and gave up. She wrapped her bathrobe around her pajamas, realized the house was cold, and went into the living room to start a fire. She crumpled newspaper, stacked it in the stove, put some kindling on top, and struck a match.

Within five minutes, the larger pieces of wood were starting to catch. Grace re-wrapped her robe about her and watched the flames through the isinglass windows of the stove, spreading her hands over to catch the first warmth as it seeped through the cast iron.

The weather was getting colder. Winter was coming. Winter, with its happy holidays and long dark evenings and reduction of farm chores that kept her so mercifully busy. And Patrick? How long would he stay? She didn't know much about writers, had no idea how long it took to write a book. No doubt he'd be gone by Christmas, and she would spend it alone, once again.

She closed her eyes and probed her mind. Kristopher was awake. He was thinking of her. Prickles ran down her arms, and she hugged herself and rubbed them away.

Depressed, she wandered into the kitchen, filled the teakettle with water, and set about making coffee. She heard the characteristic squeak of hinges on Patrick's screen door, and was not surprised when he tapped on the kitchen door a moment later.

"Morning," he said.

"Morning yourself."

He had circles under his eyes and his hair was tousled. "Couldn't sleep either, eh?"

"Not a wink."

"Thought I'd come in and beg for a cup of coffee."

"I've got the water heating right now. I started a fire, too. It's getting cold in the mornings."

"I've noticed."

"I guess I'd better check the stove, see if I need to put more wood on."

"Okay."

She wandered out into the living room, opened the side door to the stove, added another log, adjusted the damper, and then she and Patrick stood in front of the stove, staring with mesmerized fascination at the pretty flames flickering through the darkened living room.

They stood in silence. Grace wondered if his body throbbed in tingling awareness and his mind screamed with frustration. Like hers.

Finally he heaved a sigh, turned, and dropped into an armchair nearby. "Damn, damn, damn," he muttered.

A small smile hovered on her lips. "My sentiments exactly."

"So where do we go from here?"

"Go? We go nowhere. We can't."

"Because you're worried about him coming after you."

"Right. That's part of it."

"And the other part?"

She looked at him through the gloomy shadows of the living room, lit only by the flames of the woodstove and the faint light extending from the kitchen. His eyes were dark as ebony in the dimness. The pause lengthened beyond comfort, while she debated whether to tell him the truth. She finally decided.

"You said something last night that disturbed me."

"I did?"

"Yes. You said that you were in severe danger of—of falling in love with me."

"So I am."

"That's exactly what my husband said a mere two weeks after we'd met. He told me he loved me within two weeks of meeting."

Patrick's brows drew together. "I'm sorry, I'm missing something. What does that have to do with me?"

"Nothing, except the speed with which you made such a declaration. You can fall in *lust*, you can fall in *attraction*, you can fall in *like*—but fall in *love*? In such a short time? Love takes a long, long time to grow, at least to grow properly and healthily. We've known each other for only six weeks. I made a horrible mistake the last time I fell for that line. I won't do it again."

"Now wait just a minute!" Patrick jerked upright in his chair. "If you think I'm anything like Kristopher—"

Grace went pale. A resounding silence crashed into the room.

"How did you know his name?" she whispered at last, staring at him.

He paused for a microsecond before saying, "You said it at one point."

"No, I didn't. That name has been erased from my lips. I *never* said it."

"You must have. How else would I have known it?"

"I don't know. That's what I'm asking."

"Well, how else would I have known what it is?" he repeated.

Was he lying? She couldn't tell. From over by the chicken coop, she heard a rooster crow into the pre-dawn darkness. A cow lowed from far away. And the silence ticked on.

A white-hot trickle of terror inched its way up her spine. She believed him—she *had* to believe him—*did* she believe him?

She began to doubt herself. He'd never lied to her before, had he? Of course, how would she know if he had? Had she mentioned Kristopher's name at some point? She'd spent four years training herself not to speak of him, not to link herself in any way to the man she'd left behind, the man who wanted to hurt her. But then, she'd been talking about her past much more often and much more freely with Patrick than she ever had with anyone else.

So maybe she *had* mentioned his name.

Patrick was quiet until he finally said, "How can I convince you?"

Some of the blood came back to her face, slowly, and she felt less frozen. "I don't know," she said. She heard the tea kettle start to sing, and abruptly turned and went into the kitchen, pulling out an extra mug for Patrick, pouring coffee, handing him his, stirring cream and sugar into hers. They sat down at the kitchen table while the silence loomed large.

Finally she heaved another sigh, shook her head, and dropped her eyes to the mug before her. "I'm a suspicious woman," she said at last. "Another thing about me that's changed. I never used to be. I apologize, Patrick, for doubting you."

****

It was a good thing Grace wasn't looking at him, because it was Patrick's turn to blanch, this time with self-loathing. *At what point does a detective defect on a case?* he wondered silently. *When he falls in love with the subject being investigated?*

Because there was no doubt that he was in love with the woman sitting before him. He was also battling demons because of the man who was paying Patrick's bills. The fact that she'd slipped and said that magical name had confirmed her identity. But a name wasn't *proof*, concrete proof. Scars were.

He no longer needed to see the damned scars. She had as much as admitted that the name of her ex-husband was Kristopher. That clinched it for him.

It also eliminated any possibility of getting her into bed with him. What right did he have to make love to her after the devastating emotional past she'd had? To increase her vulnerability—which sexual intimacy would naturally do—would put him in the category of scoundrel, blackguard, knave. Bastard.

He suppressed the urge to run his fingers through his hair in frustration. He couldn't remember a time when a case had affected him this way. He *never* became personally involved in his cases, and he'd done more than his share of investigating beautiful women. A modern detective, unlike the movies that tended to dramatize these sorts of things, spent a good deal of time finding out if a spouse was cheating. Usually it was a matter of trailing the person in question for a week or two, snapping some pictures, and *bam*, the case was closed. But he'd never been called upon to travel the entire country on a lead that was four years old and spend weeks living with a woman in order to confirm her identity.

Suddenly he remembered something, something Kristopher had said which sent a trickle of cold down his spine. He'd asked Lehrer if Patrick should try to convince Margo to come back with him, but Kristopher had declined.

"Just find her," he'd said. "I'll do the rest."

And now, knowing Grace and the fear in which she lived, he wondered just what *the rest* entailed.

It was definitely time to call Jim, his partner, and find out what he'd dug up on ol' Kristopher Lehrer.

"Still wondering where to go from here?" asked Grace.

"Yeah." He gave her an off-center grin. "You might say that." He gave in to the urge to run at least one hand through his hair, rumpling it even more after his restless night. "Tell me something. Go back to what you said about not getting a restraining order—was it your attorney who recommended that course of action?"

"I don't have an attorney."

If she'd suddenly stood up on the table and stripped naked, he couldn't have been more startled. As it was, he reeled back in shock, staring at her. "What do you mean, you don't have any attorney?"

"Just that. I don't." She looked at him in surprise at his reaction. "Why? Should I?"

"Did you *ever* have an attorney?"

"No."

"Ever?"

"No! I don't have the money for an attorney. Now stop gasping like a fish and tell me what this is about!"

"Please don't take this wrong, Grace, but that's about the least intelligent thing I think I've ever heard you say."

Her lips compressed, her nostrils flared, but she kept an icy control over her temper. "Are you going to tell me what this is about or not?"

He regarded her with a hardened eye. "Okay, just this: a restraining order, even when it technically doesn't work, leaves a paper trail. If you had been advised by an attorney not to seek a restraining order, even *that* would leave a paper trail recording proof of your concerns that your ex-husband posed a danger to you. By just fleeing, though, you don't *have* a paper trail. This could make things, ah, hard to prove in court should you need to resort to violence if he ever shows up."

She went pale for the second time that morning. Her eyes grew enormous, her skin white as marble. "But it wouldn't have stopped him. It wouldn't have stopped him from hunting me down."

"Are you sure?"

"I'm sure. You don't know him the way I do. He's very calculated and precise and controlled in his vengeance, but he's also remarkably thorough. Let's put it this way: if he ever found out where I lived, it would take him a matter of days to be at my doorstep. Maybe hours." She touched her waist with an unconscious gesture. "And then I wouldn't give my life a penny's worth of value."

Patrick winced, to know that he himself was part of the thoroughness of which Kristopher seemed capable. He suspected now that the child in question had never existed, that Lehrer had manufactured the baby in order to garner more sympathy and make his story of a socialite wife fleeing her responsibilities more believable. And he, the damn fool that he was, had bought the story hook, line, and sinker.

"Dammit, there's got to be some way to keep him away from you!"

"He *is* away from me. I've spent four years making sure of that."

"But that's just because you're in hiding. But legally—"

"Legally there's nothing I can do until—*until*—he commits an act of violence against me. And then, I may not be alive to press charges against him." She suddenly jerked her head around to glance at the kitchen clock. "Oh Lordy, I've got to go milk the cows. Have another cup of coffee, Patrick, I won't be long."

She trotted toward the bedroom and closed the door, then hurried back through the kitchen attired in jeans, with a flannel shirt left loose over what he had no doubt was the gun belt. She opened the back door and slipped on her rubber boots she left there each night. "Back in a bit!" she called, and was gone.

Her departure was so sudden that he sat in surprise. In the silence of the kitchen, he got up to look out the window. The eastern sky was flushing green and purple and rose, and he could just make her out as she hurried across the bridge.

Now would be an excellent time. Holding his mug, he crossed the breezeway to the guesthouse and picked up his cell phone.

****

By the time Grace returned with a pail of milk, he had the information he needed, and he felt like a damned fool for it.

Kristopher Lehrer *had* lied. There was no child, or at least no records indicating one. Margo Lehrer had a history of broken ribs and at least one broken nose. She had no family to protect her or speak for her. Kristopher Lehrer had been a careful man, with the exception of the medical history of his wife, not to break the law in any other respect. He was still considered an upstanding member of the community, a rich man who owned a number of racing cars, who raced as a hobby, who owned a string of auto dealerships, who contributed to charities and donated time and money to worthy causes and—this was the ultimate irony—had started Safe House, a shelter for battered women.

Perhaps he thought that was where Margo would flee if she ever left him.

In light of these facts, Patrick was already composing his letter of resignation in his head. His fingers itched to get to his computer, write the letter, and mail it. One thing was for sure, though. He would first mail the letter to Jim, his partner; and *then* have Jim forward it to Kristopher Lehrer. He wanted no indication of where the letter originated. For now he understood completely Grace's fear of Kristopher.

"Get a lot of milk?" he asked as she kicked off her boots and came in the door.

"A fair bit." She hoisted the bucket onto the countertop, and washed her hands. "Is there any hot water left? I could use some more coffee. It's getting chilly out there."

Patrick turned on the teakettle to re-heat the water. He wondered if he should tell her the truth about himself, now that he knew the true facts. He could assure her that he would never turn her over to Lehrer. *And then what?* he asked himself. *How long can you stay here? There's nothing to keep you here, once you mail that resignation letter.*

It was a depressing thought.

He couldn't stay. If Kristopher wasn't paying his bills, there was no way that he could turn around and pay Grace the five hundred dollars a month he had promised her for room and board. The day of reckoning was rapidly approaching for him and, God help him, he didn't know what to do about it.

The thought crossed his mind that if he could actually sell his book, maybe he could stay, but as quickly as it came he dismissed it. As ignorant as he was with regards to the world of publishing, even he knew that it took months and months—maybe even years—to achieve a book sale. And he simply didn't have that kind of time.

He wanted to do something for her that he knew she would enjoy, something that was special to her. An idea came to him, but he needed to check the phone book to make sure he could do it.

"So last night, when you were singing," he began.

She glanced at him as she began grating some potatoes for breakfast. "Yes?"

"What album were you singing to?"

"It was a CD I picked up a couple years ago in Eugene, called *Shadow of the Moon*, by Blackmore's Night. You've heard of Ritchie Blackmore? He used to be in the group 'Deep Purple.' *Smoke on the Water*, and all that."

"Yes! Boy, he's changed his music style. This sounded Irish."

"It is. Sort of. I guess you might call it Irish rock, or neo-Celtic, or something like that."

"You like that kind of music?"

"Heavens, yes." She finished grating one potato, and reached for another. "I love Celtic music."

She did, eh? Shows how much Lehrer knew about his wife's talent. Patrick had spent weeks tracing dead leads because Lehrer thought Margo had gone to Nashville to give a shot at *country* music. And here she said it was *Celtic* music she loved.

"I have a few CD's of Celtic music," she continued. "There's a store in Eugene that specializes in that kind of thing."

"What's the name of it?"

"What, the store? *The New Renaissance*, I think."

"Sounds like it might be an interesting place."

"It's fun to poke around it."

"You have a stunning voice," he said softly.

She was quiet a moment, then said, "Thank you."

"So why aren't you singing? With a group, or something?"

She looked up at him. "What, and expose myself more than I need to? You've got to be kidding."

"So you stay holed up on this farm, hiding your talents."

"No, I stay holed up on this farm, hiding for my life."

She had him there. "Yet is that what you want to do the rest of your life?"

"What choice do I have? As long as my ex-husband is alive, I have no doubt he'll take every opportunity to wish me dead."

"Well, what if he wants to get married again? He'd cut you loose, wouldn't he? Not literally, of course," he added hastily, when he saw her hands go still for a moment.

"I don't know. Since I haven't been in contact with him in four years, I really don't know."

"Well, at any rate, I think it's a crying sin that you're not singing somewhere. With a voice like that, you could weave spells."

She put the grater down and squeezed the excess moisture from the grated potatoes and plopped them into a bowl. "I think you're the first person to ever notice," she murmured.

"Your voice, you mean?" He was surprised. "My God, if I could sing like that, I'd be singing day and night."

"I sing for myself. No one else would be interested."

He knew where *that* attitude came from. "That sounds like some sort of pap and dribble that your husband—Kristopher, was it?—fed you. What did he do, convince you that this remarkable gift you have is worthless?"

She opened the refrigerator door and took out a round of cheddar cheese and sliced off a generous amount. "Something like that."

"Well, he's wrong," stated Patrick flatly. "Last night when I heard you, it was...it was..." He trailed off.

Grace turned, the chunk of cheese in her hand. "It was what?" she asked.

He met her eyes. "It was like magic," he said at last, quietly. "Like you were indeed weaving a spell around me. I don't think I've ever heard anything more beautiful."

Her eyes grew wide, and she flushed. She blinked once or twice, then turned and began to grate cheese into the potatoes. "Thank you."

"I just can't figure why you don't want anyone else to hear you."

"Sure, and have my name plastered everywhere along with it. Recognition. No thanks."

"So what if...what if you had some sort of positive proof that your husband had given up all interest in finding you? Would you sing then?"

She didn't look at him as she grated the cheese. "Are we talking hypothetical here? Like what would you do if you won the lottery? Or are we talking the idea of a real possibility?"

He thought about his impressions of Kristopher Lehrer, about Grace's years of hiding, and about what Jim, his partner, had dug up on Lehrer. "I suppose we're talking about winning the lottery," he admitted.

"Okay, if we're talking pipe dreams, then yes. I might consider doing something with my singing."

That's what he wanted to hear. "Excuse me a moment," he said. "Nature calls."

He passed through the living room on the way to the bathroom and snagged the phone book he knew lay on a bookshelf. Then he closed himself into the bathroom.

The phone book covered Eugene and some of the smaller surrounding communities. Flipping through the

119

white pages, he found the listing for *The New Renaissance*. It was a restaurant/store combination—even better. He noted the address and phone number, slapped the phone book closed, flushed the toilet, and swung by to replace the phone book on his way back to the kitchen.

Grace had the potatoes cooking as he reentered the kitchen. She was leaning against the counter sipping coffee with a faraway look in her eyes.

She looked so sexy all of a sudden that he stopped and gulped. Her hair was mussed, her blue-jeaned legs were crossed at the ankles. She held her mug against her chest, and her stunning eyes were dreamy-looking. He had a sudden urge to pull her against him and take last night's kiss further than it had gone, further than he would allow himself to go. Far enough to make her forget the hurt and humiliation and fear that Kristopher Lehrer had invested her with. Far enough to make her turn to *him* for comfort, for love, for sex...

"Penny for your thoughts?" he asked.

She looked at him and gave a wry smile. "Just daydreaming," she said.

"About what?"

"Singing." She took another pull from her mug. "I hadn't given it much thought the last few years, but I was just sitting here thinking how much fun it would be to be able to sing. Without fear." Abruptly her eyes clouded and she turned around and placed the mug on the counter. "Too bad I can't." She set about straining the morning's milk.

A wrench of pain hit Patrick in the gut.

****

He knew he couldn't call *The New Renaissance* so early in the morning, so after breakfast he retired to his room and worked on his book.

He hadn't realized, when he originated his plot, how closely the characters in his book were turning out to parallel the true facts of this case. He had made his heroine fleeing from an abusive stalking ex-husband, and at the time he had no idea that this was, in fact, a real-life situation for Grace. With cold clarity, he realized that the heroine in his book resembled Grace in more than looks. Her story was becoming Grace's story. His eyes narrowed as he considered the computer screen. Hmmm—maybe it would be satisfying to kill off the stalking husband in a particularly gruesome way. It surprised him, these feelings of vindictiveness and revenge he was feeling. He flexed his fingers and began typing.

There was deep satisfaction in having the words come out of his head, through his fingers, and emerge on the computer screen. Writing was also an ego-thing to him, he realized. He had the power. He wielded it as ever a god did, directing the lives of his characters...although sometimes his characters had a habit of taking on a life of their own and twisting their fate to suit themselves, rather than him. But he found it intriguing to breath life into these fictional people and make them walk and talk and love and scheme.

The heroine was clearly Grace—the fragile beauty, the unbelievable strength beneath the surface, the unconscious sexiness, the dignity, the intelligence...oh, she was Grace, all right.

And the hero, the detective, was him. Sure, he'd made the hero more buff than he himself was, but he figured that was the prerogative of any author. Exaggerate the appeal.

And the villain—oh, Kristopher, of course. With uncanny imagination, he was coming up with all sorts of nasty terrifying things the villain could do to make the heroine's life unbearable. Pulling from his years of experience as a detective, and using a bit of a story here and a part of a case there, he was piecing together the villain to be a damned worthy opponent for the hero. Yes, it was quite satisfying to pull these characters together on paper, making them real.

And, of course, it was his wish that the villain get killed in a particularly gruesome way, and the hero gets the girl in the end. Perhaps with a good deal of lovemaking throughout...

He paused for a moment and unfocused his eyes, and wondered just how true to the story he could make real life, particularly the lovemaking part.

Chapter Ten

Using his cell phone, Patrick called *The New Renaissance* and made reservations for dinner that night. Then he set about to convince Grace to go.

"Hey, you know what?" he asked, as they planted garlic in the garden. *Garlic was planted in the fall,* she'd told him. The day was overcast and cold, and the forecast predicted rain tomorrow, which was why she wanted to get it planted.

"What?" she answered.

"It's Saturday."

"Yeah. So?"

"So, most people go out and have a little fun on Saturday night."

"Most people don't have my problems."

"Most people haven't any idea who you are. You're completely anonymous."

"So what are you saying?"

"I'm saying it's Saturday, and I think you should have a little fun."

"Oh sure. And what do you propose?"

"Dinner in Eugene."

She was so startled she dropped her garlic. Her eyes grew huge, and she began to sputter. "Wh-wh-*what*?"

"Dinner in Eugene," he repeated. "Just for fun. What do you say?"

"I can't," she responded automatically. "I just can't."

"Why not?"

"You know why not. I simply can't risk the exposure."

"Grace, your ex-husband has no idea where you are. We'll bundle you in under cover of darkness, if you like. But I'd like to treat you to dinner."

His voice was warm and persuasive, and he knew she was tempted. "Think about it," he continued. "We can go after the evening chores are done. Dress up a little, listen to some music...and I think you'll like the music."

"What do you mean?"

"I've made reservations at *The New Renaissance*. Did you know there's a restaurant attached to the store? And they have a Celtic-type band playing tonight. We can listen to the music."

She caught her breath, and Patrick knew she was warring with herself.

"Besides," he continued, and reached out a muddy hand to touch her cheek. "I'd like to see you all dressed up."

She bit her lip and flushed a becoming rose. "Do—do you suppose it's safe?"

"Absolutely. It's just this once." He saw a quiver of desire go through her, and his voice dropped. "You'd be all dressed up," he urged. "Feeling pretty and cosseted for once. I can watch you across a candlelit table. You can admire the manliness of my five-o'clock shadow..."

Grace chucked. She picked up her fallen garlic, stuck her finger in the ground to make a hole, and planted it. "All right," she said.

****

She was excited, he could tell. For the rest of the day there was a subdued sparkle about her, a playfulness that had been absent before. It was, he realized, the first time in a long time that she had something fun to look forward to. Something besides wariness, something besides farm chores, something besides brooding while she canned peas.

He took a quick shower and used her bathroom sink to shave away his manly five-o'clock shadow. Yes, he suspected it had been a very long time indeed since she'd had fun.

The chores were done. The milk cows were in the barn, the animals fed. She had taken a shower earlier and had closeted herself in her bedroom to perform God-knows-what kind of magic on herself. He just hoped she didn't plan on wearing her holster.

He dressed in a plaid shirt in shades of brown, and over it he pulled a beige cotton-rib crewneck sweater, adjusting the shirt collar so that it peeked out. A pair of pleated-front chinos, brown leather shoes, a quick comb of his hair, and he was done. No, not quite...he reached into the top drawer of his dresser and withdrew a bottle of Bay Rum aftershave. He toyed with it a moment, then slapped on a discreet amount. He was dressed.

He slipped his wallet and keys into his pockets, and let himself into the main house.

Her bedroom door was still closed. He walked into the living room, observing how she'd gotten a fire going and had stoked the stove in his absence.

"Grace?" he called.

"Almost ready," she called back through the closed door. There was a pause of about two minutes, and then the door opened.

It was getting dark in the room, though the flickering firelight added to the illumination. She switched off her bedroom light just as she emerged, so she was lit only by the flames in the woodstove and by the flush of evening through the front windows.

He took one look and his throat went dry. Oh God, if he thought she was beautiful before...

She was wearing a long-sleeved knit dress the color of the richest burgundy wine. The cowlneck collar draped softly across her chest. The dress hung to just below her knees and was belted with a black velvet belt to a slimness that stunned him. She wore sheer black hose and black leather pumps with thin heels. A single gold-braided chain hung below the cowl and nestled between her breasts. Her hair was held back with a shimmery braided headband, leaving wispy tendrils framing her face. Teardrop earrings dangled from her lobes, catching the dim lighting with sparkles. Her eyes, those enormous beautiful eyes, were softly outlined and shadowed. She didn't need blusher on her cheeks, for they were quite pink enough. She had darkened her lips.

He swallowed hard and felt his Adam's apple bob. He couldn't tear his eyes off her.

"You're—" he began, only to stop when a croak emerged from his throat. He cleared it and tried again. "You're beautiful."

She gave him a shy smile. "Thank you." Then the smile broadened into a wide grin and she twirled around in a circle, flaring out the hem, and laughed like a girl. He had never heard her so carefree, so youthful. "It's been years, absolutely *years* since I've dressed up. Oh Patrick, I'm so glad you talked me into this!"

Impulsively she launched herself into his arms to hug him. His arms tightened around her, and they found themselves in a tight embrace.

Her laughter died in her throat as she met his eyes, shadowed in the dark of the room. His glance flicked down once to her lips, those softly outlined lips, and back up to her eyes. "Grace—" he whispered.

With a boldness he rarely saw her express, she took the first move and raised her mouth to his. She wrapped one arm firmly around his neck and kissed him as thoroughly as ever he had dreamed.

She took the lead and plundered his mouth, raising in him an instant shaft of lust that speared him hard and deep. Her tongue warred aggressively with his, their teeth making occasional little clinking noises as she sucked passion from him like a woman drowning.

Volcanic desire surged in him as she laced her fingers in his hair and drew him closer. His body sprang erect, and instinct made him yank her closer. He didn't know where this wellspring of passion came from, only that it made demands that would not be denied.

Patrick was losing control. Being kissed by a beautiful woman in a dark room while they were both dressed up after having spent the last few weeks fantasizing about her was just too much. A few minutes more of this assault on his senses, and he'd lift her into his arms and carry her to that bedroom she had so recently vacated. Lay her down on the bed, divest her of that gorgeous dress, discover the secrets that lay below...His hands roamed upwards until they reached her forearms, and then with an iron grip he circled them and yanked her away.

She staggered back, blinking. Her lips were red and swollen—the lipstick had long since transferred to him— and she looked stunned, as stunned as he felt.

Still holding her by the upper arms, he drew in a grating breath. "Stop," he said slowly. "I can't think— gotta stop—" He blinked to clear his vision, and saw humiliation flood her face.

"You don't want me," she whispered. Even in the semi-darkness, he saw her cheeks flush scarlet.

Patrick knew the pathetic words were an echo of her past, when she truly *wasn't* wanted. "Don't *want* you?" he parroted. "Dammit, Grace, I was this close to dragging you into the bedroom." He released her arms and ran a hand through his hair. "I've wanted you—physically—for weeks. I've wanted you emotionally, spiritually, intellectually, for only a short time less."

His words bolted them into silence, and they stared at each other. In the woodstove, a log broke apart, sending a shower of sparks up with little staccato sounds. She closed her lips and raised her chin. "I see," she said at last. She turned away and brushed her hair back from her face, where some tendrils had escaped the band and were dangling over her eyes.

"You don't see at all," replied Patrick in a quiet, brooding voice. "I want you, but I can't have you—you're too vulnerable—too much in the grip of your ex-husband. It would be easy, Grace, easy to seduce you into bed...but not the answer."

"In the grip of my ex-husband," she repeated in a dragging voice, not looking at him. "I've been alone for so long...alone...but you're right. I *am* too much in his grip."

Now that he wasn't touching her, Patrick was able to calm down. He closed his eyes and took a deep breath, willing himself to think clearly, to speak carefully. When he opened them, Grace's enormous forest-green gaze was fixed on him with a haunted expression.

He reached out and touched her cheek. "Let's take it slow," he said softly, "but let's think about it, okay?"

The haunted look fled. She offered a tentative smile. "Okay."

****

He opened the passenger door of the truck for her. "It's my date," he said, "So I'll drive."

She smiled. "Okay."

He boosted himself into the driver's side. "You really have to get this gas gauge fixed," he said, as the engine rumbled to life.

"One of these days. I just keep an eye on the

odometer and fill up when it reaches about a hundred and fifty miles." She leaned over and looked at the meter. "See? One-thirty-seven. We can fill up in Eugene."

"Maybe I shouldn't have returned my rental car," he commented as he pulled onto Hayhurst Road.

"You weren't using it. What good was it, sitting in the driveway?"

"Nothing, I guess. Except that this gas gauge bothers me."

Grace looked around her. "I love my farm," she said, "but by God it's good to get away once in awhile." She smiled at Patrick. "It's been years since I've been out to eat, except an occasional burger at Betty's Café."

"I have no idea what kind of food they serve at this restaurant," warned Patrick. He grinned. "But it won't matter, will it? You're right—it's fun to get out—*yikes!*"

The word came out as a yelp as he swerved to avoid a pink girl's bicycle lying in the middle of the road. In the darkness, he'd nearly run over it.

"Dammit, that thing is going to cause an accident," he growled. He jerked the truck to the side of the road and got out to remove the bike.

"Happens a lot," said Grace, when he'd returned to the truck. "I'm surprised that bike isn't flattened by now."

"I nearly hit the kid the first day I came to work for you." Patrick put the truck in gear and resumed driving. "She darted in front of me and I had to slam on the brakes."

"They're nice folks, though," Grace murmured.

They fell into silence as Patrick got on the highway and headed north to Eugene.

The New Renaissance was a funky, eclectic collection of New Age, Medieval, Irish, Shakespearean, and British Isles themes. The storefront was shuttered and dark, but the restaurant side was open and active, with a pub-like atmosphere more reminiscent of what he imagined a Yorkshire or Dublin pub might be like.

It was also hopping with activity. On a raised platform in the corner of the place was a group of musicians playing guitar, fiddle, mandolin, a squeeze box, a recorder, and percussion. A female vocalist sang an Irish ballad in a beautiful voice.

They sat at a table and ordered fish and chips and beer. Waitresses dressed as peasant wenches hoisted trays above their heads and sang along gustily to some of the more upbeat pieces of music.

Grace looked delighted. "I know it's all rather staged—the costumes, the singing waitresses, the whole atmosphere—but this is great."

Patrick swallowed some beer. "I don't know my Celtic music," he said, "but it sounds like these guys are good."

"Oh they are. Very, very good."

Patrick watched her and was exhilarated that he'd thought of this. She was so used to being subdued and careful that he hadn't even considered this other side to her—this happy, almost giddy side.

"Look at that," she said low, pointing discreetly with a piece of fish before biting into it.

He looked, then chuckled. "Eugene seems like an interesting town," he observed.

"You don't know the half of it," she said. "It's got all types."

The person in question wore black leather with metal studs, black hair spiked out to alarming proportions, and abundant jewelry. "Is it a man or a woman?" asked Patrick.

"It's a woman. No, wait, a man. No..." She paused and studied the person. "I'm not sure."

"Maybe that's the idea. Either way, it's either a very feminine man, or a very masculine woman."

"Androgenous."

"Right."

The crowds were widespread in their styles, ranging from the more fringe-type such as the person with spiked hair, to the more conservatively-dressed such as Grace and Patrick. But the common theme was the enjoyment of the food and the atmosphere and above all, the music, which continued to be incredible.

"Listen to that fiddle," Grace murmured, and took a sip of her beer. "That is *some* talent."

"And the guitar," added Patrick.

The lead singer said into the microphone, "And now a piece by *Silly Wizard* called *The Queen of Argyll*."

Grace gasped and looked up.

Saving Grace

"You know this one?" asked Patrick.

"Oh, yes! *Silly Wizard* is a Scottish folk band from the 70's. I have several of their CD's. Oh listen, they're good!"

A male vocalist stood up and, in a credible Scottish accent, launched into the stirring verses about the beauty and grace of a woman called the Queen of Argyll. It wasn't a soft, pretty love song. Instead, it was a gallant, stimulating, fast-paced piece that made Patrick want to get up and dance. He glanced at Grace. Her eyes were wide and shining, and she was singing along with the music in that beautiful voice. He listened carefully to the words—about a man who had lost his heart to this woman, and about how he must find a way to court her—and knew exactly what the songwriter meant. For he, too, had his 'heart in danger' from Grace.

And he was leaving her.

He shook his head. He wouldn't think about that tonight. Tonight was just for them.

The music crashed to a halt, and the patrons in the restaurant jumped roaring to their feet and cheered and stomped and whistled. Patrick and Grace clapped and shouted as well. It was well deserved.

The band took bows and then announced they were taking a break.

"Oh, they're tremendous!" exclaimed Grace, her eyes bright. She collapsed back against the seat back and picked up a piece of fish. "I don't think I've ever heard anything like it! Those are some difficult instrumentals—they're amazing at copying the original sounds of *Silly Wizard*."

"You'll have to play me some of that music later. I liked this piece."

"It's a wonderful band. Not well known outside the Celtic folk music circles, but outstanding."

"Do you play an instrument?"

"Me? Heavens, no."

"I suppose you could say that your voice is your instrument."

She gave him a bright smile that sent his stomach south. "I suppose you could."

He nodded toward the now-vacant stage. "That

singer—the woman. You sing every bit as well as she does. Better, in my opinion. You ought to consider auditioning."

"Yeah, right."

"No, I'm serious!"

"Patrick, even if I *am* good enough—which I doubt— I'm in hiding, remember? The last thing in the world I'd want to do is be on public display singing with a band."

He shrugged with apparent nonchalance. He was satisfied that the seed was planted. "Just a thought. This situation can't last forever, you know. You have a gift, Grace, a magnificent one. It bothers me that you won't— or can't—use it."

Her eyes narrowed, and she took a slow sip of her beer. "Why this concern about whether I sing or not? Why do you care if I use this gift, as you call it?"

There was silence for a moment or two, while the happy chatter of the crowd swirled around them. "Because life is short, Grace," he said at last. "Life is short. Grab it and run while you can."

****

Grab it and run while you can. His words echoed in Grace's mind as she leaned against the headrest as they drove back to the farm. Well, she had done the running part, all right. Too bad she could never do the grabbing part.

"That was wonderful," she said into the darkness. "Thank you."

He took his eyes from the road for just a moment to flick over her. "You're welcome. How long has it been since you've been out?"

"Years." She sighed. "And years." There was a short silence, then she asked, "So when did you get the idea of taking me to dinner at *The New Renaissance?*"

"Since hearing you sing, of course."

"You couldn't have chosen a better place."

"I figured as much. It was worth it, seeing the look in your eyes as you sang to that song from Foolish Wizard."

"*Silly* Wizard."

"Sorry. *Silly* Wizard." He tapped the steering wheel as he drove the deserted highway. "I wonder...I wonder..."

"Wonder what?"

"Oh, just hearing that guitar. I used to play a pretty mean guitar myself, but I haven't picked it up in years. Lots of years."

"Not using your gift?" she asked sweetly.

He chuckled. "Touché."

"Well, you can show me how much you've lost when we get home."

He looked startled. "Excuse me?"

"Hazel's husband used to play. His guitar is in my closet, gathering dust. I don't know the first thing about guitars, so I don't know what kind of shape it's in or if it's tuned or whatever, but you're welcome to try it."

"You're kidding!" He sat up straighter in his seat.

"Nope."

"Wow." He shook his head. "I haven't touched one in so long...it makes my fingers itch to try...I wonder if I still could."

"Why did you stop playing?"

"Oh, got busy, I suppose. Just one thing after another. I don't think I've even picked up a guitar in ten, eleven years now."

"Can you sing, too?"

He chuckled again. "Passably. I can keep a tune, more or less, but I can't sing anywhere near as well as you can."

"Hmmm. We'll see."

****

He was right. He couldn't sing near as well as she could. But he could play like a dream.

She kicked off her high heels the moment they stepped through the front door. Bending to scoop them up as she walked, she went straight into the bedroom, dropped the shoes on the floor, and rummaged in the back of her closet until she came across the dusty black case of the guitar.

She walked back into the living room to find Patrick flicking on a light. "Here it is."

He seized it and laid it on the floor. Kneeling, he unsnapped the clasps and lifted the lid. "Oh, a Silvertone!" he exclaimed.

"Is that good?"

"Not especially. They were sold by Sears, believe it or

not, years ago." He touched a string, which pinged a note. "It's a steel-string, though, which is always what I preferred. The old Silvertones are not bad instruments— good student guitars, more than anything."

He lifted the instrument out of its case and stood up. He walked over to the couch and sat, propping the guitar across his knee. He took an experimental strum and winced at the resulting sound. "Oof. Badly out of tune."

"Can you tune it up?"

"Of course." Grace watched those strong fingers move with surety around the tuning knobs and press chords and strumming strings softly while he tuned one string against another to produce a harmonious sound.

"There. That should do it." He took another broad sweep across the strings and the resulting chord was dead-on in tune.

"Oh, that's better."

"Yep." His left hand curled into the frets, and he started picking with precision with his right hand.

"Hey, you're good." Grace seated herself in an adjacent armchair, and prepared to listen.

He spent ten minutes or so limbering up his fingers, touching on arpeggios and twiddling with chords, both major and minor. He could strum and pick and move up and down scales. But none of it resolved itself into what could actually be called a song.

"What did you used to play?" asked Grace at last, loathe to interrupt him but wondering about his past.

In answer, he gave her a cocky grin and launched into a peppy rendition of the children's song *Do Your Ears Hang Low*.

She smiled in delight. She knew the words and itched to sing it, but felt too shy.

"C'mon," he urged her. "I know you know it. Sing with me."

So she did. Hesitantly at first, she began the words, then grew in volume as Patrick played louder.

Do your ears hang low?
Do they wobble to and fro?
Can you tie them in a knot?
Can you tie them in a bow?

Can you throw them o'er
your shoulder like a Continental soldier?
Do your ears—hang—low?

He joined her, singing in a rough baritone that kept tune but could hardly be called excellent. But somehow they sounded good together—he took the natural harmony while she took the melody, and the house was full of music. The silly song ended, and they laughed together.

"How about this one?" he asked, and began playing *Shenandoah*. It took her a moment to remember the words, and then her throat almost closed. It had been a favorite of hers when she was a child.

Oh Shenandoah, I long to hear you—
Away, you rollin' river,
Oh Shenandoah, I long to hear you,
Away, I'm bound to go, 'cross the wide Missouri

Grace's throat thickened as she sang with him. Patrick...was he 'bound to go' in time? Of course he was.

The song ended, and without pause he segued right into *Poems, Prayers and Promises* and began singing that as well. Without hesitation this time, she joined him.

And so it went. For at least a half-hour, she sang and he played. Then to her surprise, he launched into a slow, beautiful version of *Amazing Grace*. Grace closed her eyes, and the well of emotion in her heart overflowed, and her voice lifted in the sounds of the well-known hymn.

Amazing Grace, how sweet the sound
That saved a wretch like me...
I once was lost, and now am found
Was blind but now I see...

The song lost its religious meaning and became a statement of her life, and without knowing it, her voice swelled to such piercing sweetness that even she could recognize it.

Through many dangers, toils, and snares

We have already come...
'Twas Grace that brought us safe thus far
And Grace will lead us home.

He ended the song, and the last chord echoed around the room before dying out. She opened her eyes to see him watching her.

"That could be all about your own life, couldn't it?" he asked.

"That very thought occurred to me."

He swallowed. "Grace—"

"Don't say anything." Her voice was fierce. "Just don't say anything that will tangle me up even more than I already am."

He exhaled sharply, though in annoyance or disgust she couldn't tell. Then he said something that startled her. "It's just as hard on me as it is on you."

She felt that well of emotion that had started when he began to play fill her fuller, almost to the point of spilling out. She was hesitant to call it love. It *couldn't* be love. People like her should never fall in love—the resulting pain was not worth it.

She sighed and dropped her eyes to the floor. "I wish I could give you encouragement, Patrick. But I'm frightened of what I feel, frightened to tangle you up in something that could be much bigger and more dangerous than you may wish." Her mouth compressed to a bitter line. "Damn him. Damn him all to hell and back again."

The curse echoed around the room then faded, as the chord had earlier.

Patrick touched the strings of the guitar before standing up and lifting the instrument off his knee. "My sentiments exactly," he said. He placed the guitar in its case, closed the lid, and snapped down the clasps. "Here's your guitar back."

"Keep it." She stood and smoothed the front of her dress. "I have no use for it. You might as well take it to your room so you can enjoy it."

He stood up. "Thanks. Maybe I will..."

They stood there, fighting emotions, fighting the desire to flow into each other's arms. Patrick spoke first.

"Well," he said, and swallowed. "I guess I'll go to

bed."

"Me too."

He arched a brow. "Alone."

She offered a small smile. "Me too."

"Silly, isn't this?"

"Maybe. But you know what?"

"What?"

"You have no idea what it's done to my female ego, the fact that you don't want to be alone."

"Well, let me assure you that you've done wonders for my libido as well."

"And someday, if we can ever lay to rest these troubles—" She reached out and stroked his jaw for a moment, then let her hand fall away again. "—we're going to *blister* the blankets." Abruptly she turned. "Goodnight, Patrick."

He was left standing with his mouth hanging open.

Chapter Eleven

Over the next two weeks, Grace heard Patrick several times, playing the guitar in the guesthouse. She was astounded at the extent of his talent—she heard folk tunes, bluegrass, even some classical pieces. He might talk about wasting her gift of singing, but it seemed to her that he himself had a gift that was going to waste.

She turned the handle on the pasta machine with her left hand, and with her right hand she gently supported the emerging lasagna noodles. Even though the door to the kitchen was closed against the cool, rainy weather, she could hear him playing. There was something attractive about a man who could provide music. Something endearing, something cozy, something...sexy.

The fact that Patrick was sexy was something she was thinking about a lot lately.

She wore her gunbelt, as usual. She was rarely without it; it was a matter of habit. For the first time in a long time, she wondered at the likelihood of Kristopher coming after her. Had her loneliness over the past few years exaggerated her perception of the danger? At first, she had been nearly paralyzed with fear that he would show up on Hazel's doorstep and try to kill her. She had done a thorough job of obscuring her former identity, to eradicate all traces and links to Margo Lehrer, but she was still worried. Maybe, after four years, she could breathe easier and consider herself safe.

Safe enough to look twice at Patrick's butt.

****

For Patrick, it was a novel experience to be sitting in a darkened room of his guesthouse, lit only by the flares and dancing light of wood flames. The little windows on the pot-bellied stove let out a surprising amount of light, enough to prance in the corners of the room and add mysterious and enticing shadows behind the chairs and furniture. It was an atmosphere for dreaming, for plotting, for contemplation, for music, for thinking.

For romance.

Patrick sat slumped in one of the easy chairs, the guitar cradled against his chest, and let his fingers roam idly over the strings, picking chords and doodling around some tunes. He looked around the shadowy room, thinking about Grace.

She said this used to be her room before old Hazel had died and she had moved into the big house. All the little feminine touches were still in place. The handmade lace-and-muslin curtains. The slipcovers on two of the easy chairs. The faded picture on one wall of a farm scene in autumn, clearly cut out of a magazine and then framed in a pre-made matte. The dusty little figurine of a faun, piping a tune. When he slept at night, he knew good and well that Grace had slept in that same bed, albeit years before.

She was always on his mind. Always. When he played the guitar now, he thought how she would look while singing. How her hair glinted in the translucent fall sunlight, mousy brown but with those intriguing blond roots. How her eyes would crinkle with little lines at the corners when she laughed at him. The surety of her hands to whatever she applied them to. Those hands—equally graceful whether bucking hay or making cheese or touching his skin. The sound of her voice, clear and beautiful beyond belief. She was still shy singing before him, but he felt he could never get enough of listening to her.

And nights. Oh God, the nights, when he imagined what it would be like to hold her, touch her, sleep with his arm wrapped around her. What her hair would feel like against his face, her scent as she slumbered beside him. And her body, touching his, driving him crazy with need. Her kiss that could drive him to the point of explosion.

He slumped further down on the chair and felt his body, even now, react to the mere thought of her. He hadn't been so obsessed with thoughts of sex in years. Not since he was a teenager. Yet all he could think about lately was getting her in bed. Somehow. Anyhow.

And always, coupled with these thoughts, was self-loathing. *The woman's been through enough*, he scolded himself. *She doesn't need you pressuring her.*

Besides, he was wise enough to speculate, what future was there for him? His job, his business, lay across the country in Buffalo, New York. Her job, her life, lay here in Oregon on this farm she had maintained solely by herself for two years. Four, counting the time Hazel was alive. He might be dabbling in this writing stuff, but he was in real life a detective, a partner in a respected firm.

A respected firm in deep financial hot water.

Yet he had never felt more un-detective-like in his life. He didn't want to report to Kristopher Lehrer, he didn't want to resign from this assignment, he didn't want to do anything but linger here and know Grace.

The thought frightened him. All the things he'd thrown himself into since leaving the military—his detective work, his professionalism, his career growth—now it all seemed like he was doing nothing but marking time. Like a dull road he needed to march down until the ultimate goal, meeting Grace.

Though most detective work was fairly routine, there was always an element of danger and fear that kept his senses on alert. But he was discovering that it was just as interesting to live those thrills vicariously through the characters he was creating in his writing. After pounding out a scene, he found that his pulse would race and his breathing quicken. He might even be sweating a bit, just as if he had actually experienced the scene first-hand. It was a fascinating, unexplored concept, this idea of living the danger on paper, and not actually subjecting himself to it in reality.

But the fact remained that, once this job was over, he was going back to Buffalo, back to work as a detective. It's how he made his living. There was no way, even if a miracle occurred and his book was worthy of being published, that he could make a living writing. That is, not for many years yet. So, he was leaving Grace.

Someday.

There was a knock on his door, followed immediately by Grace opening it. "Patrick?"

He was glad the room was darkened, as it made the

physical reaction to his thoughts less apparent. He was surprised that she was even still up—it was past nine o'clock, and usually she went to bed early.

"Hi."

"Hi. I heard you playing, and wondered if you would mind company."

He didn't move from his slouched-over position, except to place the guitar a bit lower, over his lap. "Not at all—you're always welcome."

She closed the door behind her and came over to the woodstove, where she held her hands over the heat for a moment, though he knew her hands couldn't possibly be cold. She wore jeans and a sweatshirt in a cobalt-blue color. She didn't look at him, and he got the distinct impression she was nervous. He wondered why.

"Lonely?" he asked, thrumming a soft chord on the instrument.

"I guess." She gave up the pretense of warming her hands, and curled herself up on one of the armchairs, half-facing him. "It's getting dark earlier."

"Hmmmm."

"It'll be winter soon."

"Yes."

"How's your book coming?"

"It's coming great."

"Have you—have you thought about how long it will take you to finish it?"

Ah, so that was it. She wanted to know how much longer he would be here. "I don't know," he said at last. "These things are always up in the air. Sometimes I write a great deal, sometimes I can't seem to write at all." He'd heard this was typical of writers, and to his surprise he had found it to be the case with him as well.

"I see."

There was a short silence, while Patrick continued to pick quietly at the guitar, and she stared enraptured at the flames in the stove. A log fell with a small shower of sparks. The light flared on the planes of her face.

"Grace, what's wrong?" asked Patrick softly.

She jerked, as if caught doing something naughty, and he could see her swallow. She continued to stare at the flames. "Wh-what makes you think something is

139

wrong?"

"You're as jumpy as a cat. You're not in bed, though I know it's past your bedtime. You're staring at the fire as if you've never seen one before."

She looked at him at last, and he nearly froze at the expression in her eyes. Those extraordinary eyes, darkened to ebony in the half-shadows of the room, held such a look of longing that his fingertips dampened. His throat became dry, as if he were dying of thirst in the desert.

She didn't answer, merely bit her lip and continued to look at him. Finally she rose and placed her hands on either arm of his chair, bending over so that her face was level with his.

He was boxed in, trapped by her body and the guitar, breathing in the intoxicating scent of smoke and lotion and soap. Her eyes were wide and fathomless, and he was reminded suddenly of the stream goddesses of Nordic myth, goddesses who sometimes took on the form of irresistibly beautiful women. The man who looked at her would immediately forget his wife and would be doomed to slavery for the rest of his life.

Yep. That was him.

"I came here tonight for a reason," she said.

His left hand gripped the neck of the guitar as if it were a lifeline. "Ye.." His voice cracked, and he cleared his throat and tried again. "Yes?"

She leaned in and pressed her lips to his.

Instant passion flared between them, sending Patrick into the stratosphere of desire. His eyes widened, then slammed shut as sensation drenched over him. The guitar slid to the floor with a musical thud, but he paid it no mind. Instead, he grabbed her around the waist and drank of what she was offering. He had no choice. He was dying of thirst in the desert, right?

She tasted like the finest wine, the headiest perfume, like any man's deepest desire. He could no more have rejected what she was offering than he could have jumped off a cliff. Her hands came up to grasp his hair, clamping his head to hers, fusing her mouth to his. She was hot and wild, this new side of Grace, and he liked it. A lot.

But something managed to penetrate his brain,

140

something persistent that tickled at him and made him draw back until their lips separated by a hair.

"Ah, you're not wearing—you don't have your gun belt on."

"That's right." Smoothly, she straddled him, settling on his lap in a manner designed to send him into the atmosphere. "I'm not."

His hands roamed under her sweatshirt, touching skin, feeling heat, and discovered something else she was not wearing. "Grace," he groaned, "I don't think I'll be able to control myself much longer. You'd better leave before I do something I might—"

His words were cut off when she plunged into his mouth again. His hands rose up of their own accord, and he filled them with the soft flesh of her breasts, unbound and erect with desire. Lust speared him, traveling from his hands and mouth to the lap she was so enticingly sitting on. How could this be? How could it be that he had been sitting here in the dark, watching the flames of the wood stove, dreaming after her, and moments later she was straddling him and offering herself?

So dreams *do* come true.

They waged war with their tongues, dueling and crossing swords until his blood pressure was ready to go through the roof. Fueled by passion, Patrick lifted her bodily off his lap and into his arms, jerking upright and carrying her down the two small steps into the darkened bedroom. He laid her on the bed and dropped on top of her, then swooped down to claim her lips again.

They ground and wrestled with each other until Patrick felt it was essential to come up for air. "Grace, if you want me to stop, you'd better tell me now...because a little bit further and I won't have a choice."

"If I wanted you to stop, I'd have told you by now."

"But why tonight?" His hand came up to caress her breast through the sweatshirt.

Her eyes half-closed with pleasure, and she instinctively moved her hips beneath his. "Because I've been thinking about this for weeks. Because I was lonely. Because it was stupid to lie in bed fifty feet away from you and think about you all night when you were right there. Because I lo—"

She broke off abruptly, and Patrick's heart swelled. He knew what she was going to say, and it only confirmed what was growing in his own heart. Gently he reached down and started to nibble on her lips, feeling only a little bit guilty about the whole thing. He still didn't know how it would all end, but this was the here and now, she was a beautiful woman lying underneath him on a bed, and it was only natural to complete what they had started.

He half-rolled off her and pushed up her sweatshirt, marveling at the sight of her erect breasts. She slipped her arms out and he yanked the garment over her head. His own shirt followed. There was the awkward removing of shoes and pants until they were fully naked in the dark room. In the gloom, with the little tendrils of light snaking in from the woodstove flames, she looked like alabaster against his bedspread—creamy and slim and stunning. And his.

He reached out a single finger and started with her cheek. With exquisite slowness he trailed it down her jaw, her throat, her chest, her right breast, her abdomen, her hip, her thigh, her calf.

"You feel like you're on fire," she said, with a sort of gasp.

"I do?"

"You must be. You're leaving it behind on me where ever you touch."

"Hmmmm. Just don't burn up..."

He lowered himself so that he could nibble on her jaw and throat, skimming, touching, tasting, nuzzling, trying to keep himself restrained.

"Patrick, that's enough teasing—make love to me—"

He obliged by plunging into her mouth once more, and his hands, where before they had been light and gentle, became crushing and firm. He pulled her against his body and half-rolled on top of her. Back and forth they rolled—first her on top, then him—lips fused, hands groping, until she rolled him onto his back and straddled him, sitting upright.

"You're beautiful, did you know that?" he breathed, touching her breasts, stroking her arm.

She wiggled on top of him, grinding her hips onto his hardness. "You're only saying that because I'm sitting on top of you naked."

"It doesn't hurt, you bet." Not satisfied with a mere touch, he cupped both breasts in his hands, lightly pinching the tips, sending shafts of pleasure through her body.

"And if I were wearing clothes, would you be saying that?"

"What, are you nuts? You're beautiful no matter what you wear." With a smooth move, he rolled over and flipped her on her back, capturing her hands and pinioning them at her sides. "My turn," he said, and lowered his lips to her skin, touching her here, there, making his way lower, until he was able to capture her very desire.

****

Grace was awash with sensation, white-hot spears of lust moving through her limbs and midsection. His touch was magical, and she was floating through a cloud of desire. Her hands went limp as she moaned in the back of her throat, and he gripped her hips as he continued to send her toward the stars.

She could feel the pressure mounting, the exquisite sensation of rushing toward a peak, as he explored her. Her breath was coming fast now, in little pants and gasps, until she suddenly cried out his name and stiffened. Feelings poured over her, rushing like river water over rocks, a veritable cascade of sensation as he took her to paradise and back.

She melted into the bed, her body becoming soft like wax, as Patrick slid upwards. Before she could regroup, he had opened her up and filled her with himself.

"Oh!" she gasped, as entirely new feelings replaced the temporary languor that had infused her limbs. But now she tightened around him, bringing a groan to his lips as he sank into her dark depths. The tempo increased. Whereas before she had been satisfied with restraint, a passion unleashed within her that sent her wild. She wrapped her legs around his waist, laced her fingers through his, and prepared to send him to his own utopia.

"Grace—" he gasped, as she started a rotation to her hips that had him close to the edge. "What are you

143

doing—"

She flipped him over, holding him inside her with tight muscles. Then she rode him as she might a horse, bucking, rotating, dueling. She felt like a fireball, a fury, a veritable temptress. Her hands capture his and pressed him into the bed. She thrust her breasts out and saw him swallow at the sight. She leaned down and pressed those breasts into his chest, capturing his lips with hers and swallowing his groans.

She could feel him losing control, bucking beneath her faster than she thought possible, until with a wild shout that tore her mouth from his, he shot over the edge of the cliff and poured himself into her.

****

They lay quiet, exhausted, for a few minutes, limbs tangled and hair askew and skin damp. Finally he turned his head and looked at her head, resting on his chest.

"I was going to be noble and not seduce you," he teased.

"Too late." She shook some hair out of her eyes and propped her chin on his chest.

"I was going to be gentle, you know."

"I'm not fragile, Patrick."

"God, not you. You're the strongest person I think I've ever met—and I don't mean just physically."

"I felt wild tonight. Wild with you."

"You were." He felt a small stirring, which she didn't miss.

She grinned at him impishly. "What—so soon?"

"Maybe." The stirring continued, a slow uncurling of a fern frond. "It's you, y'know. You're incredible."

"I'm satisfied. Physically, that is. Well, almost." She tightened her own muscles, urging his recovery onward.

"What are you trying to do, drain me dry?"

"Hmmmm—the thought had occurred to me."

"It's working."

"I've noticed."

"It's been awhile for me, that might have something to do with it."

"It's been awhile for me too. I'm sure that has *lots* to do with it."

The fern unfolded further. Heat started pumping

144

through his veins. As if with their own accord, his hands came up and filled with the tempting breasts before him. "God, you're beautiful," he whispered, as the fire continued to fill him, inflate him. "Irresistible. Unbelievable."

"And you." She leaned into him, taunting, teasing, tasting.

This time when he rolled her over onto her back, she welcomed his weight on hers and took them both home.

****

After that, there was no stopping them. She stayed there in the bed, and they made love twice more during the night and once in the morning, when she was getting up to milk the cows.

"You've milked *me* dry, that's for sure," he muttered with a smile as she pulled on her clothes.

"Oh, I expect you'll recover," she smiled. She dropped a light kiss on his lips. "See you in awhile. Why don't you start breakfast? I'm starved."

He watched her leave in the morning light through the windows of the door. Then he lay down and stacked his hands under his head, thinking about the scars on her arms. Long, white, thin.

He only had to make love to her to prove her identity beyond a shadow of a doubt. Not that he wasn't sure already.

When she returned to the house with a bucket of foaming milk, he made sure she was greeted with the smells of sizzling bacon and toast and coffee.

"How's your milk supply?" she teased, putting the bucket on the counter.

"Getting better." He put the spatula down and seized her around the waist, noting that she was still braless, and using that knowledge to his advantage. "By this afternoon, you'd better watch out."

"Watch out?" She wound her arms around his neck and closed her eyes in pleasure as his fingers excited her. "I'll be looking forward to it."

****

As if roiling floodwaters had been unleashed, they spent days making love. Anywhere. Everywhere. Any time.

They tried the barn, the living room floor, the kitchen table. In front of the woodstove. Against the back wall of the porch. The haybarn. And the bed. Again, and again, and again.

Grace could never, in her entire life, remember being so happy. It wasn't just the physical coupling with Patrick—though that was no small potatoes. It was the ability to freely express the love that had been growing, tentatively but surely, in the two months since he'd come.

The sex would decrease in frequency, she knew. Maybe even in intensity. But meanwhile, in the here and now, she was rapacious in her appetite, and marveled that he matched hers stroke for stroke.

She never knew love could be this way. Ennobling, powerful, sweet. Not humiliating, not debasing. Everything about Patrick—from the way his jeans covered his hips to the little mole on his upper right arm—was perfect. Absolutely perfect.

****

As for Patrick, he also knew that the intensity and frequency would diminish. But not the emotion. No, never the emotion. For he was as deeply in love with Grace—or Margo—as he could imagine. The lust only speared on what was already there. He sometimes wondered if his good sense was simply overcome by his gonads, but then he would catch a glimpse of Grace doing something innocuous—straining the milk, perhaps, or reading a book, or kneading bread—and a surge of love, powerful and undeniable, would wash over him.

And he knew, inevitably, that the day would soon come when he would have to tell her why he was here. Especially now that he had his prey. He had all the *physical* evidence he needed to confirm her identity as Margo Lehrer—not just the verbal.

****

Patrick swung open the door to the woodstove and placed another log inside. He was becoming adept at adjusting the amount of heat coming out of the stove depending on the adjustment of the damper, the vent, and the size of the logs inside.

"Getting colder," he commented, straightening up and hanging the poker on its hook.

146

"Yes." Grace stretched her legs out in front of her. "It's about time to split some more wood, too. Maybe I'll work on that tomorrow."

"You cut and chop all this wood *yourself?*" He whirled. "You don't buy it?"

"Of course I don't buy it. Don't look so alarmed, Patrick. I use a chainsaw and a log splitter, so I don't kill myself."

"Still, it's damn hard work."

"Yes. But who else did you expect would do it?"

She had him there. Who else, indeed? "Well, you have *me* now."

She smiled at him. "So I do. You want to work on that tomorrow?"

"Sure."

"How's the book coming, by the way?"

"Great." It really was, in fact. He was getting more and more excited by it.

How he wished he could be a real writer, not a pretend one.

****

"Thanks for letting me use your bull," said Anna Steele. She folded her arms on top of the fence and watched her cows and Chester sniff at each other.

"No problem by me. Save yourself some A.I. costs," commented Grace.

"A.I.? What's that?" asked Patrick.

"Artificial insemination. Getting cows pregnant using a long syringe," explained Grace. The cows were in a special holding pen near Grace's barn. Chester, the bull, would service them at the appropriate time during their heat cycle.

"Think you could use *this* kind of information in that book of yours?" asked Anna in an impish tone.

"Hey, you'd be surprised," replied Patrick. "I've had more experience in the last few weeks working this place than I ever imaged."

Anna glanced at him and started to make a pithy comment back, but stopped short. For the look on Patrick's face as he watched Grace was one of raw emotion, unfettered by logic or sense. It was one of pure, stainless, undiluted love.

He was in love with Grace. To Anna, it was as plain as day. As obvious as the nose on her face. As...other clichés moved through her mind, but predominant among her thoughts was an urge to protect. God knows Grace had been through enough in the last four years—she didn't need another heartbreak.

Anna bit her lip and vowed to speak to Grace at her earliest opportunity.

The chance came sooner than she expected. Anna stayed for lunch, and afterward Patrick excused himself and went to the guesthouse to write.

The two women stayed at the table, sipping coffee.

"You okay?" asked Anna quietly.

Grace lifted her eyes. "Am I okay? Of course. Why?"

"Nothing." She flapped a hand. "Just wondering how things are working out with this guy practically living here."

"He *does* live here, Anna. He's a boarder, remember?" Grace smiled. "Worried about me?

"Of course. Just hoping things don't get—well, more confused for you, that's all." Anna picked at a carrot stick.

"Actually, things have never been more wonderful," said Grace softly.

Abruptly Anna put the carrot stick down. "That's what I thought. I saw him looking at you earlier today," she said. "The man's in love with you, Grace. I mean, seriously in love. This could be trouble."

"Why?"

"Why? You're in hiding, remember? How do you know you can trust this guy? How do you know he's who he says he is?"

"It's been over two months, Anna. He *is* a writer. I checked his references before he came, and I've caught him writing many times." A small smile played on Grace's lips. "And he's been a perfect gentleman, too. Didn't push, didn't pressure. It was my decision to go to him."

Anna was startled. "You mean—" she started, then stopped and bit her lip.

"Yes," stated Grace. She sipped her coffee. "I just did as you suggested, Anna, and took a look at his butt."

Anna garrumphed out a breath. "I'm just worried about you, is all. You've been through a lot, Grace, and I don't want to see you get hurt again."

"Actually, I feel like I'm healing. Patrick is a good man, Anna. One of the first good men I've had the chance to meet."

"That's what I'm afraid of. He's the first. That means you'll be vulnerable. Be careful, Grace."

Chapter Twelve

The call came a week later.

Fortunately Patrick was alone in the guesthouse, writing. Grace was milking the cows. The morning was chilly, and he stretched out his feet toward the flickering woodstove, grateful that its warmth made the rooms comfortable. He had split the wood himself, so he didn't feel as guilty burning it.

The sound of his cell phone ringing was slow to penetrate his mind. He was bending over the keyboard of his laptop as he thought about the unfolding of a scene. The subdued ringing, coming from the bedroom where the phone had been tossed on top of the dresser, didn't sink in at first.

When he finally realized what it was, he made a mad scramble for the bedroom, upsetting a small chair in the process. He grabbed the phone, flipped it open, and breathlessly said, "Hello?"

"Patrick, my boy!" boomed Jim through the crackling connection.

Patrick expelled a breath. His heart was pounding for some reason, all out of proportion to the incident. "Jim. How's it going, man?"

"It's going. Holding down the old fort."

"Good. Good."

There was a microsecond's pause. "How're things out there on the ol' farm?"

"Oh, they're going. Holding down the old, um, cows."

Jim gave a rusty chuckle. "I'm surprised that a city boy like you hasn't gone stark raving mad yet."

"Hey, you forget I used to spend my summers at my grandparents' ranch in Colorado, up until I was eighteen or so."

"Yeah, but that was decades ago. Don't tell me

country life is now agreeing with you."

"It might be."

Another microsecond's pause, this time in surprise. The phone crackled from the poor connection. "Whatever you say." Jim cleared his throat. "So listen...what kind of progress are you making on this Lehrer case?"

Patrick closed his eyes a moment and thought about how Grace had looked this morning in bed, her hair tousled, her cheeks pink, her body warm and inviting. He thought how it had felt during the night, spooned against each other, his arm wrapped around her slim body and gently cupping a breast while they slept. Her fragrance, fresh and wholesome, smelling faintly of Jergen's Original Scent lotion. Her neck, so vulnerable to his kisses...

"It's progressing well." It was all he could say.

"Good. Because Kristopher Lehrer is ready to spit nails."

Patrick stood up straighter, and taking the phone, wandered into the other room to stand near the woodstove. The connection cleared fractionally. "Spit nails, eh? Why is that?"

"Cause he hasn't heard from you, man. He's furious."

"I see."

There was a pause, and Jim finally exploded in anger. "Dammit, Patrick, what the hell's going on out there? Kristopher Lehrer is crazy, I tell you. Starts out all calm and cool and collected, and within minutes he's got fire flashing from his eyes and murder in his heart. He's demented, I'll tell you. Tightly controlled, but violent underneath. Came in here as polite as could be as long as you're cooperative, but the moment things don't go his way, he changes from Dr. Jekyll to Mr. Hyde."

"That's what I was afraid of." Patrick ran a hand through his hair. "I've heard similar things from the woman."

"Well, it seems she was right. And now Lehrer is mad as hell, wants to know what you've been doing all these weeks with his wife. Of course I told him to—"

"*Ex*-wife."

There was a pause. A loooooong pause. Patrick knew that the tone in his voice did nothing to fool Jim, who'd known him for years. Finally there was the sound of a pent-up breath exhaling slowly, as if his partner was trying to regain control. "Uh-oh," said Jim at last. "Does this Kristopher Lehrer have just cause to be jealous?"

"None whatever. They're divorced."

"Meaning that you've fallen for the lady."

"Like a ton of bricks."

"Well, *this* complicates things."

Patrick rubbed at his jaw. "*Tell* me about it."

"Have you told her who you are yet?"

"Are you nuts? She still thinks I'm a writer, boarding at her place while I set the scene for my book. Which, by the way, I *am* writing, so at least that part's true."

"Yeah, yeah...you always *did* say you were going to write a book. Well, write all you want, but you can't stay there forever. If nothing else, Lehrer's money will stop soon. He's paid on time up to this point, but that will change if we don't cough up his wife...er, ex-wife at some point. And if you're not planning on turning over the lady into Lehrer's tender loving care, you can kiss away any money at all."

"I'm not, so we're kissing off the case away."

"Lehrer knows you're in Oregon, by the way."

Patrick became very still. "How?"

"Elementary, my dear Watson. He hired another detective, a less scrupulous one, who's been doing his own research, but this time on *you*. All signs pointed west."

"Shit."

"No kidding."

"Who did he hire?"

"Frank Waylon."

"Shit."

"No kidding."

Frank Waylon was a detective who ran a small office in Syracuse. He concentrated mostly on family law cases, shadowing people to prove adultery, that kind of thing. He was slimy and slick and generally disliked by the Buffalo P.I.'s.

Patrick dropped into an armchair. "She can't run any more, Jim. She's got the farm, and the animals that depend on her. Do you know if this detective has figured out where in Oregon she is?"

"Don't know. I don't think so yet, but naturally he

hasn't been forthcoming with me."

"We got problems then. The woman is convinced Lehrer will kill her if he finds her, and I'm inclined to believe her. She's got a concealed carry here in Oregon, and literally wears her gun belt all the time." *Except when they were making love*, he added silently. "If we don't watch our step, we could be dealing with a homicide here soon enough."

"Crap. I figured it might be something like that. Can you put her under protection out there?"

"Again, that means leaving the farm." Patrick sighed. "Look, it's going to have to be confession time over here. I'll get back to you."

"Good luck, man. Sounds like you're going to need it."

Patrick pressed the *end call* button on his cell phone and placed it on the little table where his laptop sat. The small computer's screen glowed, showing the text of the book he'd been working on these last few weeks.

Damn damn damn. He'd been so happy here with Grace. Content. Satisfied. Peaceful, even.

He enjoyed the physical labor on the farm. Feeding the cattle. Preparing the garden for winter. Helping Grace preserve food. He liked the chickens, he liked the cows. There was something so satisfying in obtaining one's living by the sweat of one's brow. Well, he admitted, it wasn't exactly a *living*. But Grace *did* manage to produce most of what she ate, a darned impressive accomplishment.

This writing stuff was a new, fascinating joy to him. He'd always wanted to try writing a detective thriller; he'd just never gotten around to it. Developing the characters, making them breathe, making the reader want to worry and fuss and be concerned with the fate of those characters—it was a challenge and a provocative goal. He didn't know if it was any good, of course, and he wouldn't know until someone read it...

His thoughts trailed off and suddenly he went very still. There *was* a way to find out if it was any good. He could have Grace read it.

Granted, her opinion would be biased and not objective, but it might be worth a shot to learn if his writing was worth anything at all, or whether it was just junk.

He got up to add another stick to the fire, then remained standing, looking out the window at the backyard. The morning sky was leaden, and rain threatened at any moment. To his right lay the garden, heaped with compost for the winter except for the cleared-away bed of garlic they had planted that day they'd gone to dinner in Eugene. Beyond the garden lay the brook, higher now that the rains had started, and beyond that was the barn and the haybarn. Even as he watched, he saw Grace emerge from the barn with a bucket of milk in her hand.

He found that he enjoyed rural life in general. Most nights, unless he had the wood stove going, he slept with his door opened at least partially, so that the night air could wash over him. He had never really done that in Buffalo, for there was nothing special about the night air in the city. But out here—well, here he could smell the sweetness of mown hay, or the smell of the rain, or even the occasional puff of barn odor. A few times he'd woken to hear the soft sound of footsteps outside his door, and had gotten out of bed and peered at a deer or two in the backyard, making their nocturnal rounds on the lawn. One deer, he remembered, had gotten within three feet of him and never detected him. It was amazing.

By day he heard the song of birds; by night, the owls. There were no buses hurtling by, no exhaust fumes, no sounds of horns honking or people fighting, no screeches of brakes or jets overhead. There were no crowds on the sidewalks, no street people asking for handouts, no hassles in commuting or finding a parking space. He had always thought of himself as a city boy, a guy who not only didn't mind the urban life but enjoyed and thrived on it. But now...well, having experienced the contrast, he was disturbed by the thought of how easy it would be to stay here. He could stay here, bury himself on this farm and live with Grace and write books and...

And pretend. Isn't that what he'd been doing all this time? Pretending? And now the game was over, and he had to confess to Grace who he was and why he was here.

He saw Grace cross the bridge and came up behind the garden into the yard. She was swinging the bucket a little, careful not to spill. She was wearing jeans and rubber boots, soiled with cow manure and mud. She had on a blue-and-orange flannel shirt, and a scarf wrapped around her neck. Her hair was mussed, her cheeks were pink with the cold air, and she was smiling to herself, as if thinking happy thoughts.

It was an expression of sweet contentment and peace.

That little smile brought a twist of pain to his gut for what he had to do. How hard must it be, he thought, for an abused woman to regain confidence enough to happily swing a bucket as she walked, and smile little inside smiles? Damned hard, he knew. In the course of his work, abused women were a regular part of his clientele, and it was never a pretty picture. Grace, by the...well, by the grace of God, had managed to recover to the point where the contentment had returned. He knew he was part of that contentment.

How fast would that smile be wiped away, possibly for years, once he told her who he was? And yet, ironically, her life could depend on him doing just that, if in fact this new P.I. was on the case.

She glanced once at the guesthouse but didn't see him, and he watched as she walked past and up the steps into the main house. Patrick shut down his computer and followed after.

"Get a lot of milk this morning?" he asked.

"Not quite as much. The calves are getting older, so the cows don't have as much milk. I'll let Chester breed them in another month or so." She finished washing her hands, dried them on a dishtowel, and then came to loop her arms over his neck. "Good morning," she murmured, and kissed him.

"Hmmmm." He spent a few minutes kissing her back, wishing that this were just an ordinary part of his day, not an exception in his life. How wonderful it would be to write for a while in the mornings, greet her coming back with a pail of milk, kiss in the kitchen...

"Hey. I have something to ask you."

"Yes?" She turned away and, opening the 'fridge, took out some eggs for breakfast.

"I have a fair chunk of my book in rough form done. Would you like to read it and tell me if it's any good?"

155

Amazed, she turned with four eggs in her hands. "Really? You'd let me do that?"

"Yes."

"Oooh—here! You cook breakfast—I'm going to start reading it!"

"Hey, hey, wait!" Reflexively he clutched the eggs she thrust at him. "Give me a chance to spell check it and stuff. I'll let you start this afternoon. Deal?"

"Deal." She tossed some hair out of her eyes and took the eggs back, breaking them into a bowl. "What do you want in your omelet?"

"Cheese, onion, and broccoli. I'll dice." Patrick went to the 'fridge and began to help prepare the food.

"So why the change of heart? I thought I didn't like people reading your work before it was done."

"Well, it occurs to me that it was probably rude, setting the book around your farm and developing the character after you, yet not letting you read it."

Her hands stalled in the process of beating milk into the eggs. "You're—you're developing the character after *me?*"

"Well sure. I could hardly help it. Watching you day after day, it was rather natural that the female character should be you."

"I hope...well, I hope that I'm not identifiable, if you know what I mean."

"You're not." Even as they discussed it, he shrank away from what he needed to do, then berated himself for his cowardice.

****

In the evening, when the outdoor chores were finished, Patrick brought his laptop into the house and fired it up for her to read what he'd written so far. He also brought the guitar.

"I'll warn you, it's rough," he said. He shoved his hands in his pockets to hide the fact that they were damp with nervousness. "It's filled with a bunch of 'XYZ's' where I'll need to go back later and fill in a detail or a word. But it should give you the gist of what the story's about."

"Don't worry, I won't be too critical," she said. She placed the small computer on her lap, put her feet up on the coffee table, and began to read.

Patrick removed the guitar from its case and pulled it onto his lap. He needed something to do, something to keep his hands occupied while she read his work. Fact was, he was nervous as hell to have her read his writing. No doubt she would guess right away that he was not an experienced writer. And then...then he would have to explain who he really was.

Fingers picking quietly at some chords, up scales and down arpeggios, he thought back to those long, happy, hard-working summers on his grandparents' ranch in Colorado. He was young and impressionable in those days, and had spent the time he wasn't working lying in the haymow, devouring Zane Gray and Louis L'Amour books. He had wanted to write something back then, he recalled. His mind drifted back, fingers drifting over the strings of the instrument, recalling a longhand attempt at writing the summer he was sixteen. Some dramatic story about a cowboy and his adventures, with a busty woman or two thrown in for good measure. He *had* been sixteen, after all, and busty women—or *any* women—were high on his mind. He'd written a respectable amount, a hundred pages or so, and then the summer was over and life in general got in the way. But that hidden, subdued urge to write had been there for a while. If this attempt, the one Grace was reading, was no good, well...he might try again. Why the heck not.

It would give him something to do during his evenings, since Grace would no longer wish to be part of his life after he told her who he was.

He glanced over at her. Her lips were parted, she was leaning forward just a bit toward the screen, and her eyes were saucer-wide as she read. Her right hand lay on the keyboard, pressing the *page down* key. Well, so far so good. At least she didn't have a cynical or a disappointed look on her face.

He continued watching her as he picked at the guitar. What a beautiful woman she was. He wondered if she was aware of just how beautiful she really was. Those unbelievable eyes, that profile with the nose slightly crooked, the high cheekbones that captured light on their planes and cast attractive shadows on her face. The graceful neck, the strong arms and hands...

His body began to stir, and he ordered it down.

An hour went by, then another, and she remained staring at the screen. Patrick continued to putter around on the guitar. Abruptly there was a groan of frustration, startling him, and Grace looked up.

"Damn. That's all you have so far."

Patrick's fingertips were damp again. "So tell me..." he said, eyes on the neck of the guitar. "What did you think?"

She leaned against the couch. "One thing. Am I so transparent that you more or less wrote my life story?"

"No." He strummed the guitar. "It's just that...well, it's easier to write about someone when you're in love with her."

She blushed. "Well, it's an amazing story," she said. "Riveting. You're a wonderful writer."

"I am?" His eyes knifed to hers, and his fingers stilled for a moment on the guitar before he remembered to act casual about it. "I mean, thank you. I'm glad you like it."

"Your character development is excellent—especially the villain." She shivered. "In fact, it's uncanny how similar he is to my ex-husband. It was hard to read in places, since it seems to parallel my situation so closely. And the woman—well, she's like me, I can see it, although you've flattered me a little. But what she goes through...I get goose flesh, just thinking about it."

"And you're satisfied that you won't be identifiable?"

"Yes. Tell me, did you set out making her like me, or did it just happen?"

"A lot of it just happened. A coincidence. I had no idea of your circumstances when I plotted the book."

She spoke low. "I just pray that a lot of what she goes through is something I won't have to live through. Your writing can be terrifying at times, and the motives and emotions of the people just leap out from the page."

It did? He had no idea of she was just being polite or if she actually thought he wrote well. If he weren't so personally involved in it, he would have said she was being honest. Hmmmm. It was something to think about.

"...the way it is, too," she was saying. "The manner in which you describe the motivation for Cedric, the villain, is scary. The little snippets into his mind, into the working of a madman who appears sane—the most dangerous kind—well, I could see my ex-husband all over it. The urge for power, the sense of superiority, the belief that all other people are just there to serve him in some way or other..." She closed her eyes. "I don't know if I'll be able to sleep tonight, since it brings it all back, in a way. How do you plan on ending it?"

"Oh, I thought I'd kill off the villain in a particularly gruesome manner. Got any ideas?"

She forced a chuckle. "Not off the top of my head." Her expression turned thoughtful. "Though sometimes I wish art reflected reality."

He was startled. "What do you mean?"

"I mean that if you kill off Cedric, it's about the only way that Maryann will be free of him. I know it's because you have to wrap the book up, and I sometimes wish my life could wrap up as neatly as your book."

"Meaning you wish your ex-husband would die."

"Well, of course."

Again, he was startled. This seemed so unlike her. "What do you mean, *of course?*"

"I mean, it would sure be convenient if he were to just drop off the face of the earth. I'll never, ever be free of him otherwise."

"Even if he's in jail?"

"Even if. Imagine it: he'd sit in jail for however long he was committed, getting angrier and angrier, plotting more horrible revenges against me. When he was out of jail, his first thoughts would be how fast he could find me."

"And it will never end."

"Never."

His voice turned grim. "Doesn't it make you feel hunted?"

"Yes. Why do you think I wear a gun wherever I go?" She touched her waistband. "I hate doing it, but I just know that the moment I forget to wear it is the day he'll show up on my doorstep."

"Yet you speak so...casually about it."

She snapped down the lid of the computer and turned to him. Her voice was deceptively calm. "Casually?"

"Yes. As though it were just an accepted part of your life."

"A lot *you* know." The words were spit out. She rose and started pacing the room.

Patrick's hands froze on the guitar strings at her mood swing. "Grace?"

No answer. She continued to pace.

"Grace, what did I say?"

She whirled to face him. He was surprised to find the first anger he had ever seen on her face. "You said that I speak so casually about how I'll be dealing with this the rest of my life. Most women, when they get a divorce, have the option of never seeing their ex-husbands again. Me, I can only desperately hope that's the case, because he's vowed to never let me go. Never. Do you think, even after four years of hiding, that I can be *casual* about something like that?"

Shame blossomed up within him. She was correct, of course. His very presence here confirmed that. After four years, Kristopher still—dangerously—wanted to find out where Margo was, so he could complete his revenge. It was a chilling thought, that he was so much a pawn in this game.

And now, here he was, ready and willing to shatter her hard-won peace of mind, and all because Kristopher had gotten impatient and hired another, less scrupulous detective to trace his ex-wife. Patrick was running out of time.

She stopped pacing and ran a hand through her hair. "I'm sorry, Patrick. None of this is your fault. And none of this is something you can change."

Guilt twinged him once again in the stomach. Lord, if this continued, he'd get an ulcer.

"I just wish—" She stopped, and sighed with a pathos that gave him another kick in the gut. "I just wish that I was an ordinary woman, and we could...could...well, we could...y'know, move ahead like any ordinary couple."

He picked some strings on the guitar, listening to the minor chord reverberate around the room. "I wish that too, Grace, though I think I'm less worried about that than you are."

"Maybe so, but you haven't had the experience I've

had."

"Maybe not." He strove to lighten the mood. "But tell you what—live out your fantasies. You can kill Cedric off in the most gruesome way your little heart desires. You can dictate to me how that part of the story will unfold."

She smiled, a rather fiendish smile, and nodded. "Give me a few hours, and I'll think of something really nasty and vengeful."

"I have no doubt you will."

Her voice softened. "And Jason—your hero—does he get the girl in the end?"

"Of course."

"Yes, I most definitely *do* wish that art reflected reality." Her mouth turned grim. "Because I don't see any possibility of that in real life."

"You mean, any possibility of us—how did you put it?—moving ahead like any ordinary couple."

"Right." She resumed her seat and propped her feet up on the coffee table, next to his laptop.

"Not at all?"

"No."

"Why not?"

"I've already told you. Because I can't subject another person to this kind of uncertainty. And perhaps—God willing—someday if there are children, I certainly couldn't subject *them* to this kind of uncertainty. That's one of the reasons I wouldn't have a baby when Kri...when my ex-husband and I were married. How could I bring a child into that? And let's take things to a logical conclusion here. Let's say that you and I got married. A baby would naturally follow. All of that would make me so vulnerable I couldn't stand it."

"Vulnerable?"

"Of course. If my ex-husband tries to kill me, it's just *me*. But if I have a husband or children, then they're affected. Therefore, I can't have a child or a husband until—" Her voice trailed off. "Well, let's just say I can't. Won't."

His fingers fell from the strings of the guitar, hopelessly, helplessly. He was going to hurt her so badly...

"That's damned hard."

"Tell me about it."

She lifted her face to his, and he thought he'd never seen such depth of suffering, such emotion expressed in those clear emerald eyes. The churning in his stomach increased, knowing that he would be shattering whatever acceptance she had accrued over the past four years.

"But that's a depressing subject." She straightened her spine and gestured toward the computer. "As far as your manuscript goes, I think you've got a winner. Except..." She trailed off, and he could see her shiver.

"Except what?"

"Reading it, reading about Cedric..." She touched the computer, with her fingertips. "Well, this might sound foolish, but it makes me think something is going to happen."

A chill trickled down his neck. "What do you mean?"

"I mean, I get the feeling he's coming after me."

"Your ex-husband?"

"Yes."

"What makes you say that?" How *could* she know?

"I...well, let's just say I have my ways. You might call it a gut instinct, maybe. I always knew he would come after me. But reading your manuscript makes it come alive. Almost like it's opened a sort of floodgate in my mind, a sort of realization that I've become too complacent here, too relaxed. If Cedric can act like that, why couldn't my ex?"

"A creepy thought." In more ways than she could possibly know.

"Yeah. No kidding." She gave a wry sort of half-laugh. "But here I am getting metaphysical on you. Your book is good, Patrick. Really good."

He forced his mind to the topic at hand. "You really liked it?

"Oh, absolutely. But you're a well-known author. You don't need me to confirm that."

It was the perfect segue. It was time to stop stalling, stop delaying the inevitable. Patrick took a deep breath.

"No, actually, it's good to hear it from you. You're the only person ever likely to read it."

She looked puzzled. "Until it's published, you mean?"

"I've never been published before. This is my first writing attempt."

If possible, she looked even more puzzled. "First writing attempt—what are you talking about? You have two other books out, don't you?"

"No. I don't."

There was a brief silence, and he watched the expression on her face. There was no suspicion, just confusion. "Patrick, what are you talking about?"

"I'm talking about the fact that I lied to you. I'm not a writer, Grace."

The first dregs of alarm began to widen her eyes, and she took her feet off the coffee table and sat up straighter. She met his eyes. After a few moments, she said, "If you're not a writer, would you mind telling me who the hell you are?"

"I'm a detective. Kristopher Lehrer sent me to find you."

Chapter Thirteen

Her world imploded, collapsing upon her like buildings in an earthquake, showering her with debris, causing pain and confusion and injury. She sat like stone and stared at him. Icy fingers of dread clamped her heart with steel bands, making it thud painfully in her chest. The pain caused her to stop breathing for a while, and her brain screamed.

Detective he's a detective detective detective, Kristopher sent him to find me he's a detective...

****

When she didn't move, Patrick wondered if she'd understood him. He reached out a hand imploringly. "Grace..."

The explosion came in the form of movement rather than words. In the blink of an eye she had burst off the couch and was full on the other side of the room, her hand on her back, grasping the hilt of her revolver. Patrick sat very still and didn't move.

She was panting as if she'd been running hard, and her eyes had a wild, frantic light in them he'd never seen before. She stood frozen with fear, hand poised to pull out her gun, but she didn't. She didn't.

"Grace, I can explain," he said. Slowly he placed the guitar on the floor, leaning it against the chair. He kept his hands visible.

When she spoke, he was astounded at the change in her voice. Its coldness rivaled the arctic in temperature. "Your whole presence here was a lie," she spat. Her eyes narrowed. Her hand stayed on the hilt of the revolver.

"Yes."

"You were here to confirm my identity in order to report my whereabouts to Kristopher."

He hesitated. "Yes."

"And this investigation included sleeping with me."

He winced. "No."

"Yet you did. Many times."

"Yes."

She gave a bitter guffaw. "A true love-'em-and-leave-'em scenario if I ever heard it."

Patrick made an inarticulate sound. "Grace, you know it wasn't like that." He stood up, and her eyes widened in panic. But he didn't go toward her. Instead, he turned and walked to the front door. He turned the deadbolt at the door, and then walked into the kitchen, where he locked the back door too. He knew the locks wouldn't deter her for long—just long enough to catch her should she choose to run.

When he went back into the living room, he found she had drawn the gun. It wasn't pointed at him, but it was in her hand, ready.

"What are you doing?" she whispered.

"You'll bolt," he stated simply, "before I have a chance to explain. I'm trying to keep that from happening."

"Patrick, open those doors."

"No."

"Yes!" He heard traces of fear creep into her voice, and saw how she forced it down.

"No."

"Yes!" This time there was near hysteria in her voice, and her fingers tightened on the revolver.

"Look, I'm not letting you out of this house until you listen to me!" he shouted, suddenly furious. "You're determined to think the worst of me. Now put the damn gun down and let me explain."

She flinched, the panic of a trapped animal flaring in her enormous eyes. He realized what he was doing to her, and shame washed over him. This was not the way to deal with an abused woman.

"You'll bolt," he murmured. He walked back into the kitchen and unlocked the door, swinging it wide open to the cold night air and the rain. Then he walked into the living room and stood at the far end, giving her an easy escape route.

"I won't stop you," he told her.

She looked at him with wide, terrified eyes, gasped once, and ran.

****

Patrick sat slumped on the couch in the living room, his head in his hands. Well, he'd certainly bungled that little investigation. *Good going, Patrick.*

First, he falls in love with her. Then he sleeps with her. Then he suddenly dumps out who he is, why he's here. Then he locks her in the house, trying to force her to listen...oh yeah, good technique. Right up his ol' detective alley.

Damn damn damn.

Where could she go on this rainy night? She didn't have her purse or her keys, so she couldn't drive anywhere. He doubted she would run to a neighbor's house. He didn't know where her friend Anna Steele lived, but he doubted she'd call her. Grace didn't have a phone, if nothing else.

All she had was a gun.

A cold chill ran down his spine. A distraught, hunted, trapped woman with a gun...would she...?

Good God, what had he done?

And what could he do now? He could don boots and grab a flashlight and start beating the bushes for her. And what would that do? Make her feel more trapped, more hunted. More vulnerable.

He could go away, and leave behind a terrified woman who had no idea of his intentions, no way of knowing that he had no plans to notify Kristopher of her whereabouts.

Or he could stay and pray desperately that she would return after she'd sobbed out her fears in some dark corner of the barn...

The barn. Of course. It was a logical place to run and hide, at least until daylight. He stood up and would have donned his boots and grabbed a flashlight, but common sense made him stop. *Don't do it, Patrick*, he told himself. *Let her work through it herself.*

It was the hardest thing he'd ever done, but he sat back down.

****

Grace was, indeed, in the haybarn, coiled up like a

fetus high among the hay bales, shivering not with cold but with fear.

Should he come after her, she could slip among the bales and keep ahead of him. Hide, like an animal. When daylight came, she could take off, slip down the road, get to a neighbor's house, call Anna.

An hour passed, then two. Her convulsive grip on the revolver lessened as no sounds disturbed her, no sounds except the mice and rats which inhabit every barn. Mice didn't bother her, and she tried not to think about the rats.

Except the very large, two-legged one now in her house.

She felt a surge of anger, towering anger that swamped her impulse to flee. Why should she up and leave everything, again? Why should she leave behind all that she'd worked for during the past four years? Her farm, her house...her animals.

She groaned and shut her eyes, not that it made any difference in the pitch blackness of the haybarn. Cold terror swamped her anew. Too late, she realized how she'd trapped herself with a farm, for she couldn't leave her animals. They depended on her to care for them, much as a child depends on his mother.

Even through her panic, a wry expression touched her mouth with grim humor. She, who had spent her married life avoiding pregnancy because she didn't want to subject a child to Kristopher's insanity, had now saddled herself with a dozen four-legged children, which made her just as vulnerable.

She shivered, this time with cold. She was only wearing jeans and a flannel shirt, comfortable for indoor wear but less so for forty-degree nighttime temperatures. She was wet, very wet, from the rain and from the fall she'd taken, trying to maneuver through the darkness to the barn. She became aware of pain in her right knee, and she flexed it, wincing. She'd fallen on her knee, and the heavy, sticky stuff on her skin and on the torn denim could only be blood.

Well, nothing could be done until morning, until she could see. Keeping the revolver encased in her right hand, she propped her left elbow on a bale of alfalfa and slumped her head down on her forearm. She had long ago—with Kristopher—learned to put aside the simple misery of her physical body and live only in her mind, until whatever abuse was happening to her body stopped. It was a technique she might as well use now.

From habit, she focused inward, looking for "prickles." The feedback nearly floored her with its intensity, flattened her with hostility—Kristopher was furious, Kristopher was focused on her, looking for her...

Because he didn't know where she was.

A grim smile curled her lip. So Patrick *hadn't* betrayed her to her ex-husband. At least, not yet. She'd give him credit for that.

One by one she relaxed her clenched muscles. There was nothing she could do right now. Nothing at all. She closed her eyes and slept.

****

Patrick awoke with a start from an uneasy slumber. His neck was cramped from his night of sleeping in a chair.

He blinked and rubbed his neck, noting that the dawn was just starting to lighten the eastern sky. He checked his watch. Six-thirty.

With a jolt more effective than caffeine, the events of the evening before flashed in front of him and bolted him upright. He strode into Grace's bedroom and checked. The bed was empty and hadn't been slept in.

He sighed and slumped and rubbed his hands through his hair. The bed was still made up from yesterday. He looked at it and recalled the powerful nights he'd spent in it with Grace—cupping her soft warmth to his body, teasing and loving and snuggling and tasting each other. He leaned against the doorway and worked a hand over his neck. He wondered if he would ever sleep with her again.

The house was cold. He opened the door to the wood stove and poked among the ashes, noting that there were probably enough coals left to start a fire without newspaper. He added thin shavings of wood, feeding it until flames started licking at the larger sticks he added. Within five minutes, the fire was going well enough that he closed the door and adjusted the damper.

He watched the flames through the windows and thought about what a mess he'd made of things here. He had taken what he'd thought was a simple case, in which a rich man wanted to find his wife—well, ex-wife—and child, and opened up an enormous can of worms. Abuse, obsession, beatings, stalking, lying...the list went on.

But there were discoveries, too. Writing. He glanced over at the laptop computer, still on the coffee table where she'd left it last night. And rural life. What a change that was, after living in Buffalo for so long. And cows. Who'd have thought he'd grow fond of cows, for crying out loud?

And Grace, of course. The haunted, hunted woman he'd come to love more than he ever thought possible. He expelled a breath and stumbled into the kitchen to make coffee.

As he stood looking out the window, watching the sullen rain, waiting for the kettle to boil, he wondered if he should just pack his stuff and get out of here. He'd spent enough time ruining Grace's life...he should do her a favor and just leave. Maybe write her a letter explaining his intentions. Maybe find Anna Steele and explain how things were to her. Maybe...

He lifted his head and stared. Grace was just crossing the bridge over the brook, walking toward the house.

He turned and prepared a second mug for coffee.

In a few minutes he opened the door, hearing the rain beat on the breezeway roof. He stood on the back step, waiting for her.

When she saw him, her hand went to her lower back, then returned to her side. Patrick understood. Her revolver was sheathed, but she was prepared to us it if necessary.

"Good morning," he said.

Her hair was soaked and plastered against her head. Her shirt was wet. Her jeans had a hole in the right knee, with an impressive bloodstain on the skin. Blood had soaked into the denim as well. Seeing the bedraggled mess in front of him, Patrick felt more shame than he ever had before in his life.

Her eyes were wide and unsmiling, and she stopped at the bottom of the steps, under the breezeway.

"I imagine you'll want to start with a hot bath," he began.

"No."

He lifted an eyebrow. "Why not?"

"Because a bath would require me to remove my gun belt. And right now, that's the last thing I intend to do."

He heaved a sigh but didn't argue. "How about some coffee, then?"

"Coffee would be fine. You go first."

So he walked into the kitchen. In a moment, she followed, keeping her back to the wall, her eyes on him. The stance of a fugitive.

They stared at each other for a few moments in utter silence. Finally he could stand it no longer.

"Grace, you're cold and wet and injured. Let me help you." He took a step forward.

"Stay away!" Her voice rang out, cold and authoritative, laced with hatred. He stopped dead in his tracks.

"Let me make one thing perfectly clear," she said, with steel calmness. "I don't trust you, Patrick. I don't trust you at all. You know perfectly well I'm willing to defend myself. But I won't—under any circumstances—be betrayed by you. You will *not* tell Kristopher where I am."

"It may be too late for that. That's what I've been wanting to tell you."

Her face paled. "What do you mean?"

"I mean my partner called yesterday morning and told me that Lehrer was furious because I wasn't reporting in. He wondered what the hell was taking me so long, that kind of thing. And then—" The kettle shrieked, and he turned and flipped off the burner. He poured the water over the coffee grounds into the mugs.

"—and then?" Grace prompted.

He spared her a glance, then returned to the coffee. "And then he hired another detective. One who's less scrupulous. That detective has traced me to Oregon." He put the kettle back on the stove and turned to face her, his arms crossed.

She swayed and clutched the countertop. For a moment he thought she was going to faint. "Oh my God," she whispered, and closed her eyes.

"Yes. And now...will you let me tell you my side of the story?"

She opened her eyes and looked at him. "You don't look like you've slept either."

"No."

She sighed. "I think first...first I'm going to take a bath. With the bathroom door locked."

His smile was grim. "I'll keep the coffee hot."

****

Fifteen minutes later, she emerged wearing clean denim jeans and a baggy sweatshirt in a forest-green color. Patrick had no doubts what lay under that shirt.

Her hair was wet but combed. There were dark circles under her eyes, like black thumbprints on alabaster. She came into the kitchen where Patrick was frying bacon.

"Coffee's on the table," he said, jerking a thumb over his shoulder.

She sat down and pulled the mug toward her, taking a long and grateful sip. "Thank you."

He adjusted the bacon and turned to lean a hip against the counter. "I imagine it took a lot out of you, to say thank you at this particular moment."

"I won't deny it." She curled her hands around the mug, as if seeking warmth.

"Did you milk the cows?"

"No. I let the calves in with their mothers. I'll skip it today."

"Should I apologize now, or later?"

She lifted her chin. "Why don't you start with your side of the story? I think I would find it more interesting than any apologies you could manufacture."

Well, he couldn't say he didn't deserve that. He turned and, using a fork, lifted the cooked bacon from the pan and placed it on paper towels to drain. He removed the pan from the burner and switched off the heat. Carrying the plate of bacon and his mug of coffee, he sat down.

"Okay, here's the scoop." He planted his elbows on the table, mug in his hands. "About five, six months ago—I can find the exact date if you're interested—Kristopher Lehrer came to me. Was desperate to locate his wife, not

171

so much for her but because his wife had taken their baby girl when she left. Four years ago, he told me with tears in his eyes. He hadn't seen his baby in four years. He struck me as being upfront and honest. Detectives are usually pretty good about noticing things like that." He gave a self-deprecating snort. "This time my instinct failed me."

"No, you can't blame yourself for that. The man is good. Good at lying, good at acting, good at convincing others." She scrubbed a weary hand across her face. "I should know."

"I can imagine. What's this about a kid, though? Why did he insist that I look for his daughter, if you never had one?"

"Kristopher is desperate for a daughter. He's gotten to where he already has her, in his mind. I have no doubt what kind of father he'd be, of course—that's why I never got pregnant—and it's become a sort of torture for him that I was barren, as he called it. I had to hide my birth control pills. If he'd found them, I don't think I would have survived his anger." She shivered.

Patrick shook his head. "I can't believe how duped I was. No, let me rephrase that...I can't believe how anxious I was to get his money. My agency is going under," he added, "and Kristopher's money would have kept my head above the water for another five, six months."

"He's rich."

"Yes. I know. Well." He took a sip from his mug. "I asked what kind of leads Kristopher might have on you. On Margo." He watched as Grace winced at the mention of that name. "He didn't have much. Some photographs, all your relevant data such as social security number, birthdate, that kind of thing."

"Which have all been changed."

"But I didn't know what. He said that you may have gone to Nashville to pursue a life-long dream of singing in a country band. So I went to Nashville."

"I never liked..."

"I was just going on what he told me, and he said you liked country music. He hinted that such music was below you, of course. Or maybe it was below him. At any rate, I went to Nashville."

"What happened there?"

"Nothing. I spent three weeks chasing down an aspiring singer named Margo who turned out to be entirely unconnected with Kristopher. There were so many similarities, including her appearance and the fact that she was new to Nashville, but when I showed her photograph to Kristopher, he hit the roof."

"I can imagine he did."

"That was the first hint I had that he wasn't normal. He didn't scream and shout obscenities as another man might. Instead, he was very cold, very controlled, as he told me what an incompetent idiot I was. He said he was giving me one more chance to find you before changing agencies."

Grace sipped her coffee, her eyes on his.

"So then," he continued, "I figured you must have changed your identity. I didn't mention that to Kristopher, but I followed that assumption. And Kristopher gave me a vital clue from something I don't think you realized you left behind."

She became very still, her hands stalling over her coffee cup. "What?"

"An issue of the *Housesitter's Handout*."

Her eyes grew wide, and he could see her swallow convulsively. Her gaze became unfocused, as if looking back over that chaotic time four years before. When she spoke at last, it was in a hoarse whisper. "So I did." Her eyes closed. "Oh my God. One mistake. One little mistake, that's all it took..."

"I took the issue home and looked it over carefully," continued Patrick. "I'd never seen a newsletter like that before—a national publication for people interested in finding caretakers for their homes or properties."

"It often has ads for someone to house-sit a vacation home in remote locations," Grace murmured, her eyes still closed. "I figured that was my best chance to stay hidden. And I found Hazel."

"But Hazel didn't want a house-sitter..."

"No. She needed farm help. But when we spoke on the phone, we had an instant rapport." She opened her eyes and looked at Patrick. "She took a chance and took me in. She gave me not just refuge but a chance to heal. God, I miss her…" Tears sparkled.

"She had no children?"

"No. Her only son was killed in the Viet Nam War. She became as close as a mother to me, though. She changed her will to leave the farm to me as…as a sanctuary."

There were a few moments of silence in the kitchen.

"But how did you find me?" asked Grace at last. "There must have been a hundred and fifty listings in that newsletter."

"Yes, and I contacted every one of them."

"But you never contacted me—I would have remembered."

"No, because when I found Hazel's phone had been disconnected, I automatically started searching the probates. That's when I discovered that the property had been left to a Grace McNeil. And then I started doing searches on a Grace McNeil, and learned that she didn't have much of a background. No credit history, no work history, nothing. It was just enough to pique my instincts. So I made arrangements to fly out to Eugene. It was just pure dumb luck that I saw you that day in Staples in Eugene."

Her eyes widened and she stared at him. "You saw me in Eugene?"

"Yes. On that day, you were having some copies made, and they announced over the store's loudspeaker system for you to return to the copy department. So naturally, when I heard that, I went too, hoping to see a woman who resembled the pictures I had of Margo Lehrer."

She winced again at the sound of her old name. "But I don't—"

"—look anything like your old pictures?"

"Yes."

"You're right. You don't. Your ears had been pierced twice, but you'd let one hole heal over."

"And my hair—"

"Was dyed brown. I saw the blond roots a few weeks ago. Your profile was different, too."

"My profile?"

174

"Yes, particularly your nose was different than the photos I have."

"That's because Kristopher broke it a day or two before I left."

Now it was Patrick's turn to wince. "Ouch."

"Yes. I went to the emergency room, but I had to have additional work done on it once I arrived here."

Patrick recalled the medical documents he'd come across in her file cabinet but refrained from mentioning them.

"Also, you're thinner than you are in your photos."

"Yes, I used to be rather chunky."

"But not any more."

Her voice was dry. "Living in terror will do that for you."

He nodded slowly. "Yes, I imagine it would."

"So you knew it was me that day in Eugene?"

"No. That was the trouble. I expected you to have a child, a four-year-old girl, which threw me off a great deal. But your eyes—" Patrick closed his own momentarily. "Well, I was half-hiding behind a display in the store when you passed by, and I saw your eyes. You have remarkable ones, Grace—unforgettable. And they were haunted, cautious eyes. *That's* what set me to thinking it was you. Of all the physical characteristics, that was the one thing that most resembled the photographs."

"And the one thing I couldn't change."

"I agree."

"So what happened then?"

"Why, I followed you home, of course."

"You did? I didn't see you..."

"It's part of a detective's job not to be seen when he doesn't want to."

"Yet it was Dirk Van Winden at the feed store in Faucet who said you were in town, looking for a place to stay."

"That's right. When you were driving through Faucet, I saw you slow down and talk to him from your truck. Figured I'd better get to know the guy better. After I saw where you lived, I drove back and planted a seed with that fellow—Dirk, was his name?—that I was looking for a place to live. The rest you know."

175

"Yet you had references, which I checked out."

"Former detectives, men I used to work with. They're now retired. They were prompted on the story."

That little bit of information seemed to silence her as nothing else had. She sat at the table, hands wrapped around the warmth of the mug, eyes closed. "One fateful day," she murmured. "A rare trip to Eugene. With disastrous results." Finally, she opened her eyes and they shimmered with tears. "So you lied the whole time."

He nodded, trying not to let the sight of those weary, beaten tears rip him to shreds inside. "Yes."

"You're a remarkable actor."

"Detectives frequently are. It's a highly underrated aspect of the profession."

"Tell me—what *didn't* you lie about while you were here?"

He thought for a moment, then said, "Two things. One is that I really *did* spend my summers on my grandparent's ranch in Colorado. I loved every minute of it, too, and working here made me realize just how much I enjoyed it. And two...I didn't lie when I said I loved you."

She made a strangled sound deep in her throat and dropped her eyes to the table. "Somehow you'll have to forgive me if I find it hard to believe at this moment."

"I understand."

She traced the top of her mug with a forefinger. "Careful..." she murmured. "I thought I had been so careful..."

"And so you were. But even the most careful person does something that every human on the planet does."

She raised her eyes. "And what's that?"

"They leave a footprint. A behavioral footprint."

Her brows furrowed. "A behavioral footprint? I don't understand."

"Even the most unstructured person will always do something by habit again and again, whether it's walking your dog at the same hour every morning, or milking your cows, or having lunch in the same restaurant. It's part of a detective's job to learn that footprint and exploit it to his advantage to solve a case. Your footprint—at least the part I caught—was your acquaintance with this Dirk Van Winden."

"But Dirk doesn't know anything about my circumstances!"

"He doesn't have to. All he had to do was *know* you, and by knowing you it meant that you had been in his feed store enough times to greet him as you drove through town. I just happened to be behind you, and saw it."

"But if you were so sure of who I was, why did you go through all this elaborate effort to move into the guesthouse and pretend you were a writer? Why not just look at my picture, look at me, then go tattle to Kristopher where I was?"

"Because I knew you were Grace McNeil. I didn't know if Grace McNeil was Margo Lehrer. *That's* what took me so long to prove."

"Why?"

"Because one major thing threw me off. Kristopher wanted me to find you so that he could get his child back."

"But I don't *have* a child!" If possible, she went more pale.

"No, you don't. And that puzzled me."

"We never had children. I couldn't do that to a child, having one under those circumstances. Kristopher hated me for it, called me barren and sterile and all that stuff..."

"I know that now. What confuses me is why Kristopher was so insistent that I find the kid in the first place."

Her words were simple. "He's twisted. He lied for sympathy. It's his way."

"Well, if he hadn't lied, I might have solved this case a lot sooner. But then... if I had solved it sooner, I wouldn't have spent so much time here, and fallen in love with you."

"Patrick—"

"*Now* will you believe me if I tell you that I had no intention of falling in love with you? And even before that, when I became aware that you had been abused, I had no intention of turning you over to Kristopher?"

She began to tremble. "Why won't you turn me over to him?"

"Look, I knew within days that you were hiding, that you had been abused." He spoke almost angrily. "It was written all over you, all over your face. Even your eyes are

177

haunted. I called my partner and started him investigating Kristopher Lehrer. What he learned confirmed the truth. And I don't turn abused women over to their abusers."

"Gee, thanks."

"Dammit, Grace, you know I wouldn't do something like that!"

"No, I *don't* know!" she shouted. Her face contorted with fury. "I learn that you've been living a pack of lies for the last two months, and now you want me to believe anything you tell me?" Her hands jerked on the mug, sending coffee splashing over the rim onto the tabletop. "Well, your credibility has been shot, as far as I'm concerned." She slammed to her feet and began pacing the kitchen, running a hand through her hair in distraction. She whirled around to face him. "For all I know, you're lying right now, and you've already contacted Kristopher and told him everything." Her voice took on a sneer. "Does he know you've been sleeping with the enemy?"

"Grace—"

She threw her hands up and addressed the ceiling. "God almighty, how could I have been so *stupid!*"

"You *haven't* been stupid!"

"Oh yeah? Then why are you here?"

There was a brief silence as they glared at each other. Abruptly the anger drained out of her face and her shoulders wilted. She turned and stalked back to her seat.

"Well," she announced, "I'm not leaving my farm and my animals. If Kristopher comes after me, he'll just have to try and kill me, that's all." She picked up her mug and took a sip of the cooling beverage. "Unless I get to him first. I'm tired of running."

"He won't come after you. At least, not because of me."

"Yeah, sure. But tell me...there's one piece of the puzzle I don't understand."

"And what's that?"

"You said that you were thrown off by the fact that I didn't have a kid. But what was it about me that confirmed my identity? I thought I'd hidden everything."

"You hid everything you could. But there was one thing about you, besides your eyes, that was unmistakable."

She went still, and her manufactured insouciance faltered. "And that is...?"

"The scars on your upper arms. Kristopher mentioned them. He said you had fallen through a plate glass window when you were eight years old."

She gave a bitter laugh. "Ha. That's another lie. Kristopher gave them to me. Remember how I freaked the first day you were here, when I saw that six-pack of beer in your room? Well, it was Kristopher's favorite brand of beer, too. He'd drink a couple on Friday nights, then bash off the necks. Two slashes if I kept quiet. Four slashes if I screamed."

Patrick swallowed. "Oh God...the bastard..."

"So let me guess. You needed to see those scars before you were positive I was Margo Lehrer."

"Yes."

"And, since I always cover my upper arms, you had to have sex with me in order to prove my identity..."

"It wasn't like that."

"Sure it was. It all makes sense." Her eyes were staring, not at him but at some point in the middle distance. "What a logical solution. And fun, too. Imagine killing two birds with one stone—good sex, and solve the case. Terrific."

"Grace, can you really imagine that what we shared—what we had between us—was...was...was merely an occupational hazard?" Patrick slammed his mug down on the table, adding his share of coffee to what was already spilled. "You know that wasn't the case."

But she wasn't listening. He watched her face close down, and pain metastasize up. Then she did what any normal woman would have done under the circumstances: she laid her head on the table and sobbed.

Chapter Fourteen

"Grace, Grace...don't cry. I'm here, I'll protect you, don't cry..." He knelt down beside her chair, stroking her hair, feeling helpless in the face of such despair.

"P-p-p-protect me?" she stuttered between sobs, keeping her face buried in her arms. "You're the one I n-need p-p-protection f-from!"

"No, I'm not." He hauled her into his arms. She collapsed across his chest, sobbing, burying her face in his shirt, wetting it with her tears. "I didn't want to hurt you, Grace, God knows I didn't."

"I'm f-frightened, Patrick...so t-terribly frightened."

"Shhhh...I know. I know." He rocked, smoothing her hair down, soothing her as he might a child. "But I'm here. We'll make it through together."

"I *never* c-c-ry...I gave that up years ago..."

"Everyone cries. Everyone."

"Not m-m-me."

But for five minutes more she was inconsolable, weeping as if her heart would break. Which, he reflected grimly, it might have. His leg was cramped from his awkward position kneeling next to her, but he wouldn't have moved for the world. For four years she'd been holding this in. He could let her cry for five minutes.

At last the storm abated, and she became still against him. He waited a few minutes more, then peeked down and was astonished to find that she'd fallen asleep. He felt his own eyes start to sting as he looked at her vulnerable, tear-ravaged face. What had he done to her?

Gently he stood and swung her into his arms, feeling the bulk of her revolver snug against her lower back. He walked into the bedroom and laid her on the bed.

She rolled away and into a coiled-up position. A fetal position. Patrick watched her, horrified, for he remembered hearing somewhere that humans tend to revert to that position under circumstances of extreme stress. And it was all his fault.

Well, at least partially.

He watched her a few moments more. He couldn't leave her. He stoked the fire, fetched his laptop from the guesthouse, and sat down on the floor in her bedroom.

After the morning's violent emotions, he had the urge to write. He found himself with a whole new dimension to add to his storyline.

He ended up pouring himself into the story, pounding out page after page, skipping ahead of what he had written before in order to fill in the scene which he and Grace had just experienced, making sure that his fictional detective made just as many stupid blunders as he himself had done. He was completely involved with the writing when he heard a sound coming from the bed. He looked up into Grace's eyes.

He removed his hands from the keyboard and examined her face. The dark circles beneath her eyes were still there but the storm seemed to have passed. "You okay?" he asked.

"Yeah. I guess."

Patrick closed down his computer.

Grace spoke from the bed. "Why are you writing in here?"

"I didn't want to leave you alone. And somehow I found fuel for a whole new twist to the story. Namely it involved writing down a fictionalized account of the last twenty-four hours, including all the idiot blunders I made."

"So you really *are* giving this writing stuff your best attempt."

"Heck yeah." He managed a lopsided smile. "That part at least was true. After all, you read all of what I had so far."

"And it really *was* good. I think you have something there, even if it *was* scary for me to read."

Silence fell. At last Patrick spoke.

"Am I forgiven?" he asked softly.

She heaved a sigh and rolled back to stare at the ceiling. "I don't know. I'm just so damn tired." She closed her eyes. "Tired of fighting, tired of hiding, tired of running. Tired of looking over my shoulder all the time. Y'know, last time I was in Faucet, I happened to catch sight of an older couple walking down the street. They were ordinary-looking people. He had a bald spot and a paunch, she had middle-age spread and wore polyester pants. And they were holding hands. Just holding hands, as they walked. Their fingers were linked together, like this—" She opened her eyes, lifted her hands, and threaded her fingers together. "Then at one point he lifted their hands and dropped a kiss on her fingers." Her head dropped back again. "I was eaten up with envy. It seemed so simple, so right. And so impossible."

"It isn't impossible. It happens to people all the time. Find the right person, get married, have a long and productive life together, and grow old so you can walk down the street holding hands."

"It didn't happen to me, though," she said, still addressing the ceiling. Then she lifted her head and looked at him. "And it doesn't look like it will, either."

He felt a twist of pain for the woman in front of him whom he wanted to make his wife.

"You have no hope for the future?" he asked, gesturing vaguely forward.

"What is there to look forward to? If this other detective has traced me as far as Oregon, as you say, then it's only a matter of time until he finds me. And then Kristopher will come."

"If he does, we'll deal with it together."

She stared at him. "Don't you have a job to go back to? I can't imagine Kristopher is paying you for doing what you're doing now."

"No, he's not. Not any more. So let's call it—a working vacation."

She started to smile but couldn't quite complete the effort. Instead, her brows drew together. "The one thing I don't understand is how this detective managed to trace me here. I mean, if *you* found me only because of the issue of the *Housesitter's Handout* I left behind, and that took you months, how did this other detective find me? And so quickly?"

Patrick suddenly felt very, very old. He averted his

182

eyes and slowly lowered the clamshell lid of the computer. He steepled his fingers and touched the index fingers to his nose. "He found you because of me," he said at last.

Her brows shot into her hairline but she didn't say a word, waiting for his explanation.

"He followed me," continued Patrick. "Naturally I took no special steps to cover my trail, and so it was a fairly simple matter for this detective to investigate airline records and rental car records and pinpoint Eugene and Cottage Grove. I doubt he knows you're here at this exact location, but I also have no doubt that he'll find out eventually. And then you and I—together—will need to figure out what to do. You may need to leave..."

"You've been nothing but trouble for me, do you know that?" The tone was mild, but the words were biting.

Patrick flinched. "I deserve that, I know. And I can't disagree with you."

"Leave," she snorted. "As if I'd leave my animals."

"Maybe Anna could watch them for you—"

"Anna has a life of her own. A family, a business. She can't come trotting over here because of your stupidity."

"Dammit, Grace, I had no idea these developments were going to take place!" shouted Patrick, suddenly angry. He jerked to his feet and began pacing the room. "I can only apologize so many times! What I'm saying now is that what's done is done, and now we need to deal with the consequences."

"Oh sure. That's easy for *you* to say." Grace rose into a sitting position on the bed, and snarled the words. "*You're* not the one whose hard-won peace of mind has been shattered. *You're* not the one whose livelihood is going down the toilet because a madman is hunting me. No, *you've* only got to deal with the fact that this whole thing is your *own damn fault!*"

He halted his pacing and glared at her. "And I'm sorry for it. Now what do you want me to do?"

She opened her mouth, paused, then snapped it shut again. She glared back at him.

"That's what I thought," he said into the lengthening, tense silence. "You're just as stumped as I am."

"Well, surely you've come across other scenarios with abused women."

"With other abused women, I get them into shelters or to a different location. You're refusing to do that."

"More running, more hiding, more living my life looking over my shoulder..."

"Look, *you're* the one who married the bastard!"

She staggered back as if he'd struck her, and her face went deathly pale. And Patrick felt about as big as a worm.

"You're blaming me for all this..." she whispered, her hands at her throat.

His anger drained, leaving behind shame. "Oh God, Grace, of course I'm not...aw, honey, don't look like that. I'm more sorry than I can say. It just came out..." He sat down on the bed and enfolded her stiff body into his arms, comforting in the only way he knew how. She sat rigid in his arms, unable to relax into him.

"You're blaming me for all this..." she repeated, staring with vacant eyes at his left shoulder. "I'm to blame..."

"No. You're not. Don't even *think* that," he said fiercely. He gripped her by the shoulders and tried to force her to look at him. "Don't *ever* think that. It's just what Kristopher would want you to believe."

"But I *did* marry him. I *did* choose him for my husband..."

"And how much of his charming personality came out before you were married?"

She blinked once or twice and lifted her eyes to his. "None. I had no idea he would be this way. But I should have recognized the signs."

Her body yielded enough for him to be able to fold her back into his arms. Instinct told him that it was time for a cathartic confession on her part. "Grace, I've told you my side of the story. Now tell me yours."

She stiffened. "I can't."

"Come over by the fire," he said, leading her into the living room. He seated her on the couch and opened the door to the woodstove to stoke it. "Just tell me everything. It may help me to know what he's like, in order to figure out what steps to take next."

She sat and slumped over, her elbows on her knees. Patrick sat nearby, hands clasped in front of him, and waited.

In a few moments, she started to talk. "I met him when I was twenty-four. I had just moved to Buffalo. I was finished with school, and I had a job there at a pharmaceutical research company. My job was mostly human-resources related, and it included a lot of desktop publishing, since I was doing the company newsletter as well as the publication for the stockholders."

She sat up from her slump and leaned back against the couch. "My parents were gone—dad died when I was a teenager, and my mom died of cancer when I was twenty-two. I have no other relatives, and when I moved to Buffalo I had no friends, either. I was more or less alone, in a new city, and it was flattering when Kristopher began to pay attention to me."

"How did you meet him?"

"He was one of the stockholders in the company. His business is cars, both selling them and racing them, but he has investments in a variety of places, including my company. I met him at a convention. He cornered me—not threateningly, but in an interested manner—in the hall where the buffet dinner was being held. We ate dinner together, and he asked me out. He was fifteen years older than me, and I was flattered that a bigshot executive-type like him would even look at someone like me."

She ran a hand through her hair. "I fell madly in love with him, and he apparently did the same with me. I thought I'd met my soul-mate. He told me that I was his soul-mate as well. And when he started asking me to marry him within a month of meeting, naturally I saw no reason to refuse. He was rich, powerful, well-known, attentive...I mean honestly, what more could a young woman want?"

"And let me guess," said Patrick grimly. "He was also controlling, jealous, wanted to keep close tabs on your whereabouts at all times, expected perfection..."

"Oh yeah. The classic signs. Of course, he convinced me that those were all *good* qualities, and that I should be flattered that he loved me enough to want to mold me to a higher ideal. His ideal. The perfect wife for a high-powered career man. I was his possession, his trophy. And his punching bag, though he didn't leave marks at first, at least none that could be seen. The broken noses didn't come until later."

"How long did it take to start?"

She wrinkled her brow as if trying to remember. "A few weeks after we were married, I guess. He began by telling me how to dress. Then how to do my hair. What color nail polish I should wear. What type of shoes to buy. The way I should greet people. The way I should say good-bye to people. The way I should deal with people between the greetings and the good-byes."

Patrick nodded. "I've heard about those types of men."

Grace gave him a grim smile. "So then you know that all infractions were punished. Wearing the wrong-colored hosiery was punishable. Wearing the wrong kind of earrings was punishable. Shaking hands with the wrong people was punishable. The list was endless, and it changed hourly. I never knew when I would be doing something wrong. I began to live in terror of making a mistake. I grew obsessed with pleasing Kristopher. His smiles and praise were tremendous, and his anger and punishment were just as huge."

"So you were a puppet dancing on strings for him."

"Yes. Margo Johnson disappeared. In her place, Margo Lehrer was born—a plump, shadowy, faceless stranger." The same grim smile came and went. "But I've done some reading since leaving him, and I've come to realize that Kristopher is different somehow. He's always calm, always controlled. Even when being violent, he never raises his voice. He prides himself on his self-control, you see. Nothing—*nothing*—would cause him to lose control. And of course it was a natural extension to control those around him."

"Especially you."

"Especially me. But it was beyond a simple matter of control. Kristopher has an utter lack of conscience, and an ego that is beyond belief. I've learned that those are classic signs of a psychopath. A dangerous, stalking psychopath. So when I got the strength to break it off, it was so unexpected that Kristopher couldn't believe it."

"At what point did you decide to leave him?"

"The first time he broke my nose. I went to the doctor

and lied, told him that I'd run into a doorframe or some such malarkey. I don't think the doctor believed me, but I stuck to my story. But I realized that things would only get worse. If he broke a nose this time, it might be a skull or neck the next time. So I started making plans to run."

"What kind of plans?"

"Well, I knew by then that he wouldn't let me go, and that even if I did manage to succeed in getting a divorce, he'd continue to haunt me. So I went about obtaining a completely new identity, down to the social security number."

"How did you learn how to do all this stuff? About disappearing and hiding so completely?

Her voice was dry. "There are books on the subject. Mostly underground books, I might add."

He nodded. He knew very well about the types of books she meant. "So you followed all the instructions."

"Yes. I filed for divorce and moved out. Of course, he didn't want a divorce. And in New York, there is no process for granting a no-fault divorce where only one party wants the divorce."

"But it wasn't a no-fault—"

"Of course it wasn't. There was evidence of battering, even though I'd told the doctor that my nose was broken because I ran into a doorframe. But when we appeared in front of the judge and I explained my story, he granted the divorce immediately, although Kristopher was furious in his calm, controlled way. That's why his violence took a whole new turn when I succeeded in getting the divorce— something was taken away from his control. Did I tell you, by the way, that he set fire to the presiding judge's house after the judge granted the divorce?"

Patrick stared. "He did?"

"Yes. He waited a month or two after the divorce so nothing would be associated with him, and it goes without saying that he left no evidence that he was the culprit."

"Wait a minute....Judge Kocinsky's place, four years ago..."

"That's the one."

"It was all over the Buffalo papers."

"And no one was ever caught, I'm assuming."

"No."

"He was beyond furious that the judge took something away from him. He told me in no uncertain terms that I would regret the divorce. A week after it was granted, he caught up with me and broke my nose again. That's when I ran."

"And where did you go?"

"Why here, of course. Indirectly. I had already made arrangements with Hazel, and was planning on coming to Oregon, but that second broken nose accelerated my plans by a couple of weeks. I had spent the last six months or so of my marriage squirreling away money, cash, in places outside the house where I could retrieve it when I needed to. When he came after me that second time, I knew I had to leave before he pulled a knife or gun on me. It took me a while to get to Oregon because I criss-crossed and left a confused trail and of course traveled under different names. Mostly I traveled by bus, different bus lines and under a different name each time. Paid in cash, that kind of thing. I'd already had my new social security number under my new name, and I've been careful to create as little documentation as possible, even after moving here. I shared Hazel's bank account, and even now I pay for everything I can with cash, and when I write a check it's under the name of the farm."

"You were a good student of those underground books," he said.

"You betcha. You would be too, if your life depended on it."

"And you probably would never have been found if it hadn't been for that one issue of the *Housesitter's Handout* you left behind."

She closed her eyes as if in pain. "I can't believe I made a blunder like that. I realize now that I'd left it among a pile of magazines in our library, women's magazines, on the belief that Kristopher wouldn't search there. Then when I left the house and filed for divorce, I simply forgot it was there because of all the chaos."

"Lehrer is an intelligent and thorough man. It took him a while to find it, but he did. He must have gone through the house with a fine-tooth comb, searching for clues as to where you went."

"I told you, he's brrigtilliant. A sick, dangerous kind

of brilliance. It catapults him ahead in business, which gives him the financial resources to spare no expense for whatever project he has in mind. And his project, after we were divorced, was to make sure that I no longer plagued the face of the earth."

"A bug that needs squashing."

"That's it exactly."

"You know what I find amazing? I can't believe you're as strong as you are."

"What do you mean?"

He made a helpless gesture with one hand. "Being a detective isn't always pretty. We deal mostly with people's darker sides. Do you have any idea how many abused women stay in the abusive relationship? They become shadows slinking around. If they have the courage to leave, they often go back. I've never understood it. But you—you left. Completely. Started a whole new life. And now you're one of the strongest women I've ever met. It's a helluva thing you've done here, Grace."

Her voice was steely. "I was weak before. I won't ever be weak again." Then she gave a faint smile. "And it only took me four years to get that way." She sighed deeply and dropped her head back again. "I actually feel better now, do you realize that? I've carried this burden around for so long, telling no one here except Hazel and Anna. Even though I'm still scared about when the showdown occurs—because it *will* occur—I feel like a rock of concrete has been taken off my chest."

"They say that confession is good for the soul."

"I guess. I've just never had anyone I could do it with, except Hazel. And, to a lesser extent, Anna." She pinched the bridge of her nose. "It's funny—Hazel taught me that the best defense is a good offense. Not only in taking the steps to hide myself, but becoming as self-sufficient as possible so as not to expose myself to discovery any more than necessary. Ironically, of course, ignoring this wisdom was my downfall. Not only by doing business in Eugene, where you saw me, but in bringing you on board here on the farm. You were the first chink in my armor, and the deadliest. So Hazel was a wise woman."

"You still realize, of course, that this chink in your armor loves you?" he asked softly.

189

She raised her head and looked at him. There was a lengthening pause, an energy that vibrated between them. "Yes," she said at last. "And because of that, I *do* feel hope, for the first time. It's a remarkable feeling...it's just that I'm too wary to accept it."

"Understandable." He dropped his head and regarded his clasped hands. "I only hope that the time comes when you can accept it. Because Grace—I want to marry you."

In the silence that followed, he raised his head and met her eyes. They had grown enormous, and looked almost black in the shade of the room. "Marry me?" she whispered at last.

"Of course. I think I fell in love with you that first time I saw you in the store in Eugene."

Her lips felt stiff. "You know, of course, that Kristopher asked me to marry him within a couple months of meeting him."

He felt a flare of anger that he would be compared to Kristopher, but he clamped down on it. It was understandable, in her position.

"Then don't say yes. Give me a year, two years, to prove it. I won't pressure you, Grace, and I would never corner you into accepting me. I'm not Kristopher. I don't have to beat a woman into submission or bully her into becoming some sort of shadow of her former self."

He saw tears spurt to her eyes and she hesitated. Finally she offered him her hand. "If you'll give me time, Patrick, time to see how all this resolves, then maybe someday I can say yes."

He raised her cold hand to his lips and kissed it.

****

The next few days passed warily. They slept in separate beds. They were polite and even affectionate. But there was a tension in the air, an aching, growing tension that had nothing to do with their relationship.

For Grace, the nights were worst. She might have shared them with Patrick, but somehow she couldn't. Sex was the farthest thing from her mind these days.

But there were times, when three a.m. would slowly turn into four a.m. and she would lay sleepless, that she thought she might creep into his bed solely for comfort. The nights were conducive to thinking, and her thoughts

190

were inevitably dark. She could imagine Kristopher coming. Finding her. Kidnapping her. Torturing her. Killing her.

Her 'prickles' numbed her body. She could sense Kristopher's obsession.

Patrick's presence was a tremendous help. She was no longer facing this alone. It was ironic that she should feel more secure near him, considering that he was the one indirectly responsible for her present worries. But she trusted him.

Perhaps it was foolish, putting that kind of trust in a detective hired to find her, but there you go. She had been so frightened when he'd first told her he was working for Kristopher. So frightened that she couldn't think coherently, couldn't reason, couldn't see logic. She knew damn good and well that Patrick would never turn over her location to her ex-husband. Yet the experience of learning who he was—a private detective who'd spent ten weeks investigating her—had left scars.

Grace sighed and rolled over. It seemed sometimes that life did nothing but leave scars.

She looked at the window and saw dawn creep through the curtains. She turned her head and glanced at the clock. Six-thirty. Time to get up and milk the cows.

She sniffed the morning air as she slipped on her boots and made her way past the garden and across the bridge. The day was overcast, with the special smell that meant rain was on the way. It was cold, possibly cold enough for the rain to become snow.

Forty-five minutes later, emerging from the barn with the bucket of milk, she paused and looked over her land.

Her land. Hers. Not Kristopher's...hers. Peaceful, not subject to brutality and bullying. Hers.

Patrick was standing in the doorway to the guesthouse when she returned, waiting for her. She felt a thrill in her stomach at the sight of him, slightly sleep-tousled and devastatingly handsome.

"Morning," he called. His breath fanned out white in the frosty air.

"Morning."

"It's cold. You must be stiff—want some coffee?"

"I'd love some."

He was like that. Courteous of her comfort. Respectful of her choices. Friendly in his offers. Had Kristopher *ever* been like that?

He made coffee while she strained the milk.

"How are you holding up?" he asked, pouring the grounds into the filter and turning on the burner to heat the water.

She shrugged. "I'm holding. I'm waiting. Waiting for something to happen, I guess. I just get the feeling that we're in for a show-down somehow."

"Yeah, I know what you mean."

Grace turned and looked at him. "You're feeling it too?"

"Yes." He pulled two mugs out of the cabinet. "Pressure. Like something squeezing down on me."

"I didn't know you felt it as well."

"I do. You're not alone in this, Grace."

She glanced out the kitchen window, where there was no morning sun to gild the frost. Instead, it was gloomy, with low swollen clouds in swirls of gray. Her hands stalled over the strainer. "It's funny," she mused. "I was looking over my property this morning, looking at this peaceful environment I had created for myself, and wondering how on earth anything evil could ever infiltrate it. I'll see the frost sparkle on the ground, the leaves all colored and bright, that wonderful smoky smell I always associated with autumn, the sound of the jays quarreling in the trees, the cows mooing, the way the sunlight can shine through the remaining leaves on the black locusts...and I marvel that I can still be jumpy and on guard after all these years."

"Well, no one can say you don't have a good reason for being jumpy—"

Unexpectedly, and completely out of the blue, there was a knock at the front door.

Grace was so startled that she knocked the milk jars over, into the sink. There was deathly silence in the kitchen except for the glug-glug-glug sound of the morning's milk emptying down the drain.

Her eyes met Patrick's, wide and terrified.

"I'll get it," he said grimly. He touched his side, and

she understood that he was armed.

She went to stand by the back door, ready to flee at a moment's notice.

Her heart was pounding, thudding against her ribs. It couldn't be Kristopher—it couldn't! She'd felt the prickles, but they didn't indicate he was near...She felt her fingertips grow sweaty, and trickles of perspiration formed under her arms. And she damned Kristopher for making her feel this way about a simple knock on the door.

She heard Patrick's footsteps approaching the front door, and a short pause while he undoubtedly looked through the peephole. Then came the immediate sounds of the door opening.

"Good morning, Anna!" he said loud enough for Grace to hear clearly.

Her shoulders wilted with relief.

"Morning, Patrick," said Anna. "I thought I'd come and see if there was any coffee ready."

They came into the kitchen where Grace was already lifting down another mug.

"Good morning, Grace," Anna said. "I knew I could come by early, seeing how you milk at dawn. I'm on my way to Eugene, so I wanted to swing by before I left town."

Grace felt a twist of jealousy that Anna could just up and go to Eugene without another thought. No fears, no concerns about being seen, no shrinking from contact with strangers. How nice it must be. *I was like that once,* she thought.

Normally Anna was like a balm. She had a sunny, happy personality that made it hard to feel worry or concern when she was around. And yet today, her eyes darted between Grace and Patrick in a way they never had before. This time, Grace was certain, Anna was not particularly interested in Patrick's butt.

They exchanged pleasantries over coffee and some scrambled eggs she'd quickly made. Grace got the impression Anna wanted to talk to her without Patrick present.

Finally she put her mug down.

"Now tell me what's up, Anna?"

Anna's eyes once again darted to Patrick and back. "I was, ah, wondering if I could talk to you. Privately."

Gravely she met her friend's eyes. "Patrick knows everything," she said quietly. "Everything."

Chapter Fifteen

Slowly Anna nodded. "I thought that might be the case, but I didn't want to presume."

"Oh, it gets better," said Patrick. Grace watched as he speared some egg on his fork. He didn't lift the bite to his mouth, instead slowly twirling the fork around in his fingers. "You may be interested to know that I'm not actually a writer. I'm a private investigator hired by Grace's ex-husband to find her."

Anna's fork clattered to the plate and she lifted her hand to her mouth in shock, staring at Patrick. Then she turned to Grace.

"Don't worry, we've already duked it out," said Grace. "Patrick will *not* be informing Kristopher of my whereabouts. When he took on this case, he didn't know the true situation about what my life with Kristopher was like. But ironically, his presence here may spell my doom, because Kristopher hired *another* detective to follow *Patrick's* trail which, of course, leads to me."

"Oh God." Anna had grown pale.

"We've been, ah, expecting someone any day now," said Grace. "In fact, I didn't hear you drive up. I was so startled when you knocked on the door that I accidentally dumped all the milk down the sink."

Anna continued to stare beyond what seemed to Grace to be a normal response time. To her surprise, she saw her friend's eyes start to well with tears. Alarmed, she reached across the table and touched her arm. "Hey, what's the matter?"

Anna closed her eyes and gave a minute shake of her head. "That's what I came here to tell you," she said in a voice that shook. "There's a man in town who's asking questions. Grocery store, post office, hardware store, library—he's showing a picture of you, or a picture of

195

what *used* to be you, and asking if anyone's seen you."

Grace made an inarticulate sound and jumped to her feet so quickly that she upset the chair backwards to the floor. Patrick jumped up at the same time and rushed around the table to her, throwing an arm around her shoulders as if to brace her up.

"Oh God oh God oh God," she stuttered, hands over her mouth, staring at Anna. "He's found me. He's found me already."

"No he hasn't. This isn't Kristopher, Grace—it's just the detective," said Patrick

Anna rose to her feet to. She didn't look panicked, but she had an expression of grim determination on her face.

"You'll come stay at my house," she said firmly. "I'll take care of your animals—"

"No, *I'll* take care of the animals." Patrick looked at Anna. "I may not be any good at milking the cows, but they can go a few days without, can't they?" He gave Grace's shoulders a squeeze. "Just let them in the pastures with their calves and they'll be fine. You go stay at Anna's until this guy comes—which he will. I'll handle him."

From the tone of voice in which he said those last three words, Grace knew that she had less to worry about than before. She slowly lowered her hands, and the wild, haunted look in her eyes diminished somewhat. She nodded, drew a deep and shaky breath, nodded again, and said, "Thank you."

She was packed within ten minutes, throwing clothes and toiletries into a suitcase with uncaring haste. "I'll drop you off," said Anna. "I'll explain to Dave—that's my husband," she said as an aside to Patrick. "I'll explain to Dave that you'll be there for, oh, let's say a week or so. I still have to run into Eugene this morning, but I won't be long. You can have Cynthia's room. She won't care, she's at college."

With Anna carrying one small suitcase and Grace carrying another one, she emerged from her bedroom. Patrick took her by the shoulders. "Don't worry," he said quietly. "I'll do everything I can to convince this guy that he doesn't want to inform Kristopher of your whereabouts."

She nodded. The frantic, bird-like beating of her heart continued, but she was able to take a deep breath. "Okay."

"I love you, Grace," he whispered, and kissed her long and hard on the mouth before releasing her and giving her a tiny push toward Anna.

Anna kept her eyes fixed firmly on the window facing the back yard until Grace was ready to go.

****

After their departure, Patrick stood in the living room of the quiet house, wondering what the hell to do with himself. The clouds had finally reached capacity and begun to drop rain. He looked more closely and realized that the rain was mixed with snow, the type that wouldn't stick but that made it much more pleasant to be inside than out.

It was a good day to build up the fire, find a good book, and stretch out with a mug of something hot at his elbow. Or better, snuggle on the couch with Grace, reading or talking or making music.

A gust of wind hit, sending rain pattering onto the window. Patrick shivered and turned to stoke up the woodstove. He was a little more worried about this showdown with the other detective than he had let on. He knew a bit about Frank Waylon, having met him once or twice. He knew more about his reputation. Waylon was a man interested in money, and Patrick had no doubts that Kristopher had promised him plenty in return for the whereabouts of his ex-wife. It was Patrick's concern that persuasion, no matter how forceful, would not work on Waylon. Patrick knew he would be unable to physically prevent the other man from betraying Grace's address.

And dammit, leaving this farm was just not an option. He muttered a curse under his breath and stared at the flames in the woodstove. He understood Grace's deep connection to this place. It had been her haven, her refuge, her sanctuary. Beyond the physical responsibility to her animals, this place had given her strength when she needed it, independence when she required it. And now, because of his casual acceptance of Kristopher's case half a year ago—for money—that sanctuary was gone.

It was time to commit murder and mayhem. Patrick

197

strode out of the living room, through the kitchen, out the back door, and into the guesthouse. He picked up his laptop and returned to the house. Opening the manuscript on the computer screen, he paged down to the end of what he'd written last. On behalf of Grace, he would relish committing the most disgusting atrocities he could upon Cedric.

****

For three days he held down the fort. He checked in with Grace daily, calling Anna's house on his cell phone. Sometimes he had to trying calling several times before he got through, since cell phone coverage was spotty at best. She was holding up, though tense. Patrick didn't dare go see her.

It was strange, being on the farm without her. Her personality seemed to infuse the very soil, and he was amazed how different the feel of the place was without her.

It wasn't just the labor she did, though that wasn't inconsiderable. It was the atmosphere she created, a seamless flow of work that often did not seem like work. The labor around Grace's farm was often more a joy, a celebration of independence, a statement of emancipation and liberty. It might be back-breaking, it might be arduous, but it was her *choice* to do something back-breaking or arduous. She took great joy in her autonomy, and it showed.

But he tried, of course. He fed the chickens and gathered the eggs. He watered the livestock. He gazed for a long time at the rows and rows and rows of colored jars of canned food in the pantry, marveling at the amount of time involved in the production. And he waited.

He read a great deal, dipping into her extensive library and learning perhaps more than he wanted about parturition in cows and the diseases of chickens. He delved into an M.M. Kaye novel and was more impressed than he thought he'd be. He tidied her house, vacuuming and dusting and washing dishes. He tried his hand at cooking, and was satisfied with his results. He tried his hand at baking cookies, and was appalled with the results. And he waited.

He played the guitar a great deal, reflecting that,

until he'd come here, it had been a long time since he'd had the opportunity to play, just play, for hours at a time. He remembered the happy hours he'd spent with the instrument in his hand, especially during the summers at his grandparent's ranch. The sound of the chords lessened some of the loneliness of the house. Gradually it occurred to him that yes, indeed, he *was* lonely. And he wondered how Grace had made it, entirely alone, for the two years since Hazel had died. And he waited.

He wrote a great deal, filling in the gaps in his manuscript that he had created while trying to capture the emotions of the scenes that Grace had played out. He was pleased with the results, emerging from an hour or two of creative and intense thinking and typing to find that what he'd written—he hoped—was pretty damn good. He wondered what the next step should be, when he finished this project. Find an agent? Submit to a publisher? He wasn't sure. And he waited. Still.

Early in the evening of the fourth day, when he was rummaging around the guesthouse for all the dirty clothes he could find with an eye toward doing some laundry, he thought he heard the dim rumble of an engine. He stood upright. Was that a car? In the driveway?

He dropped the soiled clothes and darted out of the guesthouse and made his way into the main house, cautiously approaching the window that faced front. Yes, there was a car, all right, a late-model Buick sedan in a subdued burgundy color. The windows were darkened, and he couldn't see the driver.

The vehicle paused in the driveway, engine idling. Patrick waited, muscles tense. He unsnapped his Smith & Wesson .38 revolver from its holster.

After five impatient minutes, when the car didn't move and the engine continued to idle, Patrick was ready to go out into the driveway and confront the driver. The driver beat him too it. Just as Patrick's hand reached for the doorknob, the engine cut off and he heard the parking brake engage.

Patrick stood back and waited, watching. When the driver emerged from the car, his eyes narrowed. It was Frank Waylon, all right. Greased-back blond hair, lanky,

199

wiry build, five feet eleven inches of tough city private detective. Grace, he knew, would have wilted under an assault from this man. The very thought made him clench his teeth.

He waited until Waylon walked through the gate, up the front walk, and to the door. There was a brief pause, and then a short staccato knock, sharp and authoritative. Patrick let a moment or two go by before he opened the door.

He stood in the doorway, gazing at Waylon with an expressionless face. He had the satisfaction of seeing surprise flare in the other man's eyes, before the emotion was suppressed.

"Well, well, well. Hess, isn't it? Patrick Hess?"

"That's right." Patrick gave a grave nod of his head but did not offer his hand. "How are you, Waylon?"

"Fine." Waylon's eyes flicked once or twice to the room beyond Patrick. "Heard you were out this way."

"I imagine you did, since I'm the one you followed."

Frank Waylon shrugged. "Maybe I did, maybe I didn't." He curled his fingers around and examined the nails. "You gonna invite me in?"

"No. It's not my house. I don't have the right to invite anyone else in."

"So. It's not your house. Can I conclude, then, that this house belongs to Margo Lehrer?"

"No. It belongs to Grace McNeal."

"I had a feeling that was her alias."

"You slimed your way all the way out here just to confirm that, eh?" asked Patrick.

"Well, you must admit that Lehrer's compensation was extremely generous."

"No doubt."

Waylon finished the examination of his fingernails, crossed his arms on his chest, and leaned with apparent nonchalance against the wall. "So...where is she?"

"Gone."

Annoyance flared the other man's nostrils for a moment. "Gone?"

"Yes."

"At your recommendation?"

"Damn right."

"And may I ask why?"

"Because Lehrer will kill her if he catches up with her." Patrick nodded.

"Yeah, right. Do you really think that it would come to that?"

"Yes."

"C'mon, Hess, all he wants is his wife back."

"His *ex*-wife."

"And his kid, too."

"There is no kid. He lied."

Waylon's brows drew close. "Yeah? He lied?"

"Yeah."

"You *sure* about that?"

Patrick elevated his own brows. "You doubt me?"

"Maybe."

"Check the birth records, Waylon. There's no kid."

"Okay, so he lied. He still wants the woman back."

"He wants her back so he can kill her. I'm not aiming to be an accessory to murder. I suspect you don't want that either."

"I think you're over-dramatizing the situation."

"And *I* think you're so focused on your paycheck that you're willing to disregard Lehrer's mad obsession with her in order to line your pockets."

Waylon adopted a sneering look to his face and a condescending tone to his voice. "Sounds to me, Hess, like you're talkin' from your balls, here. Have a more intimate stake in the matter, do you?"

Patrick reached out, deliberately folded the front of Waylon's sweater into his fists and slowly, inexorably, hauled the man closer, right to his face. "Sounds to *me*, Waylon, like you have an apology to make. I don't like the tone of your voice."

He was gratified to see the man gulp, though he kept his voice cool. "Put me down, Hess."

His grip tightened. "That didn't sound much like an apology to me."

"I could get you for assault and battery."

"I'm not assaulting you. I am merely requesting an apology for an innuendo that I don't appreciate being made about a woman who has suffered terribly at the hands of the man who's paying you."

"All right, all right...I apologize. Sheesh."

Patrick unflexed his hands and released Waylon's sweater. Waylon made a great show of dusting himself off.

"So..." Waylon cocked an eyebrow in a supercilious fashion. "Where do we go from here?"

"Go?" Patrick imitated the eyebrow movement. "Why, we go nowhere. You'll leave, trot home and tattle to Lehrer where you think his ex-wife is. She, meanwhile, will go about the tedious necessity of creating an entirely new identity and fleeing to some other part of the country in order to avoid being murdered. You'll pocket Lehrer's fancy paycheck, and all will be wrong with the world. Does that spell it out enough?"

"I suppose it does." Waylon stroked his chin. "Well, I suppose I'll depart and commence this ball rolling. Sorry, Hess, just doing my job."

"Though of course, when Lehrer finishes *his* job— that is, killing his ex-wife—I'll be more than happy to haul your ass into court as an accessory to first-degree murder. Think about *that* when you're cashing the check."

It might have been his imagination, but he thought he saw the other man's cheeks pale a bit. "Right. Yeah, well so long, Hess. It's been a slice." He turned and walked away.

Patrick waited until the other man had driven away before sagging against the doorframe. He closed his eyes and pinched the bridge of his nose, feeling an intense hatred in his heart against Kristopher, against Frank Waylon.

And Grace...he saw no option for her except to do just what he had suggested to Waylon—obtain a new identity and start a new life somewhere in another part of the country. Oh Lord—why must she do this? Why must she spend the rest of her natural days running, hiding, looking over her shoulder? If it were him in her position, he knew he'd have ulcers like crazy.

He sighed deeply and straightened his back vertebrae by vertebrae. Well, might as well get it over with. He had to call Grace and let her know how badly this meeting had gone.

Walking like an old man, he went into the kitchen, picked up his cell phone, and called Anna Steele's number.

"How did it go, then?" asked Grace.

"Badly. I suppose there was no *good* way for it to go. I don't like the man, don't trust him worth spit. He's only interested in the money Lehrer is paying him, and doesn't give a diddly-damn that he could be putting you in danger. I threatened him, of course, about some of the legal consequences—" He refrained from mentioning that those consequences would be a fallout from murder. "—but he seemed less than impressed. Grace, I want you to seriously think about starting over. Sell the farm, get a new identity, hit the road to somewhere else."

"No." She had been quiet during Patrick's explanation, and her voice was calm, the deadly calm of the terminally ill. Composed, full of acceptance, yet laced with the steel that he'd often noticed in her. "No, I won't. I'm coming home."

"You realize, of course, that Waylon is even now probably informing Kristopher of your whereabouts."

"I do. But I'm tired of running, Patrick. I'm tired of looking over my shoulder all the time. I gave up everything once, in coming here. I won't do it again. I'm coming home."

He felt a stab of alarm. "But Grace, I don't know that I can necessarily protect you—"

"I don't expect you to. You have a job to return to, Patrick. I can't expect you to spend the rest of your life shielding me from a madman. If Kristopher gets me, he gets me. I'll fight tooth and nail, but have no guarantee of the outcome. But there comes a point when even death is preferable to the kind of life I've been leading. I believe I've reached that point."

"Dammit, Grace, that's not right!" he exploded. "How can you sit there and calmly inform me that you're willing to become a sitting duck for the man?"

"*Patrick.*" The single word lashed out of her mouth before she regained control, and it silenced him. "Patrick," she said again, more quietly. "Do you remember I once told you that *calm* is the last thing I feel about the situation? That's still the case. I am not *calm*, I am *determined*. And part of that determination is to face the danger, not be a coward and slink away with my tail between my legs."

He swallowed a sudden lump that smacked suspiciously of tears. Through his very real fear for her safety, he found he admired her courage.

He gentled his voice. "Do you want company?"

"Oh, Patrick." Her voice thickened in a way that suggested she, too, was close to tears. "Of course I want company. But you have a home to return to, a business. You can't stay and guard me the rest of your life."

"Yes I can. I asked you to marry me once, Grace. The offer still stands."

There was a silence on the phone, and then her voice, very gentle, very quiet. "I can't, Patrick. Not until I know how this thing will be resolved."

"But do you *want* to?"

Again that brief silence. Then, "Yes. I do. With all my heart."

He forced himself to slow the rapid beating of his heart. "Then I'll be happy with that. Grace, come home, then. I miss you. We'll face this together."

He hung up the phone, while a phrase kept repeating itself in his mind. *Sitting duck...*

****

She was home within an hour. Patrick spent that time making dinner, a savory chicken, baked with a red wine sauce, lined with some of her canned carrots and freshly-grown potatoes.

When he heard Anna's car pull up in front of the house in the dusky evening light, he went out to greet her. Her eyes had dark smudges underneath and she looked pale, but she had that same aura of calm acceptance laced with steel that he'd sensed earlier. He noticed that the bones seemed more sharply defined in her cheeks and chin, as if she'd lost some weight.

"You realize that I'll find some way to return the favor," she was saying to Anna, pulling her suitcases out of the back seat.

Anna's face was a study in concern. "You'll do nothing of the short," she snapped, then tempered the words with a shaky smile. "You would have done the same thing for me. Don't think another thing about it."

Grace nodded. "Thank you, Anna," she said quietly.

"I'll keep in touch."

"Bye, Grace. Good luck." She drove away.

"Helluva friend," she said to Patrick, who had come to her side. She kept her eyes on the back of the car as it departed.

"You have a lot more of them than you think." He turned her around. "I'm glad you're back," he said, and planted a gentle kiss on her mouth.

Her lips gentled under his, though neither felt inclined to linger with the caress.

He pulled back and gave her a small smile. "Hungry?"

She considered for a moment. "Yes, actually. Starving. I haven't been eating well lately."

"I can imagine. I've made some dinner. C'mon in."

She had lost her sparkle, he noticed. The special glow that was Grace had been diminished until she was a shell of her former self. She was going through the motions, of course, but it alarmed him to see her deadly acceptance. It boded ill for when—not if—this showdown with Kristopher Lehrer came.

"How'd you do taking care of the animals?" she asked, moving into the kitchen. "Oh Patrick, whatever you're cooking smells wonderful."

"Sit down, I'll serve. The animals are fine. I thought about trying my hand at milking, but I figured the cows wouldn't let me. So we're a little low on milk. Actually, we're out of milk entirely. The stuff doesn't last long."

"That's because it's not pasteurized. You're probably right about the cows not letting you milk them. They're creatures of habit, and don't take easily to changes in routine. As it is, I'll probably get less than my usual amount tomorrow morning."

Dinner might have been delicious—certainly she said that it was—but it could have been sawdust as far as he was concerned. Possible timetables kept going through Patrick's mind.

If Frank Waylon had called Lehrer as soon as he returned to his motel, then Kristopher could possibly purchase a plane ticket within an hour, and could assumedly fly out within a few hours after that. With plane changes and layovers, the time it would take to rent a car, and the flying time between Portland and Eugene, and the driving time between Eugene and the farm, Kristopher could—conceivably—be here within eighteen hours. Or longer. Possibly shorter, but he doubted it...

"Hellooooo?" said Grace softly.

Patrick blinked and emerged from his thoughts.

"Where'd you go?" she asked.

He gave a sharp sigh and stabbed at a potato. "Just imagining a timetable," he admitted. "Wondering what the shortest possible time it would take for Lehrer to show up."

"And what did you conclude?"

"About eighteen hours minimum."

She nodded as if this news didn't surprise her. "That's about what I figured."

"Do you think he'll be alone?"

"Oh yes. I'm quite certain of that. Kristopher always prided himself on his ability to handle any situation by himself."

"Then the two of us should be able to take him on." His voice was grim.

"Should we contact the sheriff?"

He considered the matter. "Yes," he said at last. "I don't know what they can recommend beyond promising to send a patrol car by every so often, but your defense will sound better if we can document our concerns with the authorities."

"Defense."

"Yes. In court."

"For killing Kristopher in self-defense."

"Yes."

She gave another one of her nods. "Assuming that occurs."

"Yes."

She forked some chicken into her mouth. "This is a good dinner, Patrick. You're quite a cook." And she said no more on the subject.

****

"What's bothering you, Patrick?"

Patrick put down his coffee. "I still think you should leave. Go somewhere. Hide."

"Well, I won't, so put that idea out of your head. This

206

is my home, Patrick, and I worked hard to keep this farm running. I won't let Kristopher chase me away."

Patrick sprang up and began pacing the living room. "But you can't know when Lehrer is coming. That's why you need to go somewhere else. I can't protect you if you can't know when he'll be here."

"Ah, but I can."

Patrick stopped. "Can what?"

"I *can* know when he'll be here."

He stared. "How the hell can you know that?"

Grace gave him a smile. "The same way I've stayed hidden all these years. The same way I was able to leave Kristopher to begin with."

"And what way is that?"

She motioned to a chair. "Sit. It's quite a story."

Patrick sat. It seemed like Grace always had a surprise up her sleeve, and this was no exception. "You have some way of avoiding Kristopher?" He gave a harsh laugh. "What is it—magic?"

"Yes."

He stared. *"What?"*

"You're entirely right. It's magic. Well, sort of."

"Grace, I'm hardly in the mood for joking…"

"Neither am I. But what I'm talking about is magic. Or something paranormal. Hell, I don't know *what* you'd call it. I only know it's saved my life."

"What's saved your life?"

She sighed. "Listen. About five years ago, Kristopher got tired of his usual Friday-night beer ritual. He'd had a bad day at work, and I made the mistake of wearing a pair of slacks instead of the skirt he apparently wanted me in. At any rate, he grabbed me by the scruff of my neck and slammed me into a wall head-first."

Patrick made a small noise in his throat but said nothing.

"That's the last thing I remember until I woke up in the hospital," continued Grace. "Actually, I didn't remember him grabbing me until months later, so at the time the hospital personnel asked me how I got the concussion, I couldn't tell them."

"How long were you in the hospital?"

"A week. Kristopher came every day, flowers in hand.

207

And here's the thing: I always knew when he was coming. It was like I could *see* him making the decision to come to the hospital. When he pulled into the parking lot, I knew. When he was outside my door, I knew. It freaked me out."

"You mean you had this sort of...what, a psychic connection or something?"

"Yes. It gave me this awful, tingly sensation. I could sense his moods, know when he was thinking of me, detect the level of his emotions. I always knew when he was getting ready to use me as a punching bag, or when he was satisfied that I was submissive enough. Oh God, the curse of that gift..." She closed her eyes a moment.

Patrick felt shaken. "So you could never get him out of your head?"

"Yeah. That's it. I was depressed for a long time. I never told Kristopher, of course, and for months it seemed to me the worst sort of curse there could be. I mean, what could be worse than to *know* when the man you're married to was thinking on beating you up? I nearly got an ulcer."

"And then?"

She smiled, slow and beautiful. Patrick swallowed. "And then, I realized that rather than a curse, it could be a blessing. The sensation never faded, but I learned to control it. I could fade out, concentrate, and know more or less what he was thinking... that is, if he was thinking of me. It's not like I could delve into his brain and read his every thought, but I knew when he was thinking about me and when he was planning on doing something."

"So you could avoid him?"

"Well, I found that I could *begin* avoiding him or placating him when he was in an especially foul mood. And I realized that, if I could avoid him at close range, it might be possible to avoid him at long-range. I started making plans to leave, careful plans. And even all the way across the country I can sense when he's thinking of me. I call it the prickles, and sometimes it's stronger than at other times."

"So do you know when he's planning something against you?"

"Sort of. It's more like I can anticipate my own personal level of danger."

"So this gave you the courage to run away?"

"Yes. I planned it carefully, as I told you before, but this time I knew when to hide, and even where to hide. And even after crossing the entire country, I could still sense him. I could anticipate his actions by his thoughts." She paused. "The only thing I *didn't* anticipate," she added softly, "was *you*."

"Grace..."

"I love you, Patrick."

He wiped a hand over his face. "Even after what I've done to you?"

"Even so. You've given me hope, you've given me courage, and you've made me feel like a woman again. What about that isn't there to love?"

How could such beautiful words make him feel so low? He shook his head. "So now you think you can predict when Kristopher will be here?"

"I don't *think*, I *know* when he'll be here. Maybe not precisely, down to the minute, but in a general sense. I can't look into the future, I can only see him in the present."

"So what's he doing now?"

He watched as she focused inward. The familiar probing, searching expression was on her face. "Trying to come to me. Trying to come here. Something about airplanes," she said.

"To Eugene?"

"I would assume so. He's thinking about me, that's for sure, and there's murder on his mind." Her voice was mild.

Patrick shuddered. "Grace, there's only one way you're going to be free from Lehrer's stalking," he said roughly. "He has to be caught in the act of committing a crime so that he can be jailed for his abuse."

"*What* abuse?" she replied. "For all intents and purposes, he's spent the last four years leaving me in peace."

"The hell he has!"

"Look, *I* know he's stalking me, and *you* know he's stalking me, but in the eyes of the law, we've gone our separate ways and that's that. My 'prickles' will hardly hold up in court."

Patrick knew she was right. "Then we have to set a trap."

"With me as the bait?"

"Yes. I'll be here at all times, but he won't know that—I hope. We'll have the sheriff standing by, ready to arrest him the moment he looks at you cross-eyed."

"Patrick, you know that won't hold up in court—"

"Dammit, Grace, will you stop thinking about what will hold up in court!"

She flinched, and Patrick felt like a low life. She was tense as a bowstring, and here he was yelling at her. "I'm sorry, Grace. I shouldn't have snapped. But I'm worried about you. Lehrer is dangerous, and I want to do everything in my power to protect you."

"I know that. And that's why having me act as bait is the best thing to do."

"This is dangerous, Grace." He closed his eyes a moment. "I don't know if I can let you."

"You can, Patrick, and you will." Grace's face set in lines of determination. "If this is what it takes to be free of Kristopher, then let's do it and get it over with. Either that, or he'll kill me. But I'm too tired to run any more."

Patrick knew damn good and well that beneath the calm tone of her voice, the tension inside her was coiled like a spring, tight and almost unbearable. But the strength she had gained over the last four years of freedom and independence made it impossible for him to gainsay her.

****

There was a desperation to her lovemaking that night. Almost, Patrick sensed, as if she expected it to be her last, or nearly so. It didn't make it any less exciting.

She seized him as soon as they had retired to the bedroom. She fused her lips to his as if wishing she could melt into his body. Patrick was stunned by her assault, and then the sharp stab of desire caught him in up in the maelstrom. It had been a week since they'd made love— only a week—yet it seemed as if it were forever. Even as his mind was occupied by serious matters, his body ached for her.

And here she was, curling her hands into fists in his hair, pressing her body against his, edging him toward insanity.

He tried to resist at first. After all, it was up to him to sustain the defense. He needed to stay alert, maintain his senses, provide protection...all of which was impossible if he was involved in lovemaking. Yes, his intentions were good. For about twelve seconds.

That's all it took to convince him that Kristopher wasn't about to invade their sanctuary that quickly, and he may as well dive in headfirst. And she, tormented by demons he could only imagine, poured out passion like wine—rich and drugging and mind-altering.

Her skin was covered with a micro-fine sheen of sweat as they fell onto the bed, tumbling the covers and shedding clothes like falling leaves in autumn. She anchored his head to hers and set him on fire with the heat of her lips. There was no time for niceties. She didn't seem to want it. There was only time to feel, and taste, and plunder, and consume.

"Grace," he managed to croak at one point. "Are you sure you want this? I mean, I—"

That's as far as he got before she assaulted him with fresh and creative ways to dim his intelligence and neutralize his good sense. He'd never seen her this way before—wild and untamed and stormy and almost feral in her greed. So he gave up, and rode the crest of the gale.

She was sensitive—oh so sensitive. Not once but twice she erupted in a shattering climax that stunned him, in part because they came from mere touches on his part. When at last he reared back and plunged into her warm depths, she cried out and shuddered once again, nearly sending him over the edge also.

The third peak left her nearly boneless, and she opened her eyes to meet his fierce ones. Encased in her sheath, he clasped her by the forearms and lay very still.

"You're wild tonight," he whispered.

She tightened around him, causing his eyes to slam shut in pleasure for a moment. "I'm uncivilized," she replied with a low laugh. "Take me home, Patrick."

And he did, moving with increasing fury upon her, feeling the thumping of her heart fueled by estrogen and adrenaline, feeling the erotic sensation of their bare skin sliding over each other. She seemed limitless in her depth, encasing him with satin and silk until the sensation was unbearable. Gritting his teeth and tightening, he lunged over the peak, flying and crying out with pleasure and finally collapsing on top of her.

They lay still for a few minutes, feeling their heartbeats slow and return to normal, feeling the perspiration dry on their skins, feeling the fusing and bonding become complete.

Chapter Sixteen

Patrick awoke at the earliest light. The sky was beginning to gray from the black of night. The sky was clear, still sporting the fading stars as the morning crept upon the earth.

He heard a tiny noise and turned his head to see Grace watching him. A small shock went through him at the probing of those sleep-clouded eyes, as if she were trying to read his thoughts or his soul. They watched each other silently.

"It will be today," she said at last. "I feel it."

Patrick felt a sharp, stabbing shot of adrenaline in his belly, awakening him fully. If it *was* going to be today, he'd be ready.

"You think he'll fly out? That he already might be flying?" he asked.

"I think he's on his way. He's coming to get me."

He groped under the covers for her hand. "If he does come today, we'll face him together," he said quietly.

He saw tears spring to her eyes, and thought he could guess the reason behind them. After the hell that had been her marriage to Kristopher, after the four years of hiding, after wondering if she would ever feel worthy of a good man...here was one next to her, one vowing to stand by her at her darkest hour.

God, what a hero she thought he was.

Well, she was wrong. He came into this situation for money. He was determined to leave it with something more.

He gave her hand a little squeeze. "C'mon," he urged. "I'm going to make some phone calls, then let's go out in this beautiful morning to milk the cows."

****

He watched her graceful movements, her gentle

213

actions as she milked the cows. He watched the calves, older now and more patient in waiting for their breakfast, although one or the other occasionally let loose with a plaintive bawl. A tiny movement caught the corner of his eye, and he turned his head slightly to watch a large-eyed mouse creeping along the wall of the barn. He sniffed the dawn's fresh air as it came into the barn, coupled with the healthy smell of straw and cow and yes, even dung.

They came back to the house, and he cooked breakfast as she strained the milk. They spoke very little.

After breakfast, they were at a loss for activities. Grace tidied the dishes. Patrick did the laundry he had meant to do yesterday. There was an instance where they both stood looking out the front kitchen window, waiting, waiting, waiting.

"This is ridiculous," he said at last. "We need to find something to do to get through this day. Do you want me to get the guitar?"

She thought for a moment. "No," she said at last. "The only thing I would be in the mood for would be something melancholy in a minor key, and I don't think I could bear it. And something cheerful would only annoy me."

He put his arm around her waist and was gratified when she leaned into him, drawing strength. "Surely there's some labor-intensive farm chore that needs doing?"

It took awhile for her to think of one. "I suppose it's about time to clean the chicken coop," she suggested at last. "That would keep us busy for a couple hours. And the coop is close enough to the house—not on the other side of the creek—that if a car drives up, we'll be able to hear it."

"Sounds good to me. Let's go!"

So they donned sweatshirts against the chill autumn air and headed outside. They shooed the birds out of the chicken yard into the garden area, where they went with alacrity. Grace located thirteen eggs, which she tucked in a basket and placed outside the coop. Then she handed Patrick a rake, grabbed one for herself, and they began to gather in the messy straw.

After a few moments Grace stopped, closed her eyes, and went rigid.

"What's the matter?"

"Nothing." She shook her head and applied her rake to the floor of the coop. "Just the prickles. Strong ones."

Patrick continued raking. "I called Sheriff Engle and explained the situation. He promises not to be further than a minute or two away all day."

"He's a good sheriff. I appreciate that."

More raking. Then Patrick said, "I called the airport to see what flights are arriving. There's a few flights from Buffalo connecting into Portland, but only one connecting flight from Portland into Eugene, landing at three-forty-five. If I give him enough time to rent his car and drive down here, I think four-thirty is the earliest we can expect him here."

"I see."

"Grace." Patrick leaned on his rake. "When he gets here, you can't hide from him. He has to see you, he has to assume you'll be alone and vulnerable. We have to catch him in the act of committing a crime before we can convict him of something."

"I can't hide…" murmured Grace. "It's been four years of hiding. That's a hard habit to break. Especially when…"

"Especially when you'll be face to face with him."

"Yes."

"Don't worry. I'll be right with you. You won't be alone, Grace. Plus, Engle will be right on top of him as well."

They were silent for awhile, each lost in their own thoughts, while they pried dried chicken droppings from surfaces and raked the coop clean. Patrick wanted to distract Grace, so he asked her, "So tell me…how did you learn so much about farming in only four years, since leaving Kristopher?"

She scooped up a flake of straw and spread it over the floor. "It was Hazel, of course, who taught me. But it was also something Kristopher would never expect me to do."

"Farming?"

"Yes. Anything rural, actually. He is a very sophisticated man, very urbane and polished. His house is full of sleek furniture and modern art. He wanted me molded after his image, and enjoying the same things he did. I tried to convince myself, but I was always a country girl at heart, I guess. And when I decided to run, I knew that living in a rural area would be safer, since it was not what he would expect me to do."

"You got that right." Patrick leaned on his rake. "When he hired me, he stressed how sophisticated you were, and how you were used to the finer things in life. A maid, fine china, that kind of thing. Oh, and your appearance, of course. Elegant, upscale."

She gave a small snort in the first degree of humor she'd shown all day. "In a pig's eye, I was. He hated my attraction to anything provincial. He hated for me to wear jeans or a T-shirt. Even my hair had to be correct—to his standards—all the time."

She spread more straw. "As for my possessions...well, I had a picture, a cheap little farm scene I'd picked up in a store one day years and years ago. I loved that picture. Naturally I wanted to find some place to hang it once we were married, but he wouldn't have it. He actually threw it away." The humor became tinged with bitterness. "I rescued it out of the trash can and hid it. For all I know, it's still tucked away in that obscure corner of the basement, but I couldn't bear to have it just thrown away." She was silent a moment. "I suppose rescuing it was a way of stating that I wasn't ready to go under yet, to become lost in the new life into which he was trying to mold me."

"So why did Lehrer tell me that you had taken his daughter? What's with the kid?"

She twiddled with some straw. "He's got kids in his mind. Not ON his mind, IN his mind. It's a little hard to describe, but he already had our children conceived and born. Part of his violence against me was that I wasn't producing what his mind had already invented, namely kids. He especially wanted a daughter..."

"Jeannie."

"Yes, he was going to name her Jeannie. That was his mother's name."

"It surprises me that he was so focused on a daughter. I would have thought a man like that would have wanted a son."

"He didn't want to have sex with a son," she said bluntly.

Patrick was so startled he dropped his rake. "You mean..."

"Yes. I don't think he had pedophile tendencies—at least, I never saw evidence of it—but I do know that he would tell me what plans he had for our daughter. Or his mother—I'm pretty sure they were linked together in his twisted mind."

"Oh God...You mean his mother..."

"...probably molested him. He never came right out and said so, of course. But I'm fairly sure that's what he wanted a girl for. His mother is dead, otherwise he might have taken it out on her. He's insane, I tell you. He's so good at hiding it, but he's just not sane."

"His *mother*..."

"Twisted, isn't it?"

"Must have been a helluva relationship he had with her." Patrick swallowed the gorge that rose in his throat.

"So I gather. I don't know anything about her—he rarely spoke of her, and she died before I met him. But you can see why I refused to bring a child into this marriage."

Patrick shook his head. "And he seemed so *normal* when he hired me for this case..."

"Oh, he's a superb actor. Always has been. A lot of psychopaths are."

They were silent again as they finished the coop. Patrick looked at the pile of soiled straw they'd raked out. "Should we put this on the garden?" he asked.

"Yes. It'll compost over the winter. By spring, when I rototill, it'll be perfect." She paused for a moment, then added in a low voice, "If I'm still here."

Patrick dropped his rake with a clatter and strode over to her. He gripped her by the shoulders. "You not only will still be here," he informed her in an intense voice, "but you'll have the prettiest garden in the county."

The clouds in her eyes cleared as his gaze bored into hers. "I love you, Patrick," she whispered.

A shudder went through him and he closed his eyes and clasped her to him, with her rake handle pressed between them.

They finished their work. When the coop was clean, Grace looked it over and said, "Beautiful."

Patrick gave a rusty chuckle. "What would Kristopher say if he saw you praising a chicken coop?"

"He'd have a fit. Poop on him," she pronounced with more spirit than he anticipated. "Besides, look at it. It *is* beautiful. It beats Tiffany's any day of the week."

"Now how many women do you know would prefer a cleaned chicken coop to a jewelry store?"

"Out here? Probably more than you think. I don't think there's a Tiffany's within three hundred miles of here. That's assuming Portland has one, of course."

"Have you ever been to Portland?"

"No."

"Me either. What should we do next? We still have hours before Kristopher is likely to show up." He saw that she was becoming drawn tight again, her mouth thin with anxiety. He recalled the first time he'd seen her, in the office supply store in Eugene. He remembered the haunted look in her eyes that had caused such a visceral reaction in him. It was nothing compared to now. Her shoulders seemed literally bent with the weight of the stress.

They went inside the house to wash up and eat. And all the while they strained to hear something—anything. A car engine, the ring of the phone, even footsteps on the front walkway. *Would* Kristopher come today? Would he boldly walk up to the front of the house and knock? Or would he slink around, peeking in windows, planning his assault?

The road outside was unusually quiet today, with less traffic than usual from the locals who lived there. Once they heard the crunch of tires in the driveway and froze. Patrick hesitated an instant before catapulting out of the kitchen to the living room window.

"It's just the sheriff!" he called hastily, and he saw her wilt in relief.

The sheriff's car idled in the driveway for a moment until Patrick stepped out on the porch and waved him off with a smile. He had been by several times during the day, and Patrick was reassured by his diligence.

After they ate, for no reason except for something to

218

do, pass the time, anything, they went for a walk.

"Are you sure?" asked Patrick.

Grace rubbed her arms as if cold. "I need to *do* something. Get out. Get away. I can't just sit here and wait—I'll go crazy."

"All right. Let's walk, then."

They bundled into heavy flannel shirts and scarves and rubber boots against the chilly day, crossed over the bridge, and walked up the road toward the north part of the property.

"It still amazes me, how you can actually go for a walk and still be on your own property," commented Patrick.

"You mean the acreage? I know what you mean. Yet out here, thirty acres is modest. The folks whose land is behind mine have a hundred-forty acres, and I think the people behind *them* have two-hundred some-odd acres."

"And most people in Buffalo are just grateful they have backyards."

"Hey, different strokes for different folks. Want to walk around the pond?"

"Sure."

The rushes around the edge of the water were brown and dead, lending them an autumn charm that was lovely. The black-locust and big-leaf maple trees had dropped both large and tiny golden leaves in a carpet around the south side of the pond. The north side, where the stream fed into it, had a small forest of ponderosa pine and Douglas fir trees interspersed with Oregon black oaks and a cedar or two.

"Oh, look...there are the Canada geese," said Grace, pointing. She tucked her hands into her pockets. "They nest here every year. I'm surprised they're still around this late in the fall."

"They're beautiful." He stood behind her and wrapped his arms around her midsection, resting his chin on her shoulder. She leaned against him.

"Maybe next spring I'll build them some nest boxes," she murmured, as the geese swam closer. "I love having them here."

Patrick noted how she spoke about the future. He hoped that was a good omen.

His arms tightened around her middle, and she suddenly spun around in his embrace, looping her arms about his neck. Her nose was a bit red from the chill air, but her large green eyes were bright with tears. She pressed her forehead to his.

"Hey," she said.

"Hey what?" He pulled her closer to him.

"I just had an idea."

"Oh?"

"Why don't you ask me again if I'll marry you?"

This was so unexpected that he blinked in surprise. "Oooookay. Will you marry me?"

"Yes!" And she fused her lips with his for seven excruciatingly desperate seconds before drawing back.

"Why—" His voice cracked, and he cleared his throat. Somehow his mind and his mouth weren't cooperating as well as they normally did. He tried again. "Why the sudden change of heart?"

"Because I don't know what the future will bring." She drew back, and he saw one single tear drop from her eye. The rest she held in. "It would be nice to say I'm engaged before..."

Her voice trailed off, and the unspoken words hovered like lead between them.

"Grace," he said gently, "I told you before I don't want you to feel pressured or trapped. I'd love to marry you, but you told me once that you didn't trust a man who declared himself so soon."

"I trust *you*, Patrick."

His expression changed and he bit his lip. "Maybe I should just shut up and accept my good fortune." He drew her close.

"Maybe you should," she said against his lips.

They stood on the shores of the pond and indulged in each other. From whatever desperate depths she plumbed, Grace used her tongue to torment him and her teeth to nibble in a manner designed to send him over the edge. He finally groaned and pulled her shoulders back a little. "Listen, Grace, I'm only human. Unless you want me to take you here on the grass—"

"The grass is dry enough." She pulled him down beside her, pushed him onto his back, and proceeded to unbuckle his belt.

Amused, aroused, he watched her. "Not the shirts?" he teased.

"Too cold. Right now, I'm just interested in the relevant parts."

His eyes widened as he was suddenly engulfed in her warm mouth. His body jerked and he groaned, grabbing a handful of her hair and only remembering at the last moment to be gentle. She was talented, very, very talented, in sending a man to heaven in this manner. He was losing himself in her, with her, when abruptly she stopped. He grunted in frustration and opened his eyes.

She was sitting on the ground next to him and impatiently yanking off her rubber boots. She jerked at the Velcro closure of her gun belt and laid it aside, then pulled at her jeans and kicked them off. Her underpants followed.

He watched these necessary ministrations and thought that something that might otherwise seem awkward in the bright light of day was somehow erotic beyond belief when he was lying on a bed of brown grass and exposed and about to be coupled with. The very thought had him jerking in expectation as she turned back.

"Now, where was I?" she murmured, naked from the waist down, and resumed her shattering assault upon his person.

This lasted until he gripped her hair in protest. "No more," he groaned. "I won't be able to last much longer— aaahhh!" For at his words, she swung smoothly over him and impaled herself to the hilt.

She gave him a taut smile as she straddled him, not moving, letting him adjust to the sensation. Then she laced her fingers with his, leaned forward, and pressed his hands into the ground while she dissolved her lips into his.

He was drowning, drowning in a world of stimulation. She rode him expertly to the point of madness, removing her mouth from his in order to rear back and take her own pleasure with gasps. He yanked his hands out of hers and gripped her by the waist, feeling the shudders run through her, the movement of her hips as she bucked on him. He gave her no respite during her climax, urging her on with the increasing tempo until he was sent spinning into a world of his own, a world in which she had the power to draw every last ounce of strength from him. He cried out and spilled his seed into her.

Wilting down, she dropped across his chest and panted while he tried to catch his own breath. The world slowly stopped spinning, and he became aware of the chill air around them, the roughness of the grass beneath them, and the questioning honk of the birds on the pond.

"Wow," he said quietly. He stroked her hair. "Think the geese were impressed?"

"Do you care if they were?"

"No."

"Thought not."

There was silence for a moment, then he gave a tremendous sigh. "What brought that on?"

"I don't know." She raised her head and propped her chin on her folded hands.

"Fear?" he suggested softly.

She looked at him a moment longer, then nodded. "I think that probably has a lot to do with it."

The intimacy was broken immediately, and with some embarrassment they slipped apart and re-dressed in the chill air.

"Don't forget your gun belt," he said.

She stared down at the wide elastic holster she'd worn daily for four years. "I hate that thing," she said at last, touching it with the toe of her boot.

"I'm glad you have it."

"It's like a chain that I have to wear. It weighs me down."

"I know. But the alternative leaves you too vulnerable."

With a heavy sigh she bent down and scooped up the revolver and holster. She yanked up her flannel shirt, pulled the belt around her waist, and pushed the Velcro tight.

"I won't wear this forever," she said with a lift of her chin.

Patrick gave a forced chuckle. "Is that a promise?"

"No." Her eyes narrowed. "It's a threat." She shuddered. "What time is it?"

Patrick glanced at his watch. "One-thirty."

"So we have about three hours yet."

"Yes. The prickles again?" he asked, watching her.

"Yeah. Big time." She shuddered again. "He's *not* in a good mood."

"Want to go back to the house?"

"Yes." She shivered. "I don't think I want to leave it again, either."

They hiked back to the house and Grace put on the kettle for tea. An unexpected knock sent her spinning around. "It can't be him. It can't! It's too soon, I don't feel him near..."

Patrick sprinted for the front door and peered through the peephole. "It's Lyle, your neighbor," he called.

Grace wilted a moment, then straightened. "Bad timing on Lyle's part," she murmured.

Patrick opened the door and gasped. "What happened?"

The old man stood swaying on the doorstep, his left arm bent at a bad angle. "I've hurt my durn arm," he muttered.

Grace peered around the door, saw the man, and exclaimed, "Lyle!"

"Fell off the tractor," he explained, his cheeks sheet-white. "I think I need a doctor."

"Into the truck with you," said Grace. "You need that arm set. Oh Lyle..."

"I'll take him," said Patrick. "C'mon, buddy, into the truck you go."

They supported the elderly man and helped him climb into the passenger seat of the truck. Then Patrick turned to Grace, a concerned frown on his face. "There's no room for you in the cab. Do you want to ride in the back?"

"No, just take him in, quick." Grace's face was puckered with worry. "The sooner you go, the sooner you'll be back."

"Okay. I'll call the sheriff and warn him that I'll be gone for a few minutes. Maybe he can park nearby or something." He pulled his cell phone out of his pocket and dialed in the number. Then, frowning, he left the truck and walked around the driveway, stopping here and there, trying to find a spot where his cell phone would work. "Have you *always* had such bad cell coverage out here?" he asked in some irritation.

"Depends," she replied. "The weather can affect things, and even the direction you're facing. Are you getting through?"

"No." He snapped his phone shut and swore. "I hadn't counted on this."

From inside the truck, Lyle gave a moan.

"Here, try mine." Grace dashed into the house, and Patrick followed her. Grace reached into the kitchen cabinet and handed him her cell phone.

Patrick dialed the number and connected. He nodded with relief as he checked in with the sheriff. "He's at the end of Hayhurst Road, and he'll keep cruising back and forth." He closed the phone and placed it on the coffee table. "Need anything else in town?"

"No. Don't linger—just get Lyle fixed up and then come back."

"You sure you don't want to come with me?"

She shook her head. "This is where I feel safest."

Patrick went to find his wallet, feeling a trace of irritation. She felt safest at home. Not with him, but at home. Wasn't there something wrong with that?

He kissed her on his way out the door. "I'll be back in half an hour," he told her. "Go have a cup of tea or something."

"I'll be fine." She gave him a dim smile. "Hurry back, Patrick."

Chapter Seventeen

Alone in the house, the demons of fear swooped down and clamped her brain. She knew Kristopher wasn't due to arrive for another three hours, but that didn't make her feel very safe. What was she thinking, letting Patrick go off and leaving her alone? She would call him and ask him to come back...She opened her kitchen cabinet and reached for her cell phone.

It wasn't there.

For a moment the unreality of it made her stare blankly at the spot she normally kept her phone. Of course—Patrick had handed her the phone in the living room. It must still be there.

She heard a noise outside and looked out the window in time to see Sheriff Engle's patrol car sweep by, lights flashing. For a moment she thought he was heading toward Patrick, until she realized that he was heading in the wrong direction, toward the town of Pincolla.

Nausea swept her. Patrick wasn't here. The sheriff was answering another call. She was alone in the house. And Kristopher...

She focused inward and knew that Kristopher was on his way. He was close.

Her head snapped up. That couldn't be. *It couldn't be!* He wouldn't arrive for another three hours!

She ran into the living room and grabbed the cell phone on the coffee table. Fingers shaking, she opened the ear piece...and realized she didn't know Patrick's cell number. Instead, she tried dialing 911.

Nothing. Static.

She stared at the phone in horror before dropping it on the floor and backing up, her eyes glued to the useless object.

Then, panicked, she fled the stifling inside of the

house and flung herself outside into the cold autumn air, breathing hard, nauseous. He was on his way. On his way. He was close. She clutched the fence of the garden, leaned over, and vomited.

She couldn't help it. She was alone. Patrick was gone. Kristopher was on his way. And she was going to die.

****

Patrick made sure Lyle was registered into the medical clinic in Faucet, then came out into the parking lot. As he opened the door of the truck, a dark blue Cadillac sedan, looking out of place in this farming community, drove slowly by. Patrick glanced at the driver and froze.

It was Kristopher Lehrer.

There was no mistaking the elegant profile. Lehrer didn't glance his way, but he was scanning the townspeople as he passed.

Patrick jumped into the driver's seat. What was Lehrer doing here? It was too soon. He should never have left Grace. He should have insisted that Grace come with him. He should have...

The truck roared to life, and he pulled an illegal U-turn and followed Lehrer as he stopped at a stop sign, then turned left on Highway 38 heading out of town toward Hayhurst Road.

Staying well back from Lehrer's rental car, Patrick plucked his cell phone out of his pocket and called the sheriff.

Dead. No cell service.

He swore and tossed the phone onto the seat beside him, wishing violently that he had taken Grace's cell phone after all.

He pounded the steering wheel in frustration. At this point, the best he could hope for was that he would pass Sheriff Engle on his way and could flag him down. As it was, he didn't dare let Lehrer out of his sight to go look for the sheriff.

At least—at the very least—he was right on the man's tail. Grace wouldn't be alone with Lehrer for more than five seconds before he would be right there too. Patrick felt his revolver on his hip and hoped that six bullets would be enough.

Lehrer slowed down at the intersection of Highway 38 and Hayhurst Road. He hesitated, then turned left. Patrick followed

Lehrer must have known he was on the right road, but he clearly didn't know exactly what he was looking for. He slowed before each widely-scattered farmhouse and looked it over before driving on. Patrick stayed far enough back that he hoped it wasn't too obvious that he had no intention of passing.

Four miles into Hayhurst Road—two miles from Grace's house—the truck sputtered and stalled. Eyes popping, Patrick glided to a wide spot on the side of the road and stopped. Beginning to panic, he turned over the ignition key and heard the truck's faithful engine wheeze to life...then sputter and die. Heart pounding, Patrick turned the key again. This time the engine gasped but didn't turn over. He pounded the dashboard. Dammit, the truck was out of gas, victim of the faulty gas gauge...and a madman was heading toward Grace.

It was too far to run. Frantically, he looked around for inspiration when, out of the corner of his eye, he caught a glimpse of a shiny pink tassels fluttering in the cold wind.

****

Grace heard the sound of a car's engine and her heart lurched. The sheriff? She knew it wasn't, but her thoughts darted frantically...*Please God, please let it be the sheriff*...She staggered to her feet and ran to peer around the corner of the house.

A sleek dark blue Seville hesitated on the road, then pulled into her half-circle driveway.

No, it wasn't the sheriff. It was Kristopher. She knew. Fear drenched her in nauseating waves.

She stared at the man, dim behind the tinted glass of the car. It had been four years since she'd been near him. Years of prickles, years of hiding, years of independence. The engine disengaged, and in the sudden silence her stomach heaved and blood pounded in her brain. What had Patrick said? *When he gets here, you can't hide from him. He has to see you, he has to assume you'll be alone and vulnerable. We have to catch him in the act of committing a crime before we can convict him of something...*

She *was* alone and vulnerable. Oh God, where was Patrick? He was supposed to be here. He promised to protect her. Something had gone wrong. She was on her own. There was no Patrick. There was no one—no one to save her.

Kristopher got out of the vehicle, his movements surgical and precise. Grace saw her ex-husband for the first time in four years, and it was as if she had last seen him only moments before. Margo came sweeping back, warring with Grace.

He was still handsome except for the cold gray eyes that were the only indication of the twisted psychosis within him.

You can't hide...

The strength of Grace—fueled by Patrick's love—rose up and brought a measure of calm. Her revolver nestled in the small of her back, warm and hard. She stepped out from behind the corner of the barn. It was time to end this farce.

She had the satisfaction of seeing Kristopher hesitate when he saw her, as if surprised. She crossed her arms, feeling the chill in her skin. "Hello, Kristopher."

She stood frozen as Kristopher smiled his charming smile. "Margo. How nice to see you." He walked around the end of the car toward her and glanced at their surroundings. "Such a dismal place you've chosen. To think that you chose a hovel like this over the beautiful home we have in Buffalo. Really, Margo, your provincial tastes *must* be corrected. We'll work on that, you and I."

"My farm is not a hovel. That's a matter of opinion."

"No, it's not. You have no opinions. You, your opinions, your thoughts, your dreams, they all belong to me."

Grace shuddered at the calm, familiar voice. He so seldom raised his voice. "We're divorced, Kristopher."

He walked toward her. "Divorced? Of course not. A piece of paper doesn't mean anything to me, Margo. You know that. We're bound for eternity—"

"Stay away!" She took two steps backward.

Kristopher halted, though the smile remained. "Margo, Margo...You're being silly. You're my wife, my soul-mate..."

"Your slave, you mean."

"No, my soul-mate."

"Soul-mates don't beat their wives."

"Beat? What an ugly word. I never beat you, I merely disciplined you when you required it." He took another step forward.

Grace backed up a step. "When I *required* it?" she spat. "Does that include pushing me down the stairs because my lipstick was the wrong color? Does that include smashing my head into a wall because I wore slacks instead of a skirt?"

"You were rebellious, Margo. You needed to learn the proper behavior for the wife of a man of my position." He took another relentless step forward.

Grace shook her head. "I'm telling you, Kristopher, I'm not leaving here. I won't go anywhere with you."

"Oh yes you will, Margo. My Jeannie wants to be born."

"Your Jeannie will never be born. Not with me."

"Of course she will."

"I won't bear a child to you, Kristopher. Never. You'd have to kill me to touch me again."

The hated smile faded at last. "You are refusing me something?"

She froze, terrified. Grace McNeil drained away and Margo Lehrer crept into her place. *You are refusing me something*...how often those words signaled his disapproval, and preceded some act of violence or humiliation or retribution. She shuddered.

Stall him, she thought. *Maybe Patrick will arrive.*

"What happens if we have a son?" she asked, trying to reason with him. She needed space and an opportunity to draw her gun without him getting to it first. "You can't name him Jeannie."

"A daughter will follow."

"What if it doesn't?"

"I *will have* my Jeannie." He took a step forward.

She took a step backward. "So you can have your mother under your control? Is that it?"

Irritation flickered in his eyes. "You're babbling, Margo. Get in the car."

"No. I don't know what twisted, sick relationship you had with your mother, but the thought of giving you a daughter so you can take revenge on your mother..."

"*Enough.*" The word was vicious, though his voice remained low. "I've had enough trouble with you, chasing you across the country like this. You've been a bad wife, Margo. I can chastise you here just as easily, if you insist."

The blow came hard. Kristopher darted forward and backhanded her with enough force that her head slammed into the barn wall. Pain smashed through her and lights burst behind her eyelids. Something warm trickled from the corner of her mouth.

"Are you whoring yourself to that detective I hired?" he inquired, his voice as composed as if they were drinking tea. "That will have to stop, Margo. You really have been bad."

Grace dragged herself upright and edged away from Kristopher. Her head felt thick, and it was hard to think. *Get away, have to get away, have to do something...*

"Don't touch me again," she said. She spoke thickly, but her mind became clearer. The gun. She had to get far enough away to draw her gun without him grabbing it. "I'm not your wife, and you don't have me under your control again."

"Foolish girl. You'll *always* be under my control." He smiled.

"Kristopher, if you touch me again, you'll regret it."

His eyes narrowed. "You're threatening me, Margo? My own wife? You know I won't tolerate that."

She stepped away, trying to put some distance between them, but he wouldn't let her. Even at such close range, she had little choice but to jerk her revolver out of the Velcro holster in the small of her back. The tearing noise of the Velcro sounded loud in the country air.

She pointed the gun at him. "Take one more step and I'll shoot."

"How cliché." But he stopped at the sight of the gun and frowned. "I would never have thought you capable of sinking to such vulgar actions, Margo. Now stop being tasteless and come home with me."

"I won't. You'll have to accept the fact, Kristopher.

I'm no longer your wife, and I'm not going anywhere with you. *Take one more step and I'll shoot!*" she cried, as he took that step.

"You don't have the nerve." He took yet another step toward her.

Grace aimed the revolver at his chest, clutched it with both hands to steady the furious shaking of her hands, and fired.

The force of the shot thrust her backward. Her ears rang. She had never fired her gun without ear protection, had never fired at a living thing before. She shook her head to clear it, and what she saw made dread coil inside her.

Kristopher had thrown himself to the side. The shot had missed. He crouched on the ground a few feet away, looking lethal and furious as a tiger.

"Stupid BITCH!" He sprang at her.

Grace backed up and cocked the revolver once more, desperate to get in another shot. But as she lifted the revolver he smashed her flat. The gun went off and the shot went wide. He grabbed her wrist and twisted until pain shot up her arm. He wrestled the gun out of her hands. Then he backed away, panting, holding her revolver.

"I didn't think you were capable of that, Margo," he said, and his voice had resumed its normal, hated, insane calmness.

Grace rose to her feet. A curious composure came over her as she stood with her back against the barn wall. So this is how it would end. Kristopher would shoot her. She would bleed to death here in the driveway of her beloved Oregon farm. She would never see Patrick again.

But at least she would be free of Kristopher.

"Hurry up and get it over with," she told him, and raised her chin.

He jerked his head toward the driveway. "Get in the car."

"No."

"Don't make me do something you'll regret."

"Returning to you is the only thing I'd regret." *Why didn't he just shoot her and be done with it?*

"I'll have to kill you, Margo."

231

"Good. I'd rather die than return to you."

"But *why?*" he burst out, and Grace blinked. It was the most emotion she had ever seen from him.

"Because you are not sane, Kristopher," she replied. Margo Lehrer retreated, and she felt the strength of Grace McNeal rise up and face Kristopher. "Your desire to control and your wish to destroy whatever gets in your way is too much. You have no conscience. You fit every description of a psychopath. I want a normal life with a normal man, and you are not normal."

His face twisted. "A normal man like this Patrick Hess, is that it? Have you been whoring with him?"

"Just shoot me, Kristopher. Get it over with."

He raised the revolver and aimed. Grace closed her eyes and braced for the shot.

When it came, she heard two reports, nearly simultaneous. But the bullet didn't hit her head or her chest. Instead, she screamed and collapsed as it shattered her leg.

She opened her eyes and raised her head through a haze of agony. She saw that Kristopher was no longer standing. He was face down on the ground, with his arms sprawled and blood on his back. In the background, she saw the flashing lights of Sheriff Engle's patrol car as it screeched into her driveway.

But it was the sight of Patrick that made her blink. He stood behind Kristopher's body with his arms still braced in the shooting position, panting hard. Beside him was the absurd sight of a girl's pink bicycle, with the wheels spinning and shiny tassels fluttering in the breeze.

"The gas gauge on the truck," he told her between wheezes, "*really* must be fixed."

Blackness and pain swirled around her, and she passed out.

****

"Patrick?" she whispered.

She heard movement. "I'm here. I'm here, Grace."

She felt pressure as he took her hand and squeezed gently, but she felt too weak to squeeze back. "Where am I?" Her voice was a mere croak.

"You're at Sacred Heart Medical Center in Eugene."

"Kristopher?"

There was a hesitation. "He's dead, Grace. He can't hurt you any more."

Tears welled from beneath her closed lids. "Free," she whispered. "I'm free."

****

The next time Grace drifted to consciousness, the pain was the first thing she noticed. Her head ached, her face ached, her right wrist ached, and her leg throbbed in agony. But the fear was gone. The prickles were gone. Kristopher was dead—that much she remembered.

She moved to push herself upright. She saw that her left leg from hip to ankle was encased in a massive cast. No wonder it hurt.

She looked around the hospital room and saw Patrick slumped over in a chair, asleep. He looked terrible, she thought fondly. There was heavy stubble on his chin, his hair was wild, his clothes filthy. "Patrick?"

He awoke instantly, blinking to clear the sleep from his eyes. When he saw her sitting up, he sprang to his feet. "Grace! You're awake!"

"Seems that way." She pushed herself further up and winced at the pain.

"How do you feel?" he asked as he grabbed another pillow and gently propped it behind her back.

"Like hell. What happened?"

"He shot you in the leg."

"Is it true? Is he dead?"

"Yes. I'll explain everything in time, but I don't want to give you too much at once. Are you in pain? Do you want some pain medication?"

She considered. "Yeah. Actually I do. And something to eat, too—I'm starved." She raised her arm and felt a tug, then noticed for the first time the IV taped to the back of her hand. She stared at it stupidly. "Wow. I must be in pretty bad shape."

"You were." Patrick yanked a chair over and sat next to her. "I'm not surprised you're hungry, either. You've been here—" He hesitated.

"How long?"

"Five days."

"Five days!" Grace jerked upright and immediately wished she hadn't.

233

Patrick pressed a hand to her shoulder, keeping her still. "You needed a lot of care." She saw him swallow. "You were pretty messed up when we got you here."

"I'll be fine, Patrick," she said gently, and she smiled at him.

His throat worked. "Grace...oh God, Grace, I thought I'd lost you..."

He dropped his head to the edge of the bed and wept with great heaving sobs. She made soothing noises as he poured out his terrors and regrets. "...should never have left you...the phone didn't work...Lehrer passed me in town, I tried to follow him..."

"Hush, Patrick, hush," she said, stroking his head. "You saved my life. That much I remember. Hush, don't worry..." In a few minutes the storm passed, and he grabbed some tissues and mopped his face. It was a sign of his strength that he didn't apologize for breaking down. Grace's heart swelled with love.

A nurse peeked in. "You're up!" she exclaimed, delighted. She took a look at Patrick's ravaged face and Grace could see her sum up the situation in a moment. "I'll have the doctor in to take a look, and you'll be hungry, I'm sure."

Half an hour later, Patrick had taken a shower. Grace had the medication that eased her pain, and she had a tray of food before her. When they were alone once more she said, "Tell me everything."

So he did. He told her how he was coming out of the medical clinic when Lehrer drove through town, about the dead cell phone connection, the truck running out of gas. "I grabbed the first thing I could," he said. "That little girl's bike that's always being left on the side of the road. I've never pushed myself as hard as I did on that damned little bike—Grace, I heard two shots before I got there, I was terrified he'd killed you, that I was too late..."

"You were just in time," she said. "I tried to shoot him but he threw himself to one side. Then he wrestled the gun out of my hands, and it went off. That was the second shot you heard."

"He hit you. Punched you," said Patrick, his voice rough with anger.

"Of course. Twice, if I remember. That's his way.

Don't worry about it, Patrick, it's done. It's over." Her voice gentled. "Thanks to you."

"The sheriff witnessed the whole thing," said Patrick. "He came just as I dropped the bicycle and aimed. He saw Lehrer about to shoot you. There won't be any charges. It was a clear case of self-defense."

"But why was Kristopher here so early? I thought his plane wasn't scheduled to land for another couple of hours?"

"He chartered a flight." She saw his face blacken. "Damn it to hell, I should have thought of that but I didn't. He chartered a flight and landed hours sooner than we thought."

"Are you going to beat yourself up for the next ten years because you couldn't predict the unknown?" she asked gently. She reached for his hand. "It's over, Patrick. He can't hurt us any longer." She smiled. "I may look like a mess, but I feel a million pounds lighter. You have no idea how airy I feel right now. I feel like I could dance!"

"Not until that leg heals. It may take awhile."

"With three pins and a shattered femur, it wouldn't surprise me." That's what the doctor had told her. She grew more sober. "His last legacy to me."

"Not quite."

"What do you mean?"

"I have a surprise for you, and a more pleasant one this time."

"What?"

"Kristopher never changed his will after the divorce. You'll inherit everything—his house, his business, his fortune. My partner, Jim, has been gathering up all the loose ends in Buffalo. You stand to receive a fair chunk of change, Grace."

She stared at him. A slow smile spread across her face. "And do you know what we're going to do with that money?" she asked softly.

"We?"

"Yes, *we*. We're going to endow that women's shelter in Buffalo. Then we'll take what's left and invest it so we can live comfortably while you get your writing career off the ground." Her grin widened. "That is, if your offer to marry me still stands."

235

"Still stands!" Patrick raised one of her hands and raised it to his lips. "I can't live without you, Grace. I'll marry you in a heartbeat." He grinned at her. "Welcome home."

Epilogue

"Don't forget, we have rehearsal tonight."

"Yes, I remember. We need to leave a bit early, too, so you can get a new string for your guitar." Standing in the bathroom, Grace pulled a brush through her baby-soft blond hair. It was starting to grow longer since she'd chopped off the dyed brown, and now reached her shoulders in its natural flaxen color.

Patrick came up behind her and snaked his hands around her belly, cradling the growing life within, resting his chin on her shoulder as he met her eyes in the mirror. "You're beautiful, did you know that?"

She smiled. "You're biased," she said. She reached up over her shoulder and cupped his cheek. "Just don't let it end."

He dropped a kiss on her neck and let her go so that he could pick up the hairbrush himself. "Tomorrow's going to be busy," he commented. "Two people coming by to look at calves—the interest in the cows has been amazing, since that article on Dexter cattle appeared in *Mother Earth News*—and Ruby's due any day for her new calf. Plus we have to get that pipe moved in the middle pasture if we're going to irrigate."

"You're becoming a fine farmer," she teased him. In the year and a half since they'd been married, he'd thrown himself into the cow breeding program with an enthusiasm that never failed to surprise her. "I guess Kristopher's money did some good after all. Do you miss the detective work?"

"Are you kidding? I was ready to give it up before I took your case. Besides, my agent wants my next book in three months, so even without Kristopher's money we would have squeaked by on my advance."

"Yeah, but I suppose that's one thing I can be

237

grateful for, to Kristopher. The fact that he didn't change his will even after four years—who'da thought?" She reached up to slip some gold stud earrings into her lobes, then lowered her hands again. "And who'd have thought marriage could be such a marvelous thing?" she added lower.

Patrick spun her around into a loose embrace. "You've grown and changed so much in two years, do you realize that? Singing for a Celtic music band, growing your hair long, having a baby in five months, selling your own cows instead of having Anna do it...and just listening to you, Grace. God, I could do it the rest of my life. Your singing, your laughter, your voice..."

She pressed her forehead to his. "Well, guess what...you *will* be listening to me the rest of your life. I don't know what I'd have done if you hadn't found me. I'd still be living in fear, thinking all men were demons, terrified to ever stretch and grow and change..."

He dropped a kiss on her lips, and it stretched and grew and changed until both their bodies were sizzling with desire. But both also knew there was no time for anything further.

"We'd better go," she whispered.

"Yeah, I know. I never thought cutting a CD would be this much work, but I can't wait to hear your voice coming over the stereo."

"And your guitar, too, don't forget."

"No one ever listens to the guitar, just the voice."

"Well, at any rate, I'm glad this will be all wrapped up before the baby comes." She gave him one last hard kiss and walked into the bedroom to slip on her coat, limping only a little now. "We're going to be so busy then, the singing might have to go on hold."

"It if does, it's just temporary. You have your whole life to sing."

She smiled. "I know that now."

A word about the author...

I live on a forty-acre homestead in north Idaho with my wonderful husband (married seventeen years) and two daughters (ages 9 and 11). Between milking cows, gathering eggs, weeding the garden, and trying to keep the young fruit trees alive, I get up at ungodly hours (often 3:30 a.m.) to write. We have a home business and I homeschool our girls, so getting up early is the only quiet time I have.

I am published in various magazines (such as Countryside, Backwoods Home, Country EXTRA, Home Education Magazine, BackHome Magazine, and Grit) and my first nonfiction is currently under contract with an agent. I'm thrilled that The Wild Rose Press has picked up my first romance novel.

I'm crazy over books and we own over three thousand of them on subjects ranging from biography to zoology. I have a master's degree in biology but don't use it much (actually, I don't use it at all anymore). I prefer to write both fiction and nonfiction, and be a full-time mom to my kids.

I am a member of RWA and our local chapter (IECRWA). I love to write, and often write when I really should be doing something more productive...like cooking dinner. Ah well, hopefully my family understands.

Much of my writing deals with rural themes. Country living continues to fascinate me, even when I'm crouched next to a cow milking in zero degree weather.

Printed in the United States
92081LV00001B/23/A